LIBERTINE
Peta Spear

Peta Spear was born in Rockhampton, Central

Queensland. She has published a book of poetry and

a collection of short stories. This is her first novel.

LIBERTINE
Peta Spear

V

VINTAGE

A Vintage book
published by
Random House Australia Pty Ltd
20 Alfred Street, Milsons Point, NSW 2061
http://www.randomhouse.com.au

Sydney New York Toronto
London Auckland Johannesburg
and agencies throughout the world

First published 1999
Copyright © Peta Spear 1999

National Library of Australia
Cataloguing-in-Publication Data
Spear, Peta, 1959– .
    Libertine.

    ISBN 0 091 83729 4.

    I. Title.

A823.3

Designed by Gayna Murphy, Greendot Design
Typeset by J&M Typesetting, Melbourne
Printed by Griffin Paperbacks, Adelaide, a division of PMP Communications

10 9 8 7 6 5 4 3 2 1

This work was assisted by a part-Writer's Project Grant from the Literature Board of the Australia Council. Invaluable support was also provided by the Post-graduate Writing Program at the University of Western Sydney, Nepean. The author gratefully acknowledges this assistance. In particular, her thanks go to Linda Funnell, Rose Creswell and Anna Gibbs, her parents, and her friends. Thanks are also due to Meredith Rose and Andrew Trevillion for their editorial advice.

ONE

The first time. The first time. When was the first time?

Soft things brush against me before it starts to come clear: the papery wings of insects, the tickle of inky hair, the fall of ash. Then I feel the claw and memory is a wild bird, beating to be set free once and for all. But this creature memory is not made of soft things. And there is the other creature, fear, the worm that entered me, that slid through a wound perhaps, or one of the natural openings of my body, and leisurely made its home in me. When the blue fades and the heat swells within me and the red planet begins to burn, the worm threads its way through me and the battle with the bird begins.

Maybe the memory will finally get the better of the fear. Maybe the bird will eat the worm.

A victory.

Yes, I would like to have that victory.

The first time I was drunk. The slippage was fantastic, seeing the lean of the world from the privilege of a happy state. Well, not always happy, but always intense, a state of the most incredible heightening. I was amplified, with soft edges that could be teased to go just about anywhere. This laxity, this dispensation, this letting go is why drunkenness is such a crime. It lets you do anything. I did do anything.

There was no regard for safety or circumspection.

To not have the regard.

Anarchic. Amoral. Bliss.

The first time, I went to meet him as arranged. It was a terrible day, pouring rain, the start of the bad weather with the streets slicked wet and the sky doubled over, gun-metal grey. The game was, I'd decided to look entirely respectable, like an office worker on her lunch break. From the start I rightly guessed certain things about him. He liked costumes. It made me laugh, getting myself up to look like I was going off to a regular job with my shirt primly buttoned up to the collar, hair twisted back and a prissy handbag to match the sober shoes. However my naked legs were oiled and perfumed under my sedate skirt and I had a fake skin on my face and throat and running up the back of my neck. I also had Soft Surrender lips, Conquer cheekbones, Ambush eyes with Lust Dust lashes. My armpits were fragrant smoothed-out shallow basins and I had pruned my bush in case he found its luxuriance alarming.

The first time, we kissed with wide open mouths and loose tongues. It wasn't at all romantic, neither was it tentative. It was almost obscenely direct, perhaps made so by the discrete gloom of the hotel room. It was after that kiss that we got down to the business of being together and took off our clothes. When I'd first entered the room I'd not seen him and I'd had a moment of doubt, I thought I'd been duped. But he was there, waiting for me, sitting motionless in a wing chair, a blot of dark abutting a wall of pale shrouded windows. An elegant, if slightly threatening, tableau. Although the room was artificially temperate there was a heaviness in the air I'd always associated with the feeling of intense cold and goose bumps rose, pimpling my skin in a portrayal of nervousness.

A terse soldier who did not bother to speak to me very civilly or once look me in the eye had frisked me thoroughly in the foyer before escorting me upstairs. There were two guards standing at attention outside the door, one of whom began to cough without let-up when the thunder rolled in. Maybe the storm that was taking the city made the man nervous. When I lifted the white gauze of curtain and glanced out a window I saw more of his men stationed at intervals along the street, stoically being lashed by rain.

When he undressed he did so in silence and with an economy of movement. He took an inordinate amount of time to hang his uniform in the closet. He was far less particular with his flesh-coloured underwear, leaving it in a crumpled heap on the floor. Turning to me, he took hold of his partially erect penis and began to caress it, after asking me to open the bottle of champagne and disrobe. I remember my surprise when he used the word 'please'. I popped the cork and we clinked our glasses together. I swallowed a few quick mouthfuls of bubbles, which tickled the back of my throat, and then I removed my outfit in a slow striptease. Underneath I wore a pair of black nylon knickers hooked with lace. When he held my hips and pulled the knickers off me with his teeth I heard the lace tearing. When I was naked we lay upon the bed, a three-quarter sized bed, not a luxurious, king-sized bed like I had expected, and we manoeuvred our faces in between each other's legs and we kissed with loose tongues again.

After all, that's what the first time was meant to be.

When I felt a strange syncopation on my labia and heard an odd murmuring washing out of his mouth and over and around my mound I shifted his penis from mouth to hand and lifted my head to better hear what he was saying. At first the words were indistinct but after a moment of concentration I caught the litany: 'Harrier, Falcon, Vulture, Phantom, Fury, Avenger, Tornado, Tomcat, Hornet, Jaguar, Mirage, Eagle, Skyhawk, Apache, Thunderbolt, Harrier, Falcon, Vulture, Phantom, Fury, Avenger, Tornado, Tomcat …' I squeezed his penis harder and upped the tempo of my fingers. The names of fighters and bombers and jet planes began to buzz wildly against me. My body started involuntarily humming, started to spontaneously sing an invocation to the machines of the air. For a fleeting moment I felt myself slipping beyond control then I asserted myself in the way I knew how. To his chagrin, he came almost immediately. I had a talent and, as I'd hoped, it shut him up.

Afterwards he dressed and I lay in the tangle of sheets wolfing down the lunch of gourmet sandwiches and opening another bottle of sweet bubbles, obliterating the odour and the echo of the words that had sprung out of me. Overhead, planes replaced the roll of thunder and roared low in formation. 'B-52s are still useful warriors,' he said, combing his hair with the practised rigour of vanity. 'They've been refitted to carry up to thirty thousand kilograms of explosives.' He was looking at me so I affected appropriate interest. 'The ideal condition for carpet bombing is a pitch black night,' he continued, 'they can come without warning, they don't need the moon to see. Computers make moonlight redundant. In fact it's a liability. And it only takes half a dozen dedicated B-52s to obliterate a square kilometre of space.'

By the time he handed me the money I was drunk and I put on a display, saying that we'd agreed I was worth more, worth much more, at least twice as much more. My audacity must have been a further entertainment for him but he remained calm and unflinching. I never saw him yield in all my time of knowing him. He was not annoyed, only amused by my little performance. I cried my crocodile tears but I took the money and said that in future I would be strictly timing it.

But of course I never did. I'd never had a benefactor before.

The General strutted in the military way. His chest would puff out and swell and as it inflated it compensated for the otherwise petite stature, the very ordinary lack of height. It was a broad, deep chest, silvered with white hair, a mat protecting the vulnerable pale skin, the pink nipples well marked and precise, like targets. His body was somewhat out of proportion to his chest for it seemed rather too modest in comparison, with the hips too slender, the legs too short, the arms well muscled but likewise stubby, while the hands were almost dainty. His penis was small, uncircumcised and narrow, easily held entire in my mouth even when achingly erect. It was most pliable and responsive. It did not reflect the size of his nose, as cocks are said to do.

For his age he was firm enough, not spilling much flesh, compact for a man fifty-two years old, and horny enough. His age showed in the emerging liver spots, the deep fan of wrinkles from the sides of his eyes, and on his slightly spotty, balding head. It was his fashion to drape strands of hair across his pink pate as a type of disguise. An old-fashioned, mannish, ineffectual thing to do, hinting at the ripe ego so capable of excess. Furthermore, he had his hair dyed the most artificial colour: ink-black. He was wide cheeked and broad nosed, where blood vessels popped and kept popping and edging across the slope of his unblunted cheeks. Arctic-blue eyed. Cold. Cold and staring, and forever engaging in the art of the skirmish.

Even in his private time, that scant time not devoted to making war, the General liked to engage in small hostilities to provide an interesting theatre of action. That's why he liked me from the start. I obliged. Oh, it was natural for me to argue and marshal wits and wisdoms and try to outflank, outmanoeuvre, or to just plain charge into situations. He liked that very much. I obliged. When he bared his teeth in order to smile, it was a ferocious grin, not wide but intent. He had an animal intent and it strained through the imperfect teeth riddled with caries and set edge against edge. In a certain light the General could look merciless and mean, but in the beginning I did not look at him too long or too often in that light.

When we first met things were very difficult for me. The long depression, the tight squeeze for money that only grew daily tighter, and my poor prospects conjoined and I was at a low ebb. Vulnerable. At risk. In the night this vulnerability ate me up as if in preparation for the nightmares which spat me out, minced and mute. It was a cycle I could not shake off and I preferred to find someone rather than lie awake wondering what to do. It was not a hard choice. I was broke. I'd been retrenched. I had no will for scrabbling for the sort of wretched, menial labour that went by the name of work. I was down to the last of my resources. It was poverty.

In my tight red matador pants, an indecently plunging neckline, a loud red hat, and with my rude red lips I defied the bad circumstance and wrangled my way into a swank party at the Department of Insignia Supplies. I needed to find someone to pick up or pickpocket, someone with the prospect of money. I was making the obligatory gestural language and flirting with a self-aggrandising, nicely drunken major who was having trouble seeing beyond my breasts when the General made a surprise appearance flanked by his coterie of men. It was the first time I'd seen him so close by, in the actual flesh. After several minutes a flustered official told me the General wished me to join him. Ushered to a chair on the perimeter of the General's group, I silently finished off a bottle of wine and watched my major stagger away.

After ignoring me the General finally threw a look in my direction. It was the sort of look I knew well. When he walked off I put down my empty glass and followed. The tight little knot of his men followed me. We left the party en masse, trotted down a long, deserted hallway with strange, pallid stains like body outlines on the walls, squeezed one after the other, with the General still leading, through a doorway concealed behind a lurid tapestry commemorating some battle or other in our history, into a poorly lit corridor to a second, heavily padded doorway through which the General disappeared. His clique came to a halt, silently clustering around the door in the postures of sentinels. I remember wondering, as I was ushered through, whether they were keeping a guard against interlopers or interning me. As the door thudded shut behind me I saw that I had entered a veritable maze of doors—army-green, unmarked, identical. Except for the one left slightly ajar. This was my first taste of the General's fondness for the clichés of melodrama.

In an airless room full of furniture transformed by grey dust covers into looming, vaguely unsettling shapes, the General and I conducted business. I sat on the edge of an oval conference table five times the size of an ordinary dining-room table. A feeble yellow light came from an antiquated standing-lamp which made us both look sickly. There were no windows, yet a thick crust of desiccated insects coated the black glass table-top. The thin membranes of their wings were scorched and weightless. The General stood a little way off, inspecting me, his odd-shaped, top-heavy body rocking as he rolled on the balls of his feet. I would come to know that action as a habit of his. After a few moments he broke the silence and said that he had decided to fuck me. He nominated a sum.

I agreed.

He said we would meet for luncheon and an afternoon of carnal pleasure. I alluded to the fact that I did this sort of thing regularly.

I lied. He knew it.

Beginnings can be too simple.

TWO

In the beginning, I liked to spend my earnings sitting in cafes and bars watching the congress of the streets, drinking the brew being passed off as beer and enjoying a decent meal if I could get one. A real bonus had come of my meeting the General. When I was with him I had food and drink that I hadn't a hope of having otherwise. Around about that time something that was supposed to be blackberry jam glutted the market, and for too long it appeared in every guise on every menu. It got so I couldn't stomach the stuff, the smell of it was enough to make me ill. My lunches with the General helped to keep me going in those early days.

There was something else I began to reject with equivalent disgust—the daily newspapers. They were not any worse than the national radio or television I suppose, but regardless of whether the paper was the outrageously propagandising *Liberation's Voice* or the pseudo-intellectualising *Chronicle*, events were so sanitised and censored, so distorted and dis-membered, that huge holes riddled the reports and chasms yawned without explanation between the lines. The most reliable thing was that the papers provided wholly unreliable information based on the mix of military bluff, bald-faced lies, some actual occurrences and pure propaganda. The problem being that the truth, if there were any truth, was from the start impossible to discern. In addition to this, the hysterical exhortations against the enemy numbed me. Page after daily page of the enemy's butchery, lawlessness and inhumanity was more than I cared to stomach.

Rumours and hearsay were as dependable a source of information as the newspapers or official news bulletins, and in the beginning I was avid for even the most uninformed street gossip. But after a while I came to appreciate that there were things I would rather not know. A single turn of phrase or a graphic manner of description could take root and plague the imagination in difficult ways. Besides, passing on gossip in itself became risky, the public mood grew extremely volatile as the war progressed—either jittery and withdrawn, or hysterical and excessive. The time for anything placid or mundane was draining away at a rapid rate. Before long, there was nothing mundane that was not superficial, although for a brief period superficiality flourished as a type of style until it, too, dissolved under the strain of true war.

I had not been surprised when I first discovered people taking bets on the war. It was illegal, but what of it? The small battles and skirmishes drummed up a lively business, like any fight. In the beginning, when the routs were sharp and savage, the results were swift. Then the battles dragged on and it became less easy to predict outcomes. A misery and meanness wafted into the city, settled like a pervasive soot, gradually blackening and distorting everything. It was not sudden. It began little bit by little bit.

The change had not been perceived as serious to those who'd become inured to going without. At first items like chocolate, biscuits, cheese, and fruit began drying up, then luxuries began to vanish. A little while later the supply of necessities became erratic. It happened in the fashion of one thing after another, and another, then all of a sudden there were bouts of multiple disappearances. Hitherto ritzy restaurants and fashionable bars and chic shopping emporiums started to become nervy places. Waves of suspicion at their brazen ostentation, surges of resentment born from the increasing privation of the average citizen, belligerent runs of feeling against any hint of side-stepping the stringencies demanded by the war effort began to lap, then bump, then push against the showy plate-glass windows, and before long those classy windows were boarded over to avoid damage to a dwindling clientele.

It was not until I entered the company of the General that I discovered what luxuries still existed. But it did not take long for this knowledge to become a frustrating titillation—I had money again but there wasn't a great deal worth buying. Shopping was no longer much of an amusement. I stockpiled food because it seemed sensible, but really I preferred to live in the moment as far as circumstances allowed. However, when I went to the stores still operating or to the black market I was always on the lookout for sheer black pantyhose. Each time I met the General I wore a new pair, and each time they were ruined.

He had a passion for black pantyhose and I obliged. He preferred a nude toe and he was especially fond of the sheen that lycra gave. I guessed it carried connotations for him of the sparkle-arkle of cabaret. I left them in hotel rooms—it was my signature, a pair of torn pantyhose forlorn on rumpled beds. He did not even look funny in them. I think they suited him.

He had okay legs, despite the veins. Shapely and firm, not overly muscled, and surprisingly hairless, like an Asian's. But I was the elegant one.

I was the hairy Caucasian.

'We will show the enemy no mercy.' The first time I heard the General say this was during a television broadcast; he was talking about the logic of retribution while looking calmly into the camera, speaking live from some battle location. He was standing before the smoking ruins of a railway station. Twisted carcasses of trains dotted the background like strange butchered animals. Black puffs of smoke clouded the atmosphere. Apparently, trains bringing injured troops home from the front had been demolished in an air attack. To illustrate the carnage, footage was shown of dead and maimed soldiers strewn amidst the wreckage. The footage looked familiar, either I was getting used to carnage or I'd seen that clip before.

The next time I heard the General say those words was the day our association shifted into a new phase—the day I agreed to meet him at 1300 hours every alternate afternoon unless otherwise instructed. He repeated the phrase again. I looked up from unlacing my boots and was caught by his eyes in the dressing-table mirror. Eyes the colour of water lodged way under ice. 'Show no mercy,' I returned. 'Why?' Instead of replying he swung his head away from me in a violent arc and cracked his knuckles. I exaggerated the lean of my body as I bent forward to smooth my pantyhose, thereby revealing my breasts to greater advantage, in case I'd asked a wrong question. I'd come to an early understanding of the tone of some of the General's moments.

'This war is a just war,' he continued. I did not say anything to that. I watched him in the mirror as I began to brush my hair. The static electricity caused it to fan out around my head. The General went and locked the door and returned to me. His hands hovered over my halo of hair. 'A necessary war.'

'A necessary war,' I repeated. I turned to him and smiled into his distance but I avoided holding his gaze by pulling off my boots and flexing my legs and pointing my toes like a dancer. He liked that.

'Do you know why that is so?' he asked. I hated such questions because it was a matter of trying to second-guess him.

'Because the enemy leaves us no choice?' I suggested.

'Because there is nothing more intoxicating than taking the blood of one's enemy.'

I perceived his line of thought and entered into the moment. 'Do you know Kali, the mother of war? She holds a sword and a bowl of blood. She likes to feed from the skulls of her victims after drinking their blood hot from their bodies.'

'Tell me more,' the General demanded.

I dredged up the memory. I had read about the Hindu's Kali in the days when I used to kill time in the library before the libraries had been closed. 'She's a dark goddess who is invoked to make war and to crush enemies. She goes into battle naked except for a necklace of skulls and a belt of severed hands, with nothing more than a sword, but her ferocity and vengeance are unbeatable. She has four arms and three eyes, one eye here,' I gestured to the middle of my forehead, 'and is the bringer of death and the dancer of destruction. She dances on top of her consort Shiva who lies like a corpse beneath her.'

'She dances on top of his penis,' whispered the General.

I continued with not a little malice. 'She also dances on

men's bellies and bites off their penises then slurps up their intestines. She eats their organs like spaghetti. She has sharp white teeth and a long red tongue which lolls out of her mouth with which she licks the corpses clean.'

'Where did you see her?'

The lie was easy. 'I've dreamt of her.'

'And did she speak to you?' I hesitated. He seemed to take my hesitation as assent, for he mumbled, 'I knew it. You've got the look of knowing it,' then he drew me to him by placing the tips of his fingers on my shoulders and swooped upon my mouth, biting my bottom lip, his tongue worming inside. 'You are absolutely morbid,' he breathed. 'Now you've given me a hard-on.'

He removed his uniform with the usual elaborate care while I found the bottle and poured out a measure. It was a proper American bourbon, something I'd not had in a long time. I swallowed it greedily and generously dipped my nipples in the spirit so he could take his drink from me the way he liked. As I put him to suck I delicately patted his bobbing head, careful not to get too much of the oil sculpting his hair on my hands. The scent of it would seep into the skin of my fingers and I loathed the smell of it. At once both sweet and bitter, it left a taste like marzipan in my mouth. A taste I detested.

'Dance on top of me,' he directed. I knew what he wanted. I slid down on him and began my rhythmic movements. His eyes fluttered shut and he held himself deathly still, his hands splayed at his sides. This would become one of the General's favourite positions, me above, him prone beneath me. I did not especially like the corpse pose, as he amusingly called it, for it was hard work and he would lie there passively letting me do my dance on him. He would even sometimes make me dust his skin with a white powder to heighten the effect. With practice he learnt to sustain his pose for a considerable length of time, but sometimes the fantasy would dislodge and he would grip me and fuck me in a wholly lively manner, ruining his pretence at morbidity.

The first time, staying still was impossible for him. A hand crept into the cleft of my buttocks and doodled with my arse. The growing insistence of his fingers suggested what he would want next. I lifted myself off him and cheekily danced over to the table and picked up his gold-brocaded military cap. I never once played with his uniform, it was sacrosanct. Then I splashed myself liberally with the bourbon and went over to the bed, flopping down upon it on my hands and knees, wiggling my hips and beckoning to him with the round of my arse. The General was behind me in a flash, his tongue lapping up the trails of liquor. I propped my head in my hands and squirmed. 'Show no mercy, sir, show no mercy.' Working him into a frenzy. He had just mounted me when I heard an alarm sounding.

Air raid?

I was all for stopping and getting under the furniture but the awful keening noise served only to increase the General's ardour. As he continued to thrust into me he began to holler loudly, 'Kill the enemy! Kill the goddamn enemy!' He was on top of me, in me, holding me tight, I was unable to get away from the yelling. My ear began to reverberate with the noise, it was like he was entering my head. But I did not want the words he was forcing inside of me. I did not want to have to think the way he wanted me to.

The enemy.

The monstrous.

A twinning which occurred easily, as if attended by grace. The type of grace which issues from surety. I'd watched people at the public rallies snarling and spitting and raging at the enemy as if in a delirium. I'd felt the lure of it, the security it gave. I could see how it could make us feel that whatever the losses, the sacrifices, the privations, we would never become as cursed, as reduced, as unnatural, as inhuman as the enemy.

How easy to yell, Kill the enemy! How seductive to split off self from other. Easy rhetoric. Easy, to name the other, that which is not a part of ourselves, that which is inhumanly human. But it wasn't so easy to shake off the bad feeling, a kind of dread, that moved through me when the General held me beneath him and screamed death at the enemy. For I could not help but feel that somewhere someone else was also yelling, Kill the enemy! Kill the goddamn enemy! And I could not help knowing that the voice was yelling at me.

At the foe that had been made of me.

THREE

The General gave me more money than I'd had in a long time. I couldn't believe my luck.

Money money money money money.

Money mattered. The war did not stop making it matter, at least that's what I thought then. It didn't matter that there was less to buy, I was at the stage where money was pure intoxication. At first I kept it in a big red biscuit tin with a picture of a parrot on the lid. I liked to take it out and lay the notes down in a trail across the floor, a circle of money spiralling out further and further around me, then choose which denominations to spend, as if it were a game. In the beginning I hadn't expected anything more than to go from one meeting with the General to the next, if there was going to be a next. I was flattered when he used the words 'we' and 'us'. As our meetings became regular, I'd still wake in the nights, the nightmares not abated by his patronage.

If he did not bring me solace he brought me money, and for that I did not have to play at being grateful.

I kept my counsel. No-one knew the true source of my new

prosperity. When I went out, dressed up, at the same time every second day my neighbours correctly divined there was a man. When a military car began dropping me back home, sometimes well and truly inebriated, that clinched the matter. I let the gossips natter, paid my rent in advance, got rid of my debts and kept to myself, as I always did. I had various acquaintances—drinking buddies and fuck-buddies were easy enough to come by, especially when I was prepared to buy them drinks. It was routine to find someone new for a day or a night, or a week at most. I avoided the lure of true friendship. A lethal hook lurked in friendship, it was a nasty way for the war to dig inside of you, loosening your own chances of sanity, not to mention survival, when it disappeared the people you cared about.

People like Sol. But then Sol had never been a friend, he and I had been lovers from the start.

It had been too long since I'd seen Sol when I encountered the General, and perhaps the hole of his absence was as much a reason for my susceptibility to the General's extended invitation to fuck him as was my idea of adventure, any other inclination of my nature, or the dire press of poverty. I told myself it would have been impossible to have refused the General, in any case. I told myself it made sense to jump on the gravy train. I told myself that I knew better than to try to sop up the jagged nights with the panacea of one person. Given the opportunity I would have wanted Sol to be that person, but the war had swept away our possibility for togetherness and I had to go about the business of my life.

Sol. Another smooth-skinned man, but a young man, a secret man, with secrets residing in the hoods of his eyes and the careful movements of his body. He was much taller than the General but more slender, with a subtle musculature and a Latin beauty which he liked to accent by wearing black. He was extremely beautiful, for instance, when he smoked, which seemed to be constantly, languidly embroidering the air with his cigarette. Smoke wreathed him and described him, he was as intangible to me as smoke. When I held him I could never seem to hold his substance; I only briefly held his smell, his taste, his shape, his cries and moans, his textures and colours.

I absorbed all these things with eagerness and pleasure, it was my way of loving him, and it ought to have given him to me but he was never fully mine. Sol could not give himself over to me. I think my desire to possess him was incomprehensible to him and it did not make it any easier for me to express my feelings to him. Telling myself that his allure was a chemical attraction, nothing more, did not help either, and Sol succeeded in doing what no other person had done—he rendered me romantic and needy. There were times when I was, frankly, desperate for him. A desperation born of, but wider than, ordinary carnal desire.

I remember the first time I saw him—he was sitting in the corner of a slummy bar I was working in, an awful bar on Bernanos Street where we diluted the wine with so much water we had to add vinegar for taste and were told not to concern ourselves with the origin or composition of the raw poison sold under the guise of spirits. He was reading a newspaper and smoking and nursing his one drink so slowly it was painful. I was tending the bar, one of those short-lived, appallingly paid jobs that involve fending off the manager, and it was one of those nights that drag one down with the tedium of it all. It was an unusually quiet night. I don't remember it as an ominous night. More like a lull. No portent of what was coming.

After I watched him a while I gave him a come-on smile and slipped him a free drink, and he shied like a nervous animal. But he was waiting for me outside when I finished my shift. He was not much more than a shifting shadow, the tip of his cigarette glowing to show me where he was.

My movement towards him and his remove from me was in us from the beginning. To have met one week, even just one night, earlier might have made a difference. As it was, I'd decided I wanted him by the time that drink slid across the table from me to him. That first night I would have taken him in a gutter, even though the air was bright with cold, but no sooner had we started walking close together, our bodies brushing up against one another then bouncing away in the awkward dance that seduction can be, than people began running out of their houses and congregating under streetlights, hurrahing and hugging and shattering the brittle night with jubilant bursts of gunfire; revving the engines of their cars and tearing around the streets, blowing their horns. Making the first sounds of war.

War.

The General had just announced it. An unscheduled live telecast.

War.

Like everybody else I'd been aware of it as a possibility, but the reality of it was unreal. Total strangers embracing in the streets in an impromptu carnival of congratulation. Bullets showering their noise upon us, raucous outpourings into the gaping yawn of sky. As the crowd tugged and yelled at us Sol stopped bumping against me and hunched deeper still into his black greatcoat. He said nothing, his breath fuming with one cigarette after another. I had the strongest sense of him moving away from me but before he could lose himself in the crowd I took the bottle of wine that someone had launched at me with a sloppy kiss, batted away a groping hand and grabbed the sleeve of Sol's coat, yelling, 'Run!' So we ran.

That night was the beginning of Sol's running. I didn't know this at the time. I instinctively knew that if I didn't take him home with me that night I would lose him. I tugged him through the streets to my hostel, forcing the wine into him as we went, not trying to make conversation except to say inane things like 'It's not far now,' and 'Almost there.' Our breaths steamed and mingled. When I took him up the four flights of stairs to my poky room, he sat on my unruly bed and lit a cigarette and offered it to me. 'I don't smoke,' I said.

'I don't believe in this war,' he said. I took a swig from the bottle of wine and passed the last of it to him, then threw off my overcoat and rummaged around in the closet that represented the kitchen. I found two tiny carrots, a tin of beetroot, a packet of two-minute noodles and a wilted stick of celery. Luckily, some rough red in a recycled plastic wine bladder.

'Relax. Take your coat off,' I told him, pouring the wine. He kept his coat on but sat down on the edge of my bed, a sufficiently intimate gesture. 'What you believe in is your business.' I handed him a glass of wine. 'Are you hungry? I'm afraid I don't have much to eat.'

He shrugged, watching me in such an absorbed, curious manner that I was suddenly self-conscious. My hair felt dirty. 'I don't even know your name,' I said. I yanked back my hair and twisted it into a knot at my neck while attempting to look casual.

'Does it matter?'

'Not if you don't want it to. Are you in the army?'

He drained his glass in one gulp, his face gleaming with an obscure satisfaction. He was perhaps becoming a little drunk. I, too, took the wine like medicine, it was that awful.

'No.'

'You'll be expected to join up.' I refilled his glass.

He drank again. 'Yes.'

'Unless you're sick or disabled or otherwise exempted.' I was probing

'I'm not sick.' His smile was a little bit crooked. Very bitter. 'Or disabled. And I don't think they'll exempt me.'

'Then they'll conscript you.' He didn't reply, he looked intently at me. 'I won't report you if you won't join up, if that's what you're thinking,' I said. 'I'm no-one's keeper. It's your decision to be part of it or not. It's up to you.' The ash from his cigarette fell to the floor. I walked over to him and slowly rubbed it into the threadbare carpet with my foot.

He dropped his cigarette into a glass of water on my bed-side table and placed the flat of his hands against my thighs and said in a low voice, 'Choice doesn't seem to enter into it.'

I pressed into his palms and the trail of tobacco scent led me towards his mouth. His arms encircled my hips and reached around my arse. 'No,' I whispered, falling into him, 'there are times when it doesn't.'

Sol's running dictated the terms of my waiting and I accepted that.

Waiting. To express my feeling for him with my body.

When I was on top of him, holding him, taking him, opening myself, I felt empowered, full of the feeling of loving him, loving the grip of his hands, the tone of his voice, the curve of him around me. But I was afraid of making such an admission of feeling. It was not in my nature to reveal too much of myself, but even so, I would have, if Sol very early on hadn't told me that he didn't believe in romantic love. He said it wasn't a motivation for togetherness, it was a rationalisation for it. In the beginning, it represented a type of challenge to me, to get him to admit to loving me in the romantic way.

When prodded, Sol called our love a sexual love or a comradely love and my attempt at romance was neatly defeated. If I inadvertently used the word 'love', without sufficient qualification, it could cause a withdrawal in him. Not necessarily a physical withdrawal, although there were times when this was so. I became sensitive to his manner of distancing himself from me if I became maudlin or sentimental about him. It was one of the first necessary lessons in loving him.

When I made love with Sol my orgasm was explosive and violent, whereas he came quietly, almost passively. I came in a loud gush of sound that I did not make when I was with others. The General, for example, did not know these noises of mine. With Sol, I came so loudly that we joked about it at first. But when his running began in earnest, my explosions would be muzzled by his hand, and afterwards my jaw would ache from the intensity of the pressure. It was one of our many unspoken agreements. We never talked about it, nor did I ever draw his attention to the soft yellow bruises those pressures sometimes created. If he saw them he ignored them. I wondered if he thought them crude evidence of some other part of my life, a life hidden from him.

And that was before there was something to hide.

In the beginning, when we said our goodbyes, tears would pool in my eyes despite my best intentions, and there were occasions when Sol must have been exhausted with the loneliness or nerviness of his circumstances, for there were one or two times when he said I could stay with him. I would think of his life: on the run, hand to mouth, hidey-holes, and fear. It was not a clear-cut issue but I was afraid of living like that. There was no guarantee that I would be able to stay with him and I wanted to believe that I had a better alternative than running. Besides, before I could even frame a possible yes, Sol would be staring at his wristwatch as if it might tell him something more than the time, or inclining his head away from me, listening to a sound only he could hear, or smoothing away all traces of our presence from the place where we had met. Getting on with the business of leaving.

'No,' I would say, 'I can help you more the way it is.'

It was a lie. He knew it.

And in the time after the General, it became easier to tell that lie because part of me wanted the easy solutions that seemed to come from being with the General, and, like a neat betrayal, that part kept carrying me back to him.

FOUR

The General had a theory that war was in the vital interests of the State. Furthermore, he assured me, it was by far the best antidote for a recession. Resources were properly dedicated; industry became revitalised and started to grow; employment went up, both at home and in the field; national advancement and prosperity were at last given a decent chance; personal and national pride were recovered; and hope for a better future reasserted itself. 'A true war gives people something to circle around and cling to,' he concluded. 'It gives them something to replace their own pettiness with. A true war forges the nation because the people pull together and learn to stand against a true enemy. And the people are thus reunited.'

As he spoke, his hand was resting very lightly on the small of my naked back, not much more than a hint of a touch, and we were looking down eight stories from the shatter-proof window onto a street full of drones below. I could feel the cool metal of his signet ring against my skin. 'Unfortunately, in any situation there are always drones,' he said in a sorrowful tone, 'which is why a grand design is required. Along with the wherewithal to see it through. It is why conscription is essential, it's not usually until people are pushed right up against the moment of life or death that they come to realise what their higher purpose is.' As if illustrating this moment, the General propelled me against the window, pressing my face and breasts against the glass. I shut my eyes to avert the feeling of vertigo. 'And drones are dangerous for everybody. They are parasites, sucking the lifeblood out of the nation.'

As for me, I was not a drone. I was too clever to be a drone. We were both too clever to be drones. Which is why we were looking down safely from the secure hotel window, fogging the clear clean space with our breaths. The pressure of his hand eased and I opened my eyes and stepped away from the window. The General raised his glass and toasted our reflections in the glass. 'To our bright and glorious future,' he said. I obediently drank. 'Now take off the rest of your clothes and dance,' he ordered.

I left on the sheer black pantyhose he liked and the stiletto shoes I liked, and with the rest of me bare I danced a type of goose-step, throwing my legs high into the air. And I pranced a little, like a mare on parade. He liked that and called me filly, in honour of my legs. After he'd rolled down my pantyhose and had me step out of my showgirl shoes he put me on the bed and his fingers drummed on my pubic bone and his mouth tramped to where it liked to camp.

When the General had finished he was in a good humour and ravenous, and he ordered up a huge lunch. The wine was clean and crisp and delicious but for some reason I had little appetite. While he ate I was drawn back to the window by the sound of a commotion down in the street. People were applauding as platoons of soldiers marched by, row after row stepping in synchronised time with one another, their weapons gleaming and ready. It had become a familiar sight, soldiers marching in formation through the city in impressively timed public demonstrations of how an army worked.

Myths of heroes erupt out of certain processes. Like the process of conducting a war. Or the process of creating one. Legendary battles and heroic deeds were trawled through the public consciousness and became bigger, more grandiose than ever. History was revised; sometimes a whole new dimension was uncovered, lost outcomes were discovered, vibrant new tones were added, a manner of speaking about us as a warrior nation was recovered. Heroes were not allowed to languish, much less be lost to the ignominy of a forgotten or defeated past.

A new department was created, the Department of Historical Warfare, and its sole task was to reinvigorate our military history, put a new gloss on it and instruct us about its contemporary relevance. It was unbelievable, the plethora of anniversary editions of newspapers celebrating the victories of our warrior past. It was wearying, the endless loops of educative discourse that dominated the radio and the television, those venerable organs of government. The Department was responsible for coining the most absurd daily aphorisms, such as 'The past battle is the present victory', and 'Strategy springs from what was, not what is', and these were transmitted at maddeningly regular intervals over the media, like flood or fire alerts, except that they were not in any way remotely useful. The initial entertainment value soon wore off. As if to complement this extravagance, screeds of unsourced military statistics would scroll across the bottom of our television screens, interrupting our patriotic dramas and melodramas and fighting with the erratic onslaughts of static.

Overnight, portraits of the war's living heroes and dead martyrs—there being a constant movement from one status to the other—invaded the city. A massive operation must have been mounted, for one morning I awoke to find the entire city decorated. Posters had been plastered on the sides of buildings, along walls and fences, over billboards, anywhere there was a good, common vantage point. Before long, small shrines began appearing beneath the bloated images and all manner of offerings were made—a plastic flower, a child's fluffy toy, a lit candle, a cooking pot, a china ornament, a smoking stick of incense, a handful of nails, a bicycle chain, bits of clothing, a book, food occasionally, polaroids of the devotees often. Certain entrepreneurs did not take long to set themselves up in the business of taking snaps of those who wanted to add their faces to this mob of heroes and patriots.

Naturally, the General's portrait appeared foremost amongst this elite crowd. Larger than the rest; our most heroic hero enlarged, airbrushed, enhanced, more regal than he was in actuality—but for all that, it wasn't a bad likeness. The photographer had captured the effect of the General's eyes upon one—they followed you no matter where you stood in relation to the image.

It was almost enough to make one feel paranoid.

When I could not answer many of the questions put to me about military history the General lectured me on some of the crucial points my education was lacking. 'At Rivoli in 1797, Bonaparte routed forty-five thousand Austrians with an army of less than half that size. Twenty thousand French crushed the Austrians, who fled leaving eight thousand of their men dead.

It was a case of bravado and brains at Rivoli. Bravado and brains. One without the other is useless, because what matters above all is the commitment to the elected outcome and that takes—'

'Bravado and brains,' I finished dutifully. He rewarded me by untying the knot in the army dress belt lashing my feet to the leg of a heavy chair—a little game of his. I remained secured by my wrists to another chair which pulled my arms over and behind my head. The floor was getting to feel hard under my buttocks and spine and I was at the stage of wanting the circulation back in all of my extremities but the General hadn't finished my lesson yet. 'How many dead French did that leave?' I asked. The General ignored my question. I twisted my wrists in their bind and counted the cracks in the white paint of the ceiling directly in my line of vision.

I had counted nineteen cracks before he spoke again. 'We are going to achieve something equally sensational,' he said. 'We may sustain some minimal damage, but their losses …' His words trailed off as his gaze riveted on something outside. By lifting my head I saw that he was admiring a spectacular flare tearing up the sky.

'Their losses' I prompted. I wanted school to be out, I'd learned enough for one day.

He returned his attention to me. 'Will be critical, but nicely contained. Our theatre of operations has been divided into a grid of killing boxes. These boxes are several kilometres wide and the same again long, in which we will localise the enemy and pound them to pieces.'

'Can you really contain a war as neatly as that?'

'Absolutely,' he said, the immaculately shining toes of his boots resting inches away from the curve of my hip. I resisted the urge to flinch. Then he knelt and inclined his body over me in an excited manner and whispered, 'We have recently acquired some of the most sophisticated killing machines you could possibly imagine.'

I can't recall exactly when the noise of the wind became the howl of a frightened man. Or a crazed woman. When the noise that seemed something far more sinister than a noise of nature began to visit the city at night. Always at night. It would start when night had split into morning, but it was black morning, the unilluminated earliest beginning of morning when there was no hint of the light that was due to come. I would lie awake listening for it to start, or else the sound would enter my sleep and wake me. I would hear whatever it was screaming and tossing branches onto roofs, ripping up tiles, throwing stones, yanking at the windows, scrabbling at the doors. Tearing at whatever lay in its path, a dizzying, rushing path of dark air and slamming forces, by turns hot like the breath from some thing's mouth, and cold like the temperature of a corpse.

Sleep would never return when the noise was bad like that and I gave up the attempt to reclaim my difficult slumber, or the pretence that those howls did not affect me. If I was not alone I'd stay put and try to find solace in the shape of the body next to me. If I was alone I'd light a candle to give some form to the shadows, and pour myself a little drink, and when I became more used to the noise I would snuff out the candle and press against the glass of the window and look at what was out there. Because of electricity rationing there was no city light at that hour and a chink of the sky between my hostel and the building next door would be starkly revealed. I would sometimes see the luminous curve of the moon and the bright blot of Venus, the love planet.

The sign of Venus, the sign of woman.

The sign of Mars, the sign of man.

Love and war.

And fear? What sign is fear?

I do remember the afternoon I went to the Long End Battle cemetery. It was soon after I had agreed to meet with the General on a regular basis. He'd even had his adjutant draw up an agreement to that effect, including a clause on non-disclosure, which amused me. It was the day I signed the contract that I went to the cemetery. I went largely out of an obscure desire to observe the General perform in his public capacity knowing that, only hours before, I had been taking his semen from him with my adept fingers. It was a foolish reason for going. It was also my first time at a graveside, in those days I was still a stranger to the ceremonies of death.

This observance occurred with the sort of pomp and circumstance which did not attend many of the ensuing deaths in that war. I should not have gone. I should have disobeyed the General's order that I attend the ceremony for the latest delivery of martyrs. Despite the solid presence of his men. Despite the careful manicuring of plots and the discreetly draped flags over coffins and the tombstones of dark, engraved granite and the simple white crosses and the masses of floral tributes and wreaths. Despite the mix of mourners and sightseers marking the first big burial in our war. Despite all this funereal normalcy, I got the whiff of something not normal.

Something that reminded me of the noise that was not the wind.

A terrible odour came to me as I stood in my new black dress watching coffins being unloaded into the ground, and with the smell I heard the rustle of something in the waiting holes. I heard something start to turn and shift. And what I was smelling was the decay of that field of corpses. And mixed in with the horrific stench of rotting was something even more terrible, a sense that the ground itself was hungry, that the earth was reaching for the corpses with an awful hunger.

Yes, hunger.

I thought the smell and the terror that came with it would have been palpable, that all those mourning about me would have been overwhelmed and panicked, but they stayed mulish and numb around the fresh graves, right in the path of the smell. At that juncture, a shadow began to crawl across the bright surface of the sun. As the light dulled I broke rank, pummelling a path through the crowd, rushing out through those cemetery gates as fast as I could, not caring where I was going. I suppose the assumption was that I had gone to bury a loved one and grief had overwhelmed me. I did not care what my departure looked like. I did not look back and I did not stop running.

I kept going until I found a wholly different crowd, inside a bar, the sort of company that smelled human and was lively and made the panic go away, after a drink or two. But when I ventured out again, drunkenly clinging to the arm of a woman who had invited me home, she led me straight back to the circle of the General. He was at the head of a slow-moving military parade forging a path from the graveyard directly into the heart of the clamouring city.

FIVE

He dreams of the Hindu Kali. He opens his eyes and sees her standing before him stuffing men's guts into her mouth. The goddess grins and winks him a smile and he has an instant recognition—he is her consort. He shivers, hot flush of happiness, thick gurgle of strength. Those hands of hers are engaged in the essential business of the cosmos: one hand is snaking food into the cavernous pleasuring mouth, ribbons of intestines—human—slipping squashy through blood-wet fingers; another hand gracefully slices apart the air with a marvellous razor-edged sword; in yet another net of fingers a hangman's noose dangles; while in her fourth hand there waves a flower, a heavy fleshy lotus. The perfume of it shudders through his frame and he recognises the moment of godhood.

He must embrace it.

Quickly.

He kneels on singing knees and his body cracks in adoration. Beauteous vision, the Lady who eats men the way carrion are scavenged, a manner of scavenging he knows well, the manner of it recalled from his seasons of battle, but now there is a new ecstasy: the image of her mouth plunging for the softest parts.

Oh succulent interiors! Oh eating!

In his new hunger he decrees that his Kali will have food and food and more food.

He will match her blade and bowl.

He is bread and blood.

He is the mark on the mountain.

He knows sacrifice, he has yielded, he is the necessary one, the one who has been chosen, the one whose warrior-roaring will roll out and out across the smudged white whispering ash of memory.

He has laboured and amassed his weapons for this moment; he has had visions of wider and wider rivers of blood surging and swelling, coursing through his battlefields, those grounds whetted with her sacred kiss. The stench of his battles have called her to him. She will move unencumbered amongst the carnage he will create, as she, reinvigorated, remembered, reinvoked, reconstituted and abetted with blood, stoops to eat, eat and eat more.

Her pot-belly pokes out at him, lascivious bulge, and he promises her that her appetite will not defeat him. He will heap her tables until they groan; he will pile up meat, mounds upon mounds of it, steaming platters straining with his gift to her, berserker guardian angel who has reared over him in visions, across continents, her tireless shadow moving over him relentless as sea and as slow, or as fast.

He has survived outrageous fortunes of war, he has held down posts in danger of desertion and enemy takeover, he has medals to show her.

He calls to her now with the jingle on his chest. The flap of war medallions has a strange tune: the rattle of bones shaking, the clap of cannon, the shriek of jets, the music of bombers, the rain of shrapnel and Gator bombs and fuel-air explosives and mustard gas and nerve gas and napalm and anthrax and a plague, hissing down.

He wakes from his dream, for once frightened.

SIX

Mars is not my god but I found his stamp on me.

It was a spring day. Still unseasonably cold, although what would once have been unseasonable no longer applied because the seasons did not mean anything anymore. But it was a rare, beautiful day, just like a spring day would have been—unblemished light; clear, cerulean sky; the subtle perfume of warmth; a sense that a change was coming. The smell of smoke was there, faintly, not enough to clog the air. Electricity and gas rationing having long ago started, it had been a time without much warmth for a lot of people. Wood for fuel was at a premium. Gardens had been savaged and the municipal trees had all disappeared. Nearly every bit of wood, be it a choice dead branch or the still-living part of a tree, had been harvested for burning. Everything edible was eagerly eaten and birds that had not ended up in cooking pots had long left the city. It was unlikely they would make a return. It was yet another thing amiss with our spring—the silence instead of the song of birds.

Yes, it had been an unseasonably hard winter.

I had fared better than many others but I, too, was wanting heat and brightness and the day seemed to promise that. It was one of my days for meeting the General and we met at a non-descript place, in a bed I suspected contained fleas. However I was not in a mood to complain, I was lazily savouring a whisky, post-coitus, warming my skin in a runnel of sunlight, feeling relatively relaxed. The General was wandering about the room wearing my petticoat—in addition to his penchant for pantyhose he liked to dress in something I had worn, not always underwear, but we began with the underwear and graduated to the outer garments. It necessitated me buying clothes larger than my usual size and I mourned my change of style. I preferred tight, hugging clothes that were a comfort in the way they held me, sheathing and contouring my body.

The General liked to spend a little while wearing my clothing after fucking, if he was not already wearing it. He rarely, if ever, washed afterwards, and the smell of my sex on his body would mingle with the cologne that scented my clothing. These smells would cling to him after he returned to his own, always immaculate, uniform. The General assured me that he was not debased, he was merely absorbing the essence of my femaleness. He realised it was an essence he could never have and that he could only emulate. I smiled and said nothing, I was not unfamiliar with the ways in which men sought to taste the female or conjure the feminine.

On that day, the General was preoccupied with something. He kept staring first at one hand, then the other. He stepped into the shaft of sun to better examine what was fascinating him, obliging me to move out of his shade. 'Hold the palm of your hand like this,' he demanded, extending a hand towards me and cupping his palm a little as if he were holding something fragile and precious, 'and tell me what you see.' I pushed my hand into the pour of light and curled my fingers and stared into the palm of my left hand. My right hand was busy holding my drink. As I manoeuvred my hand, folds of skin formed a fleshy network of lines. 'Well?' he insisted, 'What do you see?'

An answer was required. The General liked it when I got things right. 'It's a definite shape.' I wiggled my fingers and the skin of my palm coalesced and it was easy to see. 'The letter M. A capital letter M?'

He applauded. 'Nicely observed. M meaning what, do you suppose?'

'M for missile?' I joked. He chuckled and shook his head. No. 'M for military?' I joked again.

'Close,' he said. 'But that's not it. M is for Mars.'

'The planet?'

'The god of war.' He struck the middle of his palm with his fist. The sound lingered as his fist rested. 'The centre of the hand is dedicated to Mars, the place where the weapon is held. Here.'

I curled my palm again. My life line and my heart line and my head line converged in the symbol of war. I traced the letter M which I had never in my life noticed before. It was plainly apparent. 'Does every soldier believe that?' I asked.

He smiled at me. 'I don't think every soldier knows that.'

I put down my drink and curled my right hand. Yes, there it was, the mark of Mars. Not as clear as in my left hand, but still there. 'They probably think of something like that though, when they use their weapons,' I said, 'it would stop them from thinking of something else.'

'What else?'

'M for murder,' I quipped. 'Or M for madness.'

He laughed at that. 'Mars has been a forgotten god. But a part of you belongs to him, a part of you always will. Regardless of your jokes.'

'Are you reviving him?' I asked.

'No, no. I alone cannot awaken a god,' he replied. 'I am a humble warrior. My duty is to make war. To draw together the forces that will be victorious.'

'But if Mars is a god of war, then making a war might make the god,' I retorted. I was teasing him.

'I enjoy your cleverness,' he said, 'but you will come to understand there is more to war than cleverness.'

Operation Ignition was launched with a swiftness which did not faze the media and bulletins were spewed forth in the usual frenzy, keeping us informed. In fact, one of the outcomes of Operation Ignition was the final merging of all news and media services into something imaginatively called the Department of Reportage. Not only that, Operation Ignition introduced people to BDAs (bomb damage assessments), SPDs (significant population displacements), PPs (penetration points), CBIs (cross-border incursions), MSLs (mobile Scud launchers), S&Ds (search and destroys) and a host of other military terms, whilst fortifying our positions and improving our kill rates. Apparently Operation Ignition was the hors-d'oeuvre of the conflict.

The General had obtained some high-tech defence suppression and infrared detection equipment on a line of credit from a nameless ally, and this was nicely affecting the show.

All over the city, an hysterical jubilation attended the diarrhoeic reports of our successful sorties and strikes. During the height of all the hoopla and fancy side-stepping as to the actual outcome of our offensive the General informed me that he had decided to write his memoirs. 'The present must be invigorated by the past in order to surpass it,' he told me. 'Once, strategy may have simply been a General's skill in the tactical and operational art of warfare, but this war is far greater than a military event.'

'What could be greater than a military event?' I asked, tongue in cheek.

'The defining moment.'

'Of our people?' I guessed.

'Of our entire being,' he replied. 'This is the Kali Yuga, the age of iron.'

'Kali? What happened to Mars?'

'This is her age,' he smiled. One of his animal smiles. 'And I have been chosen to be her amanuensis.'

'Why is that?' I asked.

'I am her consort.' I must have shown my surprise for he smiled again, this time indulgently. 'My dream invoked her.' He felt my breast. 'As did yours. We have both been chosen, as you well know.'

It was easy enough to engage in a little pseudo-necrophilia as a sex game but I was uncertain as to how to play at being the General's partner in a fully fledged delusion. What was I expected to do?

As if on cue he breathed, 'Dance on me. Dance the way only you can.'

So I danced on him, almost eagerly, to avoid any further discussion in case there were other, less easy solutions to the situation. Fortunately, he did not speak of Kali again and I decided that my dancing was what he required of me.

*

The General took advantage of a lull in Operation Ignition to embark upon the first of his research tours. His dual mission was to invigorate our men at the front and conduct personal interviews with those who'd had successful meeting engagements with the enemy. He was sensitive to the fact that his memoirs might lack the vibrancy of first-hand accounting. Before the General left he felt it necessary to reassure me that although we had entered a fluid situation, our position was one of quantifiable safety. After toasting to the continuation of this safety, I picked up the champagne and went out the French windows onto the balcony of the hotel room where we had enjoyed a lunch of smoked salmon and Waldorf salad and watched as the General's car swallowed him, the street swallowed the car, the city swallowed the street, and the soft ash that had recently begun to infiltrate the sky ate the city. Falling like snow, except that it was soft and dark and composed of some burnt thing that kept fluttering about.

Each time a breeze blew from the direction of the fighting in the west, panes of glass weakened by the reverberation of the distant bombardments would fall without warning, making a tinkling sound that sounded perversely happy at first, until the days were attended by the skin-crawling dissonance of shattering glass. It was not the howling wind of night that brought this but one that began deceptively gently then soared in, dumping payloads of ash, covering the city in soot, strangling the asthmatics. A breeze that would not relent and became a harsh misery of grey blowing over us until there were no clear clean spaces left anywhere at all. This lack of visibility may have been a fortuitous event for the military, but in all other respects people considered it a bad finish to a bad winter, despite the difficulty of predicting what the season really was.

It was during Operation Ignition that the light became tinged with a peculiar burned-out orange hue. As if something huge somewhere were steadily glowing, letting off a monotonous throbbing colour that began washing across the sky bit by bit, until there became, by slow degree, less difference between the colour of night and day, insinuating that summer was indeed on its way. The new difference between day and night lay in the intensity of colour: daytime watered the orange down to a shade of tangerine-tinged pink, while nighttime lent to it the soft cast of oxidising iron. The change happened gradually and it was not as unnerving as one might think, it was one of the many changes occurring then, one of the many things which one was helpless to do anything about.

With the colour came the smell.

Acrid, burning, disgusting.

Something charred, rolled up in the wind. Flaring our noses and surging into our sinuses like fever. It was this smell that fuelled fears of a poison gas attack and created the first mass panic, a situation which required the deployment of troops for the reinstatement of civil order. It was later determined that death due to friendly-fire was the only morbid outcome of the smell. But after the smell's occurrence, officially described as the result of strategic burn-off, the fear persisted, people paid vastly inflated prices for gas masks, and in a suddenly fashionable display of safety went about with a mask at all times. The gas mask itself became a statement of fashion, and before long the gas mask carrying kit became an accessory, just like a pair of shoes or a money-belt.

The kit even became a rather chic item. Of course not everybody could obtain a personal gas mask and a mask became something more than a premium for survival against a possible chemical attack. It advertised the owner as having a certain status. It could even be dangerous going about alone in certain quarters carrying one's kit, advertising one's vulnerability to black-market racketeers, so I managed my own protection, selling masks I obtained from one of my fuck-buddies in military supplies and promoting them through a contact on the black market.

I believed I had a sort of immunity when I went out walking.

I considered myself anonymous. Cut off.

Protected.

The General would return from his research forays to the front with a car boot full of signed statements, an attaché case full of used micro-cassettes, and a laptop laden with data. He would deal with the urgent business of war, then he would lock himself and his research paraphernalia in his writing room. A room furnished the same no matter where he situated himself: two desks, two chairs, two desk lamps, a jar of lead pencils, an array of electronic equipment, a printer, reams of pale grey military-issue paper, a paper shredder, two camp beds, two pillows, two space blankets, and his adjutant. He left strict instructions not to be disturbed except for regular meals and essential military matters. The adjutant plugged the keyholes with shredded documents and started transcribing tapes and there the two of them stayed, insular and inviolate.

The General's mission to write his memoirs coincided with

another shift in relations between us. A soldier would arrive at my hostel at any hour of the day or night, or I would arrive home and see the car and find the soldier waiting for me in it with the message that my attendance was required. I would be advised to pack a bag and I would be taken to whichever hotel had been designated as the General's abode. This new arrangement eclipsed the lunchtime rendezvous. I was, effectively, on call but I did not necessarily get to see the General upon a summons.

During his time with his adjutant I had to stay put in the General's rooms. During this time I was not allowed to leave for any reason whatsoever. It was made clear that waiting was expected of me. It was only after I offhandedly remarked that I preferred being in a room with a view that any selectivity seemed to enter the process. The one essential element in the proceedings being, of course, that it be a place easily made secure. It was for the General's protection that the hotel was situated in a residential area. This, combined with the random pattern of his movements to ensure he was not in any one place long enough to become an easy target, meant that I never knew what view awaited me when the General's man came for me. I learnt fairly quickly that the most sordid places could often be the most secure. After being driven to the location and shaken down and ushered by the usual censorious bevy of soldiers into whichever elite suite or crummy rooms the General would be occupying, I would drink and wait.

I paraded before hotel staff, his men, unshuttered windows. I took an infantile pleasure in trailing my legs across a sofa as I hooked a young soldier with the bait of an unlit cigarette. I never did smoke. A trace of phosphorus hovered as I blew out the wavering matches close to their faces. My perfume slicked over them like a shroud. They did not see that. Yet I could see how white their bones were beneath their stiff composure, how brittle, how fragile, how impermanent.

The deal was, I had to be ready the moment the General came at me. A bull. Sleepless, unwashed, unkempt, horny. I knew those times. So did his men, they turned awkwardly away, not at all at ease. I knew to go for the cock first off. The smell of it filling the room as I hunted it to its source. A rude human smell that for a while overrode the other increasingly odd smells which seemed, every day, to proliferate, to taint the air of the city, and from which there was less and less relief.

That human smell gave me a type of solace.

Those times when it dominated everything else there was a definite comfort in yielding to the known.

SEVEN

My education began in earnest after the General installed me as his mistress proper. At the time, I did not quite realise that what delivered me into that circumstance was the desire to have a sense of control. It was a common enough desire, I don't think anyone knew what was sliding in or out of control. In fits and starts, in huge chunks or small gradual erosions, everyone seemed to be losing their sense of personal control. Not everyone would admit to this; the General, for instance, maintained that everything was under control, although one must allow for the contingencies of the battle. I suppose I wanted to cling to the possibility of having control, despite the evidence that the very notion of an individual life was being flushed away with each new surge of war. I also thought I knew what would come of a closer association with the General—a premium against the worst sorts of hardship. However, I was to learn that there were other hardships besides poverty and hunger.

This change in my situation occurred when Sol's presence in my life had become so tenuous as to be ghostly. When the war began I had unclenched my thighs and Sol had shuddered and slid out of my body and like the other lovers in the city we had held each other as the conscripts and the enlisted men were marshalled. It was clear that he wasn't prepared to fight. 'I won't be sacrificed to another man's vision,' he said, 'I won't fight for something I don't believe in.'

'What do you believe in?' I asked.

'Finding my own path,' he replied, 'and going wherever it takes me … away from here. Do you think I'm a coward for wanting to get away from it?'

'No. You shouldn't fight if you don't believe in fighting.'

'That's very simplistic,' he said. 'If you were called up, would you fight?'

'There are things I'd fight for, like staying alive, but the question seems academic. I haven't really thought about it. Being a woman, I don't have to fight.'

'But you'll suffer,' he answered grimly. 'We all will, whether we fight or not.'

To lighten the mood I took out a silver chain bracelet I'd lifted from an undiscerning gentleman and fitted it around the elegant bones of Sol's wrist. 'A memento,' I said. 'To bring you luck.'

He fondled the links of the chain. 'Putting your belief in luck can be risky,' he said.

'Maybe,' I shrugged, 'if it's all you've got to believe in.' When his cigarette burned down to ash in the silence which followed I was compelled to add, 'Believe in the fact that I will help you,' to break the feeling of excruciation that had invaded me. Then he lifted my chin and kissed smoke into my mouth and went out the door, leaving an inscription of dark hairs on the pillow. A memento. Even though I had told him I would help him, I wondered if I'd ever see him again. After he left, I opened the window and released the smell of tobacco and watched the shredding of cloud in the emptying sky and let in the sound of a city being mobilised for battle. And even though I wanted not to, I began to wait for him.

My patience was rewarded, Sol returned. The outbreak of war had closed the borders, travel beyond the city perimeters became impossible without official papers, checkpoints with a 'shoot first' policy were set up and the military had command of all routes and transit centres. The outside world faded away from us, telephonically, electronically, and in actuality. No-one seemed too interested in getting into the city. I imagine a few outside journalists tried, the start of a new war usually pulled them in, but we were just one war of many wars and we did not count for very much. Later, refugees came, but that was because they were our people and there was absolutely nowhere else for them to go. Escape from the city for those without connections, money, or a Department of Movements permit was impossible and Sol had none of these.

In the beginning, meetings were difficult but not impossible to arrange. Sol would slip into the bar where I worked on Bernanos Street and catch my eye, then wait for me on a certain corner when I'd finished work—almost like our first time. He had no address he would give me and when he heard that phones were being bugged he refused to call me at either the bar or the hostel. He also refused to commit anything to paper. In fact, Sol soon refused to visit me at my hostel and if he didn't have somewhere for us to go we would end up in dark public places, against a wall, pushing urgently into the warmth of one another.

But then I was sacked. The manager told me it was a 'war

measure' but it was because I wouldn't let him have me. If not for Sol I would probably have acquiesced, but in those days I only wanted Sol, my desire for him was that fierce. When I told him what had happened he said it would have been worth it to have kept my job, what was I going to do now? Afterwards he was repentant and said I could join him if I liked, but he had wounded the loving part of me and I could not go with him. I put my sacking to some good purpose though. My workmate was a soft-hearted woman called Mei Lien and I worked on this softness of hers and her evident relief that it was me rather than her out on the streets as a 'war measure'. She agreed to act as a go-between for Sol and myself, passing along messages when necessary. Mei Lien proved to be a loyal woman, she was lonely enough for the smallest scraps of friendship and she was thrilled when I told her Sol was an undercover intelligence agent and we had to keep our love affair a secret in order not to blow his cover. She was extraordinarily gullible and I had some fun concocting stories of Sol's nerve-racking missions.

It was not ideal, because Sol would not use Mei Lien to leave a message for me very often, but he could not offer a better alternative and at least he was staying in contact with me. By then it was all too apparent that he would not be leaving the city without an extraordinary change in circumstances. A change neither of us could imagine effecting. In the meanwhile people were being exhorted to improve their patriotism by denouncing the coward resisters and the sham conscientious objectors, and the city turned into a sort of hunting ground in this exercise of loyalty. It was a bad time. In this hysteria of denouncement Sol went underground, and even when the worst of the madness abated we could only meet intermittently. Those meetings, as fraught, as infrequent as they were, were all I did call happiness.

Whenever we met we made love.

Love, not fucking. When I made love with Sol I would arc and lock my legs around him, wanting to wring something from him I was not allowed to name. In my moment of love I gripped his flesh, that which made my love seem so real, and tried to secure him in the twist of my body.

Love.

After I began going with the General the distinction became clearer, even though the General was not deficient in technique. But it was not the fuck that distinguished Sol, it was the little things, the intimate things of lovers. I liked to play with his hair, it would fall across his face like a veil and snag and tease my fingers. It was whilst playing with his hair that I got the idea to outfit him as a woman, to distort his male form, to disguise him from harm. In fact it may have even been the General who planted the notion in me, with his penchant for my clothing.

This was the first of Sol's disguises. He did not relish it, not like the General, but then the General played it for a game, not for survival. Later Sol pretended to be lame, blind, simple, decrepit, but I think this one was his best disguise. It suited him, the female shape, in a way that the General could never match. I taught Sol how to wear flowing, concealing clothing; how to accent his lips with Firestorm; colour in the hue of his whiskers with Battalion Beige—fortunately he was fairly hairless, which allowed the ruse to work—remove the shine on his chin with Tender Triumph complexion powder; and how to contour his beautiful grey cat eyes with Secret Weapon Number 12.

I saw that man disappear in crowds of women.

A man melted and made invisible by women.

And when I drew his semen, his legs would fall open, in acquiescence, like a woman's. And his mouth would open, and it was the shape of the mouth on an ecstatic woman.

So we continued, erratically, incredibly, to meet. Surreptitious trysts in strange, out-of-the-way places that Sol found for us. Places full of silences which at times threatened to overrun us, the sort of silences that inhabit neglected and unvisited tombs. The spaces we decorated with the writhing of our bodies were usually so deadened by destitution, so devoid of anything heartening, that each time we parted I carried the unuttered hope that I had not visited a place where he was actually living. He refused to tell me one way or the other and I had learned to not ask. For the first time in my life I became bothered by rats holed up in ceilings, mould living on walls, the ingrained stench of cooking fat, the pile of rags that more often than not was our bed. Once, I would not have cared about shoddiness but when we lay limb to limb after sex, my head hooked by his shoulder, his smoke drifting across our murmuring, the juxtaposition of these places with the rooms in which I'd been fucking the General could be brutal.

Increasingly, there were long pauses between our meetings. Pauses which intensified. Pauses I had to make useful. Pauses which forced me to consider my choices—to keep going back to the General, to keep managing life as best I could, or to go with Sol.

In the beginning I was pretty much a free agent, my contractual obligations weren't too difficult to fulfil and it was a short step to seeing the General outside the arranged hours. The money dilemma had been nicely resolved and the practical benefits of keeping company with the General were evident whenever I took a drink or ate a meal. Furthermore, I was able to help keep Sol alive and in my life by giving him some of that money. The General and I had settled on a weekly fee—an allowance, it was called—and there was no more haggling over my price. I told Sol I was a handy pickpocket, which was true, although not the truth. I was good at duplicity. I felt no dilemma hiding things from Sol, it was for his own sake. At least, in the beginning I believe it was for his sake. After all, it was he who was the hidden part of my life before I had anything to keep from him.

But when Sol failed to show at several consecutive meetings we had painstakingly arranged, my hopes for his safety, let alone any sort of togetherness, plummeted. Waiting futilely in places lacking warmth or human connectiveness, I reminded myself that our capacity to meet was sporadic at best. On each of these occasions I had to battle an ugly dread. Had he been caught? War evaders were forced to make atonement in subterranean cells before contributing their services to war, rumours said, as human shields for sensitive sites and weapons stockpiles. This was the type of rumour that was dangerous to listen to, that would have you at the window looking into the noise of the wind in the middle of the night.

After these terrible, gnawing disappointments it wasn't until much later, sometimes days later, when the waiting had badly eroded my equilibrium and started tearing me up, that I would finally receive a message from Sol that he'd had other business. I think the scarring that the word 'business' gave me was as much a catalyst as anything else in my deciding to join the General's camp. Because Sol could hurt me badly, and had, and because I could not change the circumstances of him effecting such hurt, I became consumed with the notion of anything, everything, being made easier. I don't know why I thought going to the General would make things easier for Sol and me, I imagine it was my hurt and my anger trying to put Sol away from me, but I do know that I could not stand waiting for the possibility of him while he did 'business'.

In fact, what precipitated the change in my status was being kicked out of my hostel. Perhaps the coming and going of military cars had been too much for the other residents. Perhaps my occasional return in the General's car, a black shark-shaped Mercedes with tinted windows and a sleek, elite, utterly impersonal look, had had the effect of making certain people in the neighbourhood jittery, even though the General, of course, was never in it. Perhaps the soldiers who called for me, and perhaps, by extension, I, were a reminder to some that the war would be as happy in residence inside their homes as on the prescribed battlefields. Perhaps they were simply looking for a way to express their resentment at my not having the grace to get out of their neighbourhood following my evident good fortune. I did not think, then, that perhaps the General had arranged my evacuation in order to cure me of my stubbornness in still preferring to live there rather than with him.

The day I returned to find my belongings in piles on the pavement and new locks on the doors it was as if summer had come at last. The air was that odd orange colour and it was stiflingly hot, although the sky was not raining down ash anymore. As the car pulled up at my door, curtains twitched at windows shut despite the heat. There was, unnaturally, no other movement in the street. It was deserted. I got the message. 'Don't go,' I said to the driver as I slid from the General's car. 'Not yet.' No-one had looted my stuff and that made the situation crystal clear. My neighbours wanted nothing to do with me. I looked at my belongings and I felt removed, dispassionate. Dispensed with. What was really worth keeping?

My grandfather's gold fillings.

My grandmother's gold wedding ring.

Money.

I finally got to use a soldier's match, I set those piles alight. At the time, I was pleased with that gesture, leaving my past in ashes. I thought I would start anew. 'You may as well take me back to the General,' I directed.

On the drive back to his hotel I saw something on the razor wire that had risen up around the city. For the first time I took a good long look, for the first time I saw the bodies strung up on the new fences. Scarecrows flapping a warning to stay away. 'Resisters,' mumbled the driver. He had a heavy foot and he drove off fast but I saw the carrion birds coming towards us, their beaks full and their wings dipped in blood.

I looked again, they were bombers.

EIGHT

There was never a home as most people usually know it, there was a series of hotels we occupied, endlessly hopping from one to another. One day it was the Hotel Disneyland, the next day the Hotel Valentino, a week later the Hotel Flamboyant, following that the Hotel Tourist. Those hotels suited me. The desire to have no attachment, to have literally only a handful of objects of personal value, had possessed me when I found my belongings out in the street. As for Sol, I bore down on the part of me that wanted him when I got back in the General's car and drove away. It was survival. One had to do it as best one could and there was no point in getting sentimental about it. Even when I got drunk I stopped myself getting sentimental about it—it was as if I'd bitten a part of my feelings off.

There were no regular hotel guests in the places we stayed. Once a place was commandeered by the General they were shunted off elsewhere. It was like being billeted with a regiment, living in close quarters with his men. The General had a private corps, of course, in addition to a bodyguard who patrolled the perimeters of every place he inhabited. His men were all wary of me but they gradually got used to me—for the most part I think I was probably viewed somewhat like a piece of furniture, some thing the General insisted on having with him despite the circumstances, annoying, but not much more than that. When it came down to it I decided that it suited me, I did not really want them to know me in any other way.

The General appreciated it very much that I came to him in nothing but the clothes I was wearing. 'I want you in your skin,' he said. I obligingly removed my clothing and he swept it into the bin. 'From now on the woman you become will issue from me.' I began to laugh—I was stark naked, with nothing in the world but a couple of trinkets and a wad of money. 'Yes, laugh,' he enjoined, 'your smile shows the white-ness of your teeth.' The General took an interest in my clothes and it was easier to let him decide what he wanted. It wasn't because he liked to wear my clothing sometimes, or that buying women's clothing was a well-exercised passion, for he was obviously a novice at it. 'I have dreams of you,' he said by way of explanation. 'I see you joining with me and the female in you rises up in me.' I wondered if the General thought he was being romantic.

'Is that why you like to choose my clothes?' I asked, picking at the shopping bags he had had his adjutant heap upon my bed.

'No,' he replied, 'you are like a primitive, you are unaware. It is not a complaint, it is an observation, for it is not in your nature to care for the art of the couturier.' After that I rarely shopped, and when I did I bought things that I made sure the General never saw.

*

The General sweated bombs. It got so I could hear them going off in his sleep. Every drop, every hit, his payloads unloading, him flying lighter and lighter, deeper and deeper into his dream after each new strike. I saw the sweat bubble up and blister his skin. Every night it ate him away, his own body salt was acid sluicing him raw. He would cry out in his sleep at times, but not very often. Occasionally he moaned, but he was rarely restless and it took some watching before I realised that the General was riddled with nightmare. It took me a while to work it out. We slept apart. We rarely touched in the easy, intimate way of couples. Sleeping together would have left us unguarded and that was unthinkable.

After he had retired to bed I would sit and drink and wait. I would count what I took to be the surface-to-air missile launches, the far-away impacts. I would listen to mortar shells exploding in the distance, the flak bursting somewhere, sometimes the closer sound of sirens, sometimes the sound of running in the street. Picking out the sounds and learning to identify them as normal, every-night sort of sounds. Nothing to be alarmed at. When the wind blew it was more difficult, but the sound of certain things would still carry—exploding shells, for instance, carried very clearly. The wind would get behind them, pushing them over to us. One benefit of the peculiar orange that had washed across our sky was that it had stopped being truly dark anymore, at night-time everything was obliquely defined by that oxidising colour.

After I had listened enough and drank enough, I would enter the General's room. He was one of those fortunate people who fall profoundly asleep as soon as their head hits the pillow, but still, I would wait until I was quite sure that he was sound asleep. I would go into his room naked, with empty hands. There was a risk that he might wake and think me an assassin. It had happened, apparently, that he had woken to find someone moving towards him and he had pulled his gun out from under his pillow and shot them dead. My precautions were my nakedness and a story that I desired him.

He never once stirred.

I would take a chair and sit a little way from the General's bed, and once more wait. I would wait until I saw his sweat begin to boil and rise like a disturbance under the deceptively calm surface of a lake. Wait until I knew that the war had him. Then I would move the chair in very close to him. For some reason I knew he wasn't going to wake when he was in the grip of it like that and sometimes, when I reached that point, I'd all of a sudden need another drink and I'd incautiously scrape back the chair and go and get a drink and come back to him. Without any regard for an accidental shooting. In this way I prepared myself for sleep. Sitting, drinking, watching. I liked being alone with him, watching the war take him in its own way, stripping him of the pretence that he could control it. Giving him nightmares.

Yes, those were possibly some of my better times with the General, sitting there watching the war eat him like any other.

When the General started wanting me with him at his War Council powwows my days became minutely determined by the business of war. I was wildly out of my league in those disapproving male meetings. I alarmed them, I think, as the only female presence. I did not present tea and coffee and sweet biscuits and discreetly withdraw. I sat in their midst, at their table, at the General's left hand, and watched the lot of them. I was not there to do anything in particular and I learnt to affect feminine apathy. That soothed the gang. They did not ever appreciate my inclusion, but my display of indifference allowed them to ignore me and get on with it. I acted bored, as if it were all over my head, all beyond me, and I soon became nothing more than their reminder that the war belonged wholly to them. My life was in their hands and there I rested.

Balm to them and confidence to them and victory to them.

My presence in his military meetings so entertained the General that as soon as the brass filed out of the room I was under orders to spread him on the conference table and take him in his babble of maps. As I moved over him I would hear his guard twitching outside the door, maintaining the pretence of the General in conference.

Such a slut.

There was no hiding it for him. When he was in war's elite company he could get tremendously stiff. That's why I went with him to the War Council in the beginning, when the fighting was fresh and fierce and when those meetings gave him an irrepressible hard-on. Indeed, the exercise of mounting the General afterwards created a pattern of monotony for me.

I spent quite a lot of time sitting up late alone in the noisy, bombarded nights that followed those days, war strategies scrolling unprompted in my head. I did not find those night-time lullabies the soporific the General seemed to. I would take my drink and sit with my back to the windows, scribbling on the reams of stationery I had taken a fancy to at one place we had camped at. Each page stamped with a silly grinning clown-face logo of the Hotel Happy Holiday. Each page a random jotting of code-names, operations, dates and method-ologies of attack. The words all jumbled together, a mishmash of memory. I was not given the remotely useful task of taking the minutes for those meetings but I was compelled to write things out afterwards, a small gesture against the prescribed uselessness of my part.

My black loopy blossoms inked out pristine continents of paper and the regurgitation helped me regain some sense of equilibrium. What I was doing was inventing another character for myself to play in order to extend the role of the General's mistress over whose head soldiers talked. I did nothing with those pages. I amused myself selecting hiding places in which to stash them for posterity, or the cleaner. It was a bit of a joke, I did not fancy myself as a spy. It was a means of getting the War Council's chatter out of my ears, of forcing away the apathy and the enclosure of the nights and maybe getting myself off to sleep.

The days were signals: long, patient queues of women damming the doors of shops for flour, oil, sugar, rice, tea, coffee, soap, formula milk powder, unravelling onions, lean bones of meat; long, silent rows of women outside munitions factories waiting to work; long, labyrinthine streets of women selling off their bodies, bit by bit; long, measureless days and long, lousy nights of women waiting for news of their men in the battle zones. In the beginning there had been spectacular rallies, with the women cheering and the men marching and the heroes making speeches and the white burst of our insignia blooming on flags waving high in the sky. Blood-red banners unfurling like flowers in a hothouse atmosphere. Events glamorised by the Department of Reportage, but, for all that, there'd been an ardour, a happiness, on the faces of those women as their men stepped in time to the call of war and their boys strained against the leash of their youth towards the battlegrounds they were so eager to get to.

In those days, before the war began to chew on that ardour and sully it with its grind and worry and want; before the non-negotiable blackouts and rationing and gas masks; before the victories and the defeats became endlessly shifting phrases; before the whizzing blue and red lights of tracer bullets began crisscrossing the odd colour of our horizon, and the *whump! whump! whump!* as the 82s, the 120s, and the 155mm howitzers began pumping out their rounds of shells—before all this accretion there was a vast optimism. But as the war wounded, and poured its salt onto the wounds, there was a loosening of certain bonds of fidelity to it.

The decree against women in action remained in effect but this did not prevent the introduction of voluntary labour gangs to utilise citizens considered unproductive. Women who constituted a national risk—for example, those expressing an anti-war sentiment or who were disorderly in public, were shunted into tasks considered to be in the public good. This could mean something as innocuous as sweeping a street, or as terrifying as being forcibly relocated, along with their families, to sites sensitive to hostile incursion. A technique for reducing the potential of an enemy strike. Children not absorbed into the fight in this way, or let loose in other ways from their families, began roaming in packs, kicking out against war's mothering. Men too unfit or decrepit for enlistment and boys not of age for real battle started their own wars, savagely fighting each other for the right to sift street garbage and comb the rubble on the far limits of the city which took, on a reliable enough basis, direct hits from Scuds and Thrashers.

I was touring these furthermost outskirts the day I watched a grand procession of tanks move through the streets. Before the General had left for the front that morning he explained that the enemy had started bleeding the battlefield into civilian areas. But the enemy had reached a point of diminishing returns. Mop-up operations were about to commence, our strike-backs would have the superior impact. With his assurances ringing in my ears I ordered the car into an area I had never been before, Dien Bien Phu District, a civilian no-go area, which is why I wanted to go there. I had no trouble getting through the barrier in the General's car, but once inside I was disappointed, there was nothing either very awful or particularly adventuresome about the place. There was, instead, a horrible lonesomeness because the place had been abandoned.

It was a suburb of eerily empty establishments with the stark look of desertion. The gardens, a sign of wealth, had been stripped of everything, even the weeds. Even out there, the bitter smell that plagued the innards of the city was pervasive. No doubt about it, one of the most prestigious addresses in town had not been insured against going down the sewer. I liberally sprinkled my hanky with perfume, ignored the driver's exhortations to stay inside the vehicle and went walking. Those wide, swank streets were as much mine as anyone's now. The houses were, one after the other, blank with absence. The district nestled too close to the dubious charms of war, adjoining the Western Sector, once a fashionable play area with its streams and lakes and hazy chain of mountains, now nothing more than the venue where our forces were being compelled to match the enemy's latest escalatory steps.

On the way back to the hotel I directed the driver to stop the car at the first watering hole we saw. I wanted to be around people and shake off the empty feeling that had seeped out of those deserted houses and settled on me. That was where the tanks passed by in measured ceremony. I didn't crowd the doorway in silence like the other patrons. I stayed in my corner and watched the ranks of glasses shivering en masse and the rows of bottles clinking one against the other. When I put down my money for the next drink the bar-tender slopped it, there was so much movement. Then the war machines rolled off to their destination, leaving an aftermath of absolute quiet. My driver even swallowed the drink I'd bought him. I felt a spurt of fondness for him for going against the rules. Then the fool went over to the television and filled the room with its gush. As I identified the garish blare as war news, I picked up the bottle and very carefully blocked what I had no wish to hear.

NINE

A pale pink chrysanthemum sent me back to Sol. It was not much more than a bud but it was real, emerging in a place where flowers were unreal. It was in an ordinary brown plastic pot and a Seller was asking a lot of money for it. She had laboured over that plant, you could see it in the way she guarded it—fiercely, with her body, as if it were immeasurably precious. People were brazenly selling all kinds of things on the street; it was a new enterprise, not legal, but that didn't matter, a person had to make money somehow if there was no work for her to do. War hadn't injected much new life into the economy as far as I could see, businesses went bust, factories shut down and hardship increased. I didn't haggle, I gave the woman what she wanted and I, too, cradled the pot, as if it were a tiny child.

Why did taking possession of that flower unleash my yearning for Sol? He began to unfurl in me, each petal another unbidden thought, opening out petal upon petal until he bloomed fully in me once more. What was it about that chrysanthemum? New life? New beginnings? Hope? An extraordinary ordinariness? Coincidence? The plant bloomed and the part of me which I had bitten off, the part that wanted Sol, had grown again. In the end I went back to the bar on Bernanos Street. Mei Lien greeted me with the ardour of a long-lost friend. After listening to some smooth-faced lying as to my recent whereabouts she confided a message, and I saw that my going there that day was one of those predetermined or wildly coincidental things: Sol would be waiting for me that very afternoon. Although she'd told him that she hadn't seen me, that I'd been terribly wounded by him, he made it clear that he'd be waiting regardless. Excitement ran through me like a sickness.

It was so easy to go to him.

For my rendezvous I was careful. I went back to the Sellers and bought a dress from a woman on Borodino Boulevard. She was standing in a line of hawkers, items of her wardrobe dangling off her body as if she were a clothes-stand. Such intimate disclosure struck me as an act of wilfulness rather than pathos, despite her meagre garments fluttering there for all and sundry to see. That's what decided me on the dress. Also, the dress was red, a colour which I liked to think of as my signature colour before I learnt to be less eager in my associations.

I matched my new purchase with a pair of cheap red shoes and changed in the toilet of a friendly watering hole along the way, stashing my outfit in place of my usual bottle behind the bar. One of the benefits that came of having money was being able to keep a bottle of decent liquor at my favourite bars. I touched up my mouth with Vermillion Victory. Despite the reminder of the General, I wore the black pantyhose, but because my underwear comprised only expensive silks, satins and lacy things I wore none.

That afternoon the whole city seemed to be in a good mood. The length and brightness of the sun seemed to intensify, enlivening the orange sky and creating a happier sense of warmth. We were becoming accustomed to the acrid smell which had come to stay, however the subsidiary odours of the ripening, heated-up city were providing another heady bouquet, albeit a more comforting one: the everyday human smells that had risen with the heat were nothing to worry about. It was all of a sudden a day of optimism and I felt buoyant, alive with adrenaline, thrilled with anticipation, wet between the legs and quite on heat.

His head blocked the chink of light in the blackout curtain which he had pulled shut. My body felt unnaturally light, as if it might slip away from me at any moment. I was having difficulty distinguishing where my feet and hands ended, I was ballooning in the dark. We were nothing more than sounds scraping against harsh walls. Sounds falling away from each other in a tiny, containing room, insular as a well sunk deep in ground completely dried up. No other noise, no other movement, no colour except the delicate pink seep of outside light infusing our theatrical darkness. I opened my mouth and tasted a grey metal atmosphere and shut it again. I was sweating between my breasts and along the sharp line of rib running out from under my arms. Sol's words deadened the air between us. 'How can you say that you're nothing but a common whore?'

'What's wrong with you?'

He kicked the bags on the floor. I winced. Bottles clinked, the only cheerful sound. 'How come all of this? Food. Booze. This cost a lot. More than you can afford.'

'You're not one to be questioning me!' I cried, my happiness gone quite flat. 'Where were you all the times I waited for you? Have you any idea what it's like to be left waiting like that? Not knowing whether you're dead or alive. What sort of business made you too busy to see me?' We glared at each other. It wasn't supposed to go like this, we were supposed to fall into each other.

'You left the hostel,' he side-stepped. I felt a ripple of ill ease. 'You drove off with a soldier,' he continued, 'in a car that had been calling for you nearly every day.' Damn the neighbours, I thought. Damn them for god knows what they'd enlightened Sol with. At least no-one had ever sighted the General. 'A soldier came for you day and night. In the same car you went away in. Where did it take you?' At least Sol thought that it was only a soldier who took me away.

'I got kicked out.'

'You're his fuck.'

'I was broke. I was homeless. He was there. That's all there is to it.'

'How convenient.'

'Yes. Convenient. Okay? What did you want me to do? Enlist in one of the military brothels? Stand on the street? Lie down in the gutter and die?'

'It's your life,' he said, 'do as you wish.'

'We can't do as we wish, can we?' I demanded. 'This soldier, he can access supplies. I fucked him. Yes, I fuck him. In return I get gas masks. They're in short supply, people don't have them, but there're thousands of them sitting in this supply dump. So I get them and sell them on the black market or swap them for things like this.' It was my turn to kick the parcels. 'People need them. They pay whatever they can because they could die without them if there's an attack. That's how I get the money. That's how come I get things for you. I fuck a soldier. He puts a roof over my head.' It was not the full truth, not a complete lie. I did have a side interest in selling masks and I didn't have to do it for the money. I did it for diversion, some sort of entertainment. A small strike against the General and the way he liked to run me.

I had created this trouble because I'd arrived carting impossible luxuries, lugging the detritus of my life with the General into my moment with Sol. Instinct had told me not to do it but I wanted Sol to have the best, the tastiest, the finest, the most wonderful things which were available. The markets had tantalised me, I found goods that had not made an appearance in a while and there was a rare window of choice. And I had chosen with a wash of euphoria, because it had been another sign that the day was a good day, a glad day. Was. Past tense. Sol's breathing was barely audible, like his voice. 'I never asked you to do anything for me.'

'It's not always in talking that you do your asking,' I snapped.

'You think it matters to me whether you're fucking a soldier?' he spat. I waited, motionless. 'You're not with me so why should I expect anything of you?' His voice thin with emotion. Maybe love.

'I want you to expect me to do what I can for you,' I said softly. I wanted this scene to be over. I wanted to know what it was that we still had. 'It's a matter of survival. I need to survive. I need you to survive. Please.' I heard the sound of tearing bags. I heard the breaking of glass. The violent eruption of liquor fumes grounded me. I reached out and grabbed the hazy outline of Sol's arm. He jerked away and I felt the fall of liquid on my hand. I put it in my mouth and licked it, a reflex action, and swallowed heat. Brandy.

'I don't want you bringing the war to me. That's what this is.' The aggrieved tone of his voice jarred me out of my soft longing.

'You think we're not in the war at this very moment?' I turned and wrenched at the blackout curtain and it fell from the curtain rod, bleeding light into the nasty little room where Sol had taken us. He stood there shocked, blinking rapidly, clutching the broken bottle. I shoved open a window. 'Look outside, it's there, it's everywhere, it's in this room right now, it's here inside of us. Both of us. It's why we're at each other's throats like this. It's the war, treating us with contempt, treating us exactly the same as anybody and anything else. With complete disregard for feelings, wants, needs. The war doesn't give a damn how, or if, we survive.'

Sol slid his back down the wall until he was sitting propped up on the floor. Out of view. 'That doesn't make it all right.' He fingered the glass neck of the bottle. It was a remarkably clean break.

'I'm not saying it's all right. I'm saying what is.'

'Does this soldier mean anything to you?'

'No.'

He took a swig of brandy. 'Show me how you screw him.'

I did not say anything to that but went and knelt on my knees on the dirty floor beside him and took the bottle and put it aside. 'The war hasn't changed the most important thing,' I said, placing myself in the shell of his body. 'Despite every-thing, we still have each other.' I paused. 'Don't we?'

Sol's mouth gripped mine. His tongue was a memory I'd been withholding. We drank from each other, hands crawling over our covered-up bodies, looking for the comfort of skin and the response of muscle. He lifted my dress up over my hips and curved his hand between my legs, stroking my clitoris, a rhythmic thumb on my pulse. I pushed my hands inside his pants. His penis was hot and sticky. I felt again the distinctive scar of his circumcision and the characteristic bend of his shaft to the right.

I had little time to languish over his sex. In one swift movement he pulled the pantyhose down over my naked buttocks to my thighs, both of us too urgent to break apart and remove them altogether. I centred myself in his lap, knees resting on his chest, as I slid along his shaft, feeling the run of my juices. Our noses pushed together, tongues swimming in the cavern of the mouth to the back of the throat, along the sharp-smooth edges of teeth, over the sensitive slick of gums. 'Put your cock in me now,' I whispered. He grasped my hips. I lifted myself up on my haunches, tilted my pelvis back and arched as his penis dived into me. We both cried aloud.

Our movement dragged the black nylon pantyhose against the flesh of my thighs. The thrust of our bodies jerked the pantyhose harder against my skin, each plunge of Sol's cock a rasping of black nylon, a fire of friction, a Chinese burn. My thighs twisting, the nerve endings of my clitoris exquisite, swollen, inflamed.

I climaxed.

When I came I flung out my hands in my ecstasy and the edge of the broken brandy bottle penetrated my left palm.

I did not feel it, I felt only a rapture of heat as my orgasm shuddered through my frame. It was Sol who realised that I was bleeding, my blood a new motif of colour on the khaki drift of his clothing. He had come to me that day in the guise of a wounded soldier, limping and dragging his leg. He would not say where the uniform had come from, only that it was a safe way to travel about because he had papers that made him look legitimate if anyone stopped him. He pressed my ripped palm with a piece of his shirt and bound it up to staunch the bleeding. I told him it didn't hurt, that I wanted him again and so we did it again, more slowly but still strong and needy.

The pain set in later when he was preparing to leave. 'What sort of safety can you ever have?' I asked, sadness worsening the pain.

'I've got contacts,' he replied, repacking the supplies I'd bought him. 'I'm not on my own, you don't need to worry.' He patted the bundle. 'I'll sell this on the black market.'

'But I bought it for you,' I protested.

'It's money we need, not luxuries.'

'We?'

'I told you, I have friends.'

'Are there many in the same boat as you?'

Sol looked at me steadily. 'There's plenty of us who don't want to be in the General's war.' At this mention of the General I felt a spasm deep in the pit of my belly, in the vicinity where Sol's penis had leapt, and my injury began to throb badly. I dragged out my wallet and handed it to him.

'Stay safe,' I said. What else could I say?

He kissed me, the kiss I'd been wanting. Not a headlong sex kiss, a tender surface-to-surface love kiss. Then he kissed my hand, and although he was gentle, his touch set off detonations of pain.

'Until next time,' he said.

'Next time,' I murmured. But he had already gone.

TEN

The wound in war is almost always a complicated wound. Because of the way modern weapons are designed this wound is almost always a multiple of wounds.

Under the tutelage of the General I was informed that the first international agreement aimed at governing the weapons of war had been reached in St Petersburg in 1868. In 1899 the Hague Convention outlawed the use of bullets without full metal jackets, but over time the metal jacketing on bullets became so much thinner that jacketed bullets, too, came to have a devastating impact. They deformed and fragmented in the body, having the same sort of consequence as the outlawed unjacketed or dumdum bullets. But smaller, lighter, thinner-jacketed bullets were a boon for fighters, they increased their fire-power and that was of paramount importance in facing the enemy.

A case in point, the General told me, were hollow-pointed bullets. They had been designed to cause the biggest wounds possible by releasing the maximum energy of the bullet within the body, tearing up soft tissue, shattering bone, rupturing muscle. The body itself stopped the bullet and hindered it from passing through and out the other side, thus preventing damage to something other than the target. Quaintly, such advances in bullet design had been called inhumane bullets. The General considered it amusing that there had ever been any serious notion of a humane bullet.

In the striving for superior fire-power the repertoire of weaponry had been affected by fewer and fewer principles of humanitarian design. In accordance with this an epidemic of a new sort of wounding had started to occur wherein a casualty commonly suffered one primary injury with numerous complications. Like a fragmentation injury. Or an anti-personnel injury. A style of wounding which became an additional element on the battlefield.

New bullets had new consequences.

Like a reconsideration of the idea of unnecessary suffering.

The realisation that such a thing as unnecessary suffering was nothing more than that, an idea. 'Absurd, illogical, unrealistic,' intoned the General.

The Hague Convention had also held that there were laws of war, one such being that there should not be superfluous suffering. But superfluous suffering had never really been defined. And it was an idea easy to lose or misplace in the moment of battle, in the moment of dealing with the enemy, of kill or be killed. 'Besides which,' the General added, 'a badly wounded soldier is more effective than a dead soldier.' A badly wounded soldier slowed things down, created delays, affected overall morale. A badly wounded soldier was better strategy than a dead soldier. It was part of the arsenal of war. It was a good tactic. 'And that's the most important thing,' he concluded, 'to have the superior tactics.'

When I presented the General with my lacerated hand he was fascinated. He'd been waiting impatiently for me and I was relieved that my wound deflected any curiosity he might have had as to my whereabouts. I'd delayed my return because I wanted to be alone with thoughts of Sol while I doctored myself with a few long pulls from a bottle, and by the time I made my way back to the Hotel Jolly I was not very aware of my hand. By then the afternoon had turned into one of those sullen sweltering nights—not a hint of a breeze, the earlier liveliness of the city punctured by the heat which had steadily accumulated in a sky giving a good impression of a furnace. It was a warmth no longer joyful and I could smell the sourness of my own body as the General inspected my hand. For some reason this scent aroused him. Or was it the smell of Sol on me that aroused him?

I was startled when he put his mouth to my wound and began lapping it, making long sweeping strokes with his tongue, not the eager or comforting motion of a pet, a dog, say, nothing so familiar. It was a worrying sensation, not because it was painful but because it was such an excitement to him. He lifted his mouth and it was rimmed with my signature colour, looking fresh and bright after his ministrations, then he undid his fly and presented me with his erect penis.

I always had the right instinct for what the General wanted.

I held out my hand and it began to throb wildly.

He said, 'Bombs away,' and slid into the folds in that part of my hand dedicated to the god Mars. And with my stiffening fingers holding him in just the right way, I elicited his burning discharge.

*

74

Because I had not chosen the right sort of lie to tell, the General seized on the fact of my injury and presented me with an escort whose job was to accompany me wherever I went. Without thinking it through clearly I'd told the General that I'd lost my wallet to a thief and had hurt my hand in a futile pursuit. Hence I was imprisoned by my own stupidity and locked into a situation which I could not, in the short term, seem to escape. When the General told me he would not have me hurt I wondered if he was being ironic. I'd dressed various injuries already, none so dramatic as the tear in my hand, but the concepts of being hurt and being with the General went well enough together.

In one stroke my life changed. It had been bad enough having to tag along with the General to those War Council meetings, now I couldn't go anywhere without one of his faithfuls stepping on my heels. I had no wish to advertise my new status, so my usual haunts were out of the question and I was soon pining for the temper of the streets and the atmospheres of my favourite bars. Above all, I could not afford my predicament to be advertised in those quarters which might transmit news of it to Sol. Or worse, be seen by him. I did not know who he knew or where he went. I realised I knew less and less about him and I wondered whether I would even recognise Sol if I saw him in public, as he'd no doubt be disguised. And if Sol happened to see me I could only hope he would assume that I was with my 'fuck-soldier', as he called him.

I visited out-of-the-way places but sitting in public under guard—and it always looked so damn obvious—had the unfortunate effect of both drawing attention to myself and keeping people at bay. There was not much fun in it. The officers' clubs were closed to me because I was non-military personnel. I couldn't get a foot in the door despite, or perhaps because of, my standing with the General. Besides which, I wanted to go to a place where the war might not fill the pause in every conversation, mushroom in the foam of every beer. There were still a few places where people pretended there was life beyond the war and they were where I wanted to be. I enjoyed quite enough intimacy with war babble as it was.

From the start, these escorts of mine were changed about so frequently it was difficult to develop the camaraderie that might have led to me creating some space for myself. They proved annoyingly immune to bribery, but in any case I doubt my chaperons would have disobeyed the General even if I was eager to. The only time my guards were at ease was when I was safely inside the sanctuary of the hotel, where I could move about the place with relative freedom. After some subtle investigation I filched a worker's uniform from the hotel laundry basket, and over a few days ordered up bed linen and towels which I stashed in my cupboard. I then donned the uniform, wrapped my hair in a scarf like a cleaner, hefted the pile of towels and sheets in my arms, careful to conceal my injured hand, and kept my head down all the way to the laundry, a dim, steaming place in the bowels of the building. And went out a back door.

They caught up with me. And became more vigilant, more distantly courteous, more grimly attentive than ever.

Before long my sense of enclosure was acute. The phones, of course, were bugged, not that I had much interest in calling anyone from the General's quarters. The rumours had never been substantiated that all the phones—those that still worked, that is—had been bugged. Mobiles had been confiscated quite early on, only military personnel were permitted mobile phones and any citizen caught with a mobile was incarcerated as a national security risk. Net-talking and other electronic communication had never been in the reach of most people but of course that too became impossible. My own small business of black-market deals with the gas masks had been going through the sort of lull that was only natural when the General was around, but now my connections were in danger of being lost altogether.

In a petulant act of protest I refused to budge from my bed, so the General ordered me into restraints. When I was securely shackled he suspended work on his memoirs to move court to the Hotel Fantasia Delight, an ornate, slowly decaying, rambling place that was more originally gothic than anything I'd ever seen before. He deposited me in the honeymoon suite which had a splendid view of what had once been the city's financial district: streets where no-one had reason to walk because they did not lead anywhere worth going; a monotony of blank, utilitarian office buildings and a plaza adorned with scummy, non-functioning fountains and unimaginative public sculpture where the detritus of the city was trapped whenever the winds kicked. A place of emptiness and vanished commerce, decorated with those huge unsettling posters of the General.

When I took in the view from my new window I saw that my only choice was to be patient, to wait it out. I told myself that I was used to waiting. I had waited often enough for Sol. But in all the times of waiting to see or hear from him I had continued on in my own way.

The General, it seemed, was set on changing my ways.

The next day, entering the hotel lobby flanked by my wardens after a dreary stroll through that ossified part of town, it occurred to me that with the exception of Sol there may not be another person who would miss me enough to care what became of me. And that it was impossible to go to him now. That night, odd symptoms erupted in me: the feeling of a claw on my throat, a sensation of being squeezed hard, an idea that I wasn't getting enough air into my lungs. I was certain that I was choking. I had to force myself to sit very still until the panic subsided and I was again rhythmically breathing in the reliable sound of the SAMs, the distant iron dropping, the low growl of ground fire, the din of the world going on as usual, until the claw let go and I could swallow my drink.

Being in the General's camp was starting to prove bad for my health.

When the General went off on a mission to gather more material for his memoirs and oversee the dispersion of enemy prisoners into the Disposables Zone, I began to slip into the state of rigid boredom that came from being in the sole company of my humourless round-the-clock guards. Their unyielding composure and dour countenances, combined with my isolation, began to produce in me a feeling of ennui. Beautiful word, horrible disposition. Desperate for some new amusement and encouraged by a bourbon, I began to hack at the plaster cast on my hand I'd been ordered not to touch. God knows why a cast had been put on a little rip in the skin. As I unravelled the gauze from my itching wound I discovered that I had been ornamented with a brand new scar, one that perfectly clarified what I had seen, at the General's prompting, in the convergence of lines in my palm.

That inscription, that M, was now so vivid, so unambiguous, I realised that the General's medico must have deliberately carved me and stitched me in order to achieve the effect. The scar was too precise to have been an outcome of a chance encounter with a broken bottle. I even suspected that damned medico of enhancing his handiwork with red ink like a tattooer, the scar was so livid. Now no-one would doubt that I carried a signature in the palm of my hand. The wound had been sutured with fastidious, neat, black-gut stitches and they were a further ugliness. Wincing at the taut pull of flesh I flexed my fingers and tears blurred my vision. I hadn't wanted any medical attention, but the General had insisted. The medico had produced a needle and when I came to, the job, all neat, swathed with white plaster, had been done.

And it hurt like hell.

And my injury, its pain and my disabling made worse by the operation, gave cause for the General to fire off a salvo about the safety of having an escort.

Salvō jurē.

The right of being safe.

I'd laughed at that, because my right of safety had been eclipsed by his act of war. The General did not get my little joke, but he approved of my being able to laugh at pain. I didn't know if his extravagant insistence on my need for a 24-hour escort was based on a concern that I might try to shoot through, but, for my part, I had begun to realise that my options might have started to run out. Taking up with the General seemed to have been the beginning of a very serious loss of choice.

ELEVEN

The damaged sign above the doorway at the top of the stairs read 'Soak Away Stress Inc.'. A vestige of a time when stress could be managed like a dirty stain. I was surprised that baths were still a going concern, stringent water restrictions were in force. On a sudden whim I ordered the car to stop, and when I got out the guard followed me up the creaky stairs, almost stepping on me when I came to a halt at the doorway. I directed his attention to the broken blackboard propped up beside the entrance. Painted on it were the words 'By Order. Females Healthy Bathing—Women & Girls only'.

'Down boy,' I commanded, 'I'm going to take a bath.' He hesitated, looking confused. 'At ease, soldier,' I ordered, 'I promise I won't abscond. Go protect the car, you're not here to take prisoners.' Before he could reply, I turned and pushed open the door and entered a vestibule. To my surprise he didn't follow, perhaps he was as bored with my company as I was with his. Perhaps he was using his handy little mobile phone and getting the building surrounded in case I made a run for it.

The door slapped shut behind me and it took me a moment to adjust to the poor light. Three women were seated at a wonky table playing cards. They ignored me, continuing with their game. Some form of poker, I think. Pumpkin-coloured light fluttered in through high-set windows of thick, watery glass into air undulating with cigarette smoke. The atmosphere of abstract preoccupation was punctuated by the women's tonal, phlegmatic coughing. The youngest woman was jiggling a listless infant on her lap, feeding it what looked like blackberry jam from a broken saucer. Set in a far wall was a pair of large opaque swing doors with a massive crack running through the glass of each door. A long, narrow stainless-steel counter ran perpendicular to the same wall, stacked with squares of thin, worn towels. At the end of the counter was a burnished copper tray of tiny plastic bottles containing minute amounts of amber liquid soap. That tray was the only lustrous thing in the room.

There was that smell of bleach and industrial soap I remembered as particular to public bathing places. There was that combination of concrete and tiling on the floor and walls, in this case a greying white and a muddied pink. There was the impression that the room was a cool, relatively clean mausoleum. The extreme height of the ceiling from which hung a plastic imitation cut-glass chandelier on a wire as slim as a thread exaggerated the room's impersonal textures. I stood there as the women continued with their random spitting into handkerchiefs, all the while throwing down cards on the table. I was familiar with this sort of out-waiting game. The baby seemed to lapse into unconsciousness. Finally the youngest woman lifted her head and looked me up and down. 'Who runs you?' she asked. I wondered why she thought I was a whore.

'The General, I replied.' They greeted that with hoots of laughter which heralded fresh spasms of coughing. The baby slid further down the young woman's lap, its neck flopping at a bad angle as the women waved their dirty rags of handkerchiefs. 'I want a proper bath,' I said. 'Nice, clean water. All the extras.'

'Water's expensive nowadays,' commented the young woman as she appraised the cost of my get-up. I decided the three women were family, there was a facial similarity, especially around the eyes. Punched black eyes, glazed currants swollen in puffy dough. 'Well, Mother?' she prompted, confirming my thought.

Speech, for the oldest woman, had assumed the form of an articulated wheeze. 'That General pays well, eh?' I took out my wallet and fanned out some notes on the counter. The third woman, who had neither spoken nor looked directly at me, laid her cards face-down on the table, scraped back her chair, hefted her bulk out of it, came over to the counter, picked up the money, secreted it in the tent of her dress, selected a towel, reached under the counter and deposited a locker key, along with one of the plastic bottles, on top of the towel.

As I reached for the bundle, her hand swooped down and grabbed my wrist, pulling my scarred palm up to the light. 'It's healed. It's not infectious,' I explained. Flattening my hand, the woman lightly tracked along the lines of my scar with the tip of a torn, yellowing fingernail. It tingled but did not hurt. I glanced up and saw the old lady sneak a look at my examiner's cards. The woman dropped my hand and snapped her head up like a turtle, studying her fellow players, both now fascinated by their own cards. Eyes flatly, almost hypnotically fixed on the others, the woman motioned me towards the opaque doors. I was dismissed.

*

'A cunt is a cunt is a cunt.' Juanita laughed as she said that, looking at me standing in front of her, laughing a laugh that said she didn't believe it. I couldn't believe it myself. I laughed too. I impulsively lent over and kissed her on the lips. My most spontaneous act in a while. The water on her skin tasted chemical, but sweet. We were standing naked between two large tubs of water, one a spa-pool churning up green water, the other a tranquil ginseng pool tinged with yellow, which is where I'd discovered her, in a pack of gossiping women.

I could feel the heat coming off the spa curling into my back.

I could feel the frank curiosity floating our way. This capturing of something from my past both excited and exposed me. All of a sudden I felt nervous. It had been years since Juanita and I had seen each other. Maybe two years.

Juanita opened a door to a large wooden box that formed a separate small room. Steam flowed out. I followed her inside. We sat facing each other in the steam bath and considered the scrawl of time on our bodies through the wreaths wrapping up our lungs and forcing out the sweat. Juanita's pubic hair, thick and springy like her head hair, was black and frizzy with the saturation, the heat; her nipples were dark, like the flesh of blood plums. Her breasts and hips were fuller than mine, but she was slender too, and the same height, which gave us a similarity, along with the bones of our faces which offered the misleading impression that I was aristocratic and Juanita was regal. The fair and the dark connotation of the words. Something we had, of course, capitalised on.

But beyond that, there had always been a physical tension

between the two of us. When we'd been girls we'd dressed in the other's clothes and compared body parts and made each other up for the boys we fucked. We'd fucked some of the same boys. Some of the same men. From the start there'd been a competitive edge between Juanita and I, a friendly feminine edge, a manner of bonding.

She flopped her legs apart. 'Not dead, eh?'

'Not yet.' We grinned and swiped at the run of sweat turning into rivers riding our bodies. 'And you?' I asked. 'Are you okay?'

'When soldiers have money to spend I do okay.'

'So there's still enough business then?'

'Yeah. Just enough.'

'Where're you working?'

'The streets. They're safer than military brothels.'

'You work alone?' That seemed equally risky.

'Uh huh. You?'

'Sort of.' I did not quite know how to express the type of risk I'd taken. 'I've got a regular provider.'

Juanita nodded and said, 'You know, not just anyone can walk in here. You need credentials, a reference, it's a private club. It's not for anyone.'

'All you need is money.'

Juanita stared at me. Assessing me. I had an overpowering need to be with her awhile. I was not thinking of consequences or of not being known when I said, 'Let's go somewhere and have a drink.' She hesitated. Before she could say no, I added, 'I'll pay you. Your usual rate. You can come with me for as long as you want.' Juanita looked away from me then. She didn't believe me. I stood up and took her by the hands and drew her to her feet, bringing her close to me, I slicked my hands down her hot shoulders. 'It's good cunt money,' I said, 'the best.' Juanita started to laugh again.

The bottle I had with me in the car was vodka. A happy coincidence—I remembered Juanita being particularly partial to vodka. I pointed her out to the guard as she emerged from the building and started down the stairs, casting about for me. When he got out and approached her she all of a sudden looked belligerent, which was how I best remembered her. He escorted her to the Mercedes. She swaggered, out of habit, perhaps, or bravado; maybe it was something the street had taught her. Legs a little too loose, slow rolling in the hip-sockets. When she saw me sitting in the genuine luxury of the car's insides, she virtually fell in the door. I nodded and the guard closed the door behind her as she slid over the seat. It was then I noticed how her hands were patterned with small pink burns, only recently healed. If she, in turn, noticed the scar on my own hand she chose to ignore it.

The Mercedes moved cautiously forward, then leapt into the frenzy of traffic. I handed Juanita the bottle and said, 'It's a fluke meeting you, you're the first person I've seen in ages who I know.'

Juanita took the vodka with a sigh. 'This your car?' she asked.

'No, I just borrow it,' I replied.

'You're doing all right,' she said, taking a good long pull.

I picked up one of her hands and held it in my lap and continued. 'Usually I don't stop. I'm driven around until I've had enough. I see quite a lot. Sometimes I go around in circles for hours.'

Juanita relaxed into the leather of the seat and said, 'I've never had a car.'

'You want to go somewhere special?' My turn to take a swig. I felt clean and alive and I was no longer alone in the car.

'Nah,' said Juanita. 'Nowhere's fine with me.'

Juanita didn't ask whose car it was. She ignored the soldier and the driver sitting tight-arsed behind the soundproof partition in the front seat. I had lucked it and that's what mattered. We sat in a bubble of safety, sealed up with our pasts, remembering and reconstructing ourselves, skirting around the present. When I finally let her out at Krupp Place, one of the popular beats, she took my money without comment. We did not make promises to meet again, we were in the moment and the moment might not sustain a future. She mumbled, 'Thanks for the drink,' and got out of the car daintily enough, but walked off with legs so loose she couldn't keep a straight course.

The oddness of her gait made me wonder if I was starting to see double but I couldn't decide, it being that kind of hot blurred evening, a pour of movement and racket. The sky was the soft drained murk of orange. There was a liveliness in the streets, a lot of business about. There'd been a lull in air raids. The war didn't sleep but it had gone so quiet of late that, combined with the pleasant heat of the evening, people were encouraged out of doors. Some of the jangled nerves had been soothed, some of the wariness had fallen away, and there was a tangible air of release, festivity almost. A lot of soldiers were on leave and that created a comforting busyness. In the afterglow of my encounter with Juanita I felt that things could quickly return to normal, if only the lull could last and become something permanent so no-one had to face another day of fighting. But I knew that the General was in the middle of planning a new offensive and there was slaughter to come.

Thinking of the General made me realise I was not quite ready for him so I amused myself further by cruising the streets, vetting the signalling women. The Mercedes was a terrible tease, but it was harmless fun and I think even my watchdog enjoyed the episode. We drove around, encouraging the girls' come-ons, until I caught sight of Juanita again. I saw her detach herself from a fuck-wall—one of those shadowy, muttering, heaving lanes where people screwed who had no better place to do it—and greet someone she wrapped in her arms and loped off with, leg to leg. Man or woman I couldn't tell, but it was no soldier. There was something so intimate in the way they walked together, a shared rhythm that told me it wasn't just any fuck she was taking somewhere. Curious, I instructed the driver to follow at a little distance, but we lost them in the tangle of bodies.

As a headache pressed in on me I let her, it, them, the street, the encounter go, and I closed my eyes against seeing her, maybe ever again, and did not open them until I was delivered to the hotel door.

My entrance coincided with a nasty wail. A siren.

The General was back.

I saw him when I entered our rooms. He was in the dark, curtains gaping at the open window, a swollen, sick-looking moon rising above the first violent arcs of tracer. Kneeling on the dining-room table, naked, knees in the mess of a meal, playing with the cutlery. By then I was seeing double. Two figures were crouching there. With a fluid movement the General raised a large knife above his head and smashed it into the table with tremendous force, attacking the table, hewing and splintering wood. I held my breath and stayed very still, my body swaying with the effort. Then he buried the knife in the chewed-up centre of the table and adroitly rolled to the floor into a standing position. I realised that he was staring straight at me. A sensation of extreme cold invaded me.

In complete silence he turned and went into his bedroom. I felt impelled to follow. I watched him laboriously climb into his bed like a clumsy but obedient child, the pieces of food stuck to his body falling from him into the sheets. When I first heard the sound I didn't know what it was. Then I realised he was snoring. I moved closer and saw that although his eyes were wide open he was deep asleep. Bubbles of spittle were gathering in the corners of his mouth and leaking down his chin.

I was not seeing double.

Outside, the siren continued squalling. Then the explosions began, one atop the other. The war had got noisy again.

TWELVE

In his night he dreams of the place of illuminated darkness. The place of resting, the final bed, the crypt, the pit, the vault, the coffin, the catacomb. Things that have never once alarmed him in his long history of killing fields. In this place he can feel himself becoming languid and luxuriously aroused. He can hear clearly, as if for the first time, the poetry of the grave. He can hear the whisper the earth makes as bodies are enfolded and fucked one last time. He can hear, too, the whistling whisper of the blade, the creaking whisper of the rope, the slurping whisper of intestines, the vegetable whisper of the twirling lotus.

This is his new poetry, his Lady's whispers.

Vapours erupt from the consecrated darkness, the bubbling white tongues of corpses. Thin eddies of scent drift above the sea of tombstones. The smell of earth to air, the translation of countless tongues. Her name on every one of them.

Kali! He yells too. Kali!

The word falls into flat, dead air. Suddenly stinking air. His mouth is left gaping. How empty he is without the word.

How alone. He knows that he has nothing human for company. Only the wind to watch him. He falls to his knees and begins the business of pulling a fresh corpse from its bed. How easily it comes into his arms, how ardent the dead are to be found. How abundant they are, jostling for attention. An air-raid siren starts somewhere, not far away, and goes on and on, a throb of panic and determination, persistently painful.

A poignant song.

The next line in the song is simple. He takes a knife and in one movement slices the yielding throat. A huge grin. Then he anoints his hands in the stream that springs before him. A stream that issues from the corpse's neck. And his hands begin swimming in the stream in a way that is very peaceful. Meditative.

Alone with death, full of solitude, full of longing, he methodically paints his genitals with blood.

It is only after he has prepared himself in this way for her, the way of the consort, that he hears her footsteps and the long emptiness of his night is broken. In the humming of earth he hears the soft slither of night patrols, the tattoo of infantry, the constant shifting sea of troops, and his heart lurches in gladness. Joy and supplication.

His fingers slide together and his hands knot in an attitude of prayer. His head bows. He is careful not to look up. The footsteps stop behind him. He feels her breath on the back of his neck like a lick of flame, and from the dazzling behind him the hands touch him. Something bursts within him.

Oh Lady!

One hand slips the noose around his neck, squeezing it tight until he is breathless for her, one hand engulfs his stiff penis in pleasure, one hand penetrates his anus. The arse of him is fucked by her as her fourth hand places the sword between his clasped fingers.

Feed me, she says.

Held in the ecstasy of hands, he puts her sword into the swollen belly of the corpse and slices it open. Sternum to groin. The corpse whispers delight.

Now eat, she demands.

Eat.

She takes the snake of intestine in her impatient fourth hand and rams it into his mouth. He retches without waking as he receives the sacrament.

THIRTEEN

A volume of an antiquated *Encyclopedia America* provided me with a useful definition: a prisoner of war was a member of a belligerent's armed forces taken by the enemy and treated according to the Geneva Convention Relative to the Treatment of Prisoners of War. The POW had a protected status. The POW was to be detained humanely for no purpose other than to prevent participation in combat. When the convention became customary international law in 1949, the categories of people who could be classified as POWs had inflated due to the increasingly elaborate nature of warfare. Since the General was a stickler for historical detail, I delivered the words 'nineteen hundred and forty-nine' to him with some satisfaction.

That same year saw the drawing up of another convention, the Geneva Convention Relative to the Protection of Civilian Persons in Time of War, which was supposed to protect interned civilians. I'd never heard of it and as the conversation went on I realised it had been a futile and expensive gesture getting one of the hotel staff to procure the encyclopedia for me. Getting hold of the latest American gun would have been a cinch. Despite my having done my homework, the General was not interested in conceding any points that night.

The General had been citing both Geneva conventions as impacting upon the latest situation, even though he insisted that the conventions were not much more than historical curiosities. We were discussing the situation over a meal of coq au vin. I decided that the burgundy had more body than the rooster and began entertaining myself by making small mounds of bird bones on the table, to which the General was happily contributing. As he tossed a section of rib on the damask tablecloth he said, 'If you follow that line of logic, either convention confers on the prisoner a protected status. The key word being protection. The only relevant debate being the type of protection best afforded not only to the POWs, but to the victors. The commander of the occupying force determines that. He must protect his position and his men, as well as the occupied population, and eliminate all potential or actual threat.'

'It's barbaric, putting heads on spikes. It's like something from the Middle Ages.' I picked up the heavy silver-plated knife and put it down again. It gleamed at me, its polish mottled with disuse.

'In the Middle Ages POWs had no rights at all. From classical times they were ransomed, bartered, enslaved, or killed. Usually killed. Alexander the Great drowned 3000 POWs at Krokos in the fourth century BC. It was par for the course. The first treaty to formalise rights for POWs was in 1775. Prior to that, what existed was something like a gentlemen's agreement.'

'Of little value to those who were not gentlemen, of course,' I replied. The General shrugged. 'But that still doesn't mean no-one had the notion or the will to treat their prisoners humanely before then,' I continued.

He took another helping of food. 'Even the Geneva Convention permitted the execution of terrorists, spies and saboteurs.' There was a pause while I pushed the mess I had made of my meal as far away from me as I could. A greasiness coated my stomach.

'Was there a trial?' I asked.

The General searched through his mouth with his fingers hunting out the last pieces of meat from his teeth before answering. 'A closed court. Proof of guilt incontrovertible. POWs obey every law, every regulation, every order of the detaining power or they're punished. To punish is to instil discipline. To punish is to ensure compliance.'

'It's not very humane executing your POWs and displaying the corpses. On national television. It's called an atrocity. Besides, a prisoner of war has no allegiance to the detaining power.' I slopped the wine as I topped up his glass, not an accident. We both watched the red seep into the tablecloth, our breathing perfectly twinned. 'In fact it's their duty to try to escape.'

'These were not ordinary POWs. They were war criminals. They had committed terrible crimes against our people. It was imperative they be punished to show how we will not waver in our duty to justice. Being just is a necessary element in this war, it shows our natural superiority over the enemy.' He wiped his mouth with a snowy napkin, spotting it with rust-coloured stains that reminded me of the spore of fungi. 'Besides, executions are extremely effective as a control mechanism.'

'But not humane.'

'When has war ever been humane?'

I was then informed that, in the legal sense, an act of war did not necessarily constitute a state of war.

Or a declaration of war.

An act of war could be considered a just response in a domestic disagreement. An act of war could occur outside a state of war. Outside the usual laws and the customs of war. No Geneva Convention need apply. No need to pay any heed to the concept of a POW. The prisoner of an act of war had no rights whatsoever. The best such a prisoner could hope for was to be considered valuable enough to attract the price of release. If he was one of the gentlemen in the gentlemen's agreement. A situation not unlike the Middle Ages.

After a while the General stopped talking and the silence swelled out from under the low hum of the air-conditioner. It was a quiet night, in itself unusual, because usually the heat amplified the nearness of the war. The guttering candles pushed our shadows up against the walls and I suddenly felt as blurred and as insubstantial as a shadow, that trapped thing which cannot exist without a corresponding substance but which has no substance of its own. I was tired. My hand ached. I fished the bird's wishbone from a heap of chewed bones and held it with my teeth and my hand. I closed my eyes as I cracked it apart. The sound of it breaking was sharp and loud.

'What are you wishing for?' There was an intensity in the General's voice which took me aback. I was grateful I was able to tell him the truth.

'I wish I hadn't hurt it,' I said, laying my scarred hand on the table, 'it's a bitch.'

'Quite the contrary,' the General smiled at me, his fingers moving over my scar, 'in time you will understand that such a mark is a blessing.' I could not muster an answering smile.

*

The days disappeared, one inside the other, one fish swallowing another, then another fish swallowing that one, then another fish and another. And another. I was cocooned by the General's care. Following my little folly with the *Encyclopedia America* he presented me with von Clausewitz's tome *On War* and ordered me to read it for edification. We then went through a distinctly unedifying process of me having to read portions of the book aloud to him whenever he was in the mood. Fortunately the work comprised handy little sub-headings within chapters within books and I would read at random, jumping from 'Military Virtues of the Army' to 'Attacks on Swamps, Flooded Areas, and Forests' to 'What is War?' A fairly heady question, one, of course, which the General pursued.

Von Clausewitz had advanced the argument that there was ideal or absolute war and there was real war. I took the line that ideal war might be a useful concept for the war-shapers and myth-makers in the Department of Historical Warfare but real war, although supposedly a lesser form of war, was the only sort of war worth talking about because real war was actual war. 'Absolute war is an impossibility,' I suggested.

'No, no,' objected the General, 'it is entirely possible. Think of nuclear warfare.'

'I suppose a complete nuclear wipe-out constitutes absolute war, as long as there's absolutely nothing left after it. But doesn't it ruin the idea of a victory?'

'The obliterating act is the ideal of a true war. An ideal war would necessitate the complete obliterating act. True war is an ideal, it is how war ought to be.'

'Why do you call it a true war?'

'Because an absolute war is the most truthful form of war that can occur. It provides the notion of what is required. True war is pure war and the true warrior will strive for this purity. The true warrior knows that he has a calling and he dedicates himself to it. This dedication simply isn't possible unless he believes in something larger than the war at hand. Wars come and go, but war itself—not *the* war or *a* war—is a constant. War is truth.'

'It's only a warrior's truth, it's not everyone's truth. Not everyone believes in war. There're people who believe in peace.'

The General laughed. 'Until their peace is threatened. Peace as an ideal is in fact more ludicrous than war as an ideal could ever be because war is nature. Peace is like war in so far as both are a means of implementing and continuing policy. But there the similarity ends. Until those who believe in peace start to fight for peace and discover the true nature of war, which is that it serves only itself.'

'Apart from when it's serving the policy-makers,' I said sarcastically.

'Precisely.'

'Do you believe in peace?' I ventured.

'Peace is not innate like war, it is not natural. Peace is surrender,' he replied, 'nothing more, nothing less and I do not follow a policy of surrender.'

Reading that book did nothing to increase my appreciation of war, absolute or otherwise, and the activity pushed my thoughts towards Sol. I would think of him and his stand against the war every time I was obliged to discuss von Clausewitz with the General. I knew that if I didn't get a message to Sol soon I might lose him for good and the possibility of that was already tearing my armour away from me. Once before I'd done battle with myself over him. Reason had lost and I'd made the decision to keep my connection with him.

Finally I became desperate enough to decide to risk visiting Mei Lien at the bar in Bernanos Street for news. With bitter humour I realised that all I could convey in a message to him was that I was 'busy'. I sweated over a scheme: I'd do a pub crawl and make sure the bar was just a stop along the way. I'd do it on a day when I was with the guard who was the least officious. I'd prepare a good story to explain my absence to Mei Lien. I'd trust in the moment. I'd have to. I thought through all the scenarios but I didn't factor in one thing— when I finally got to Bernanos Street the bar was no longer there. It had been closed down, the place gutted. Worse, Mei Lien had lived in a room above and she'd disappeared along with every recognisable feature of the place where Sol and I had met. My one means of communicating with him had vanished.

As I stood there uselessly rattling the broken bar door I felt a powerful impulse to take off down the street, to run somewhere, god knows where, anywhere, but I couldn't at that moment think of anywhere, and besides, the watch-dog would outrun me. So I about-turned, stepping over the pieces of my smashed-up hope, and went on to the next bar as planned.

'Our ground units will make incisive cuts in enemy lines. Our air attacks will disable them. We'll slice through their supply lines. Obliterate their command centres. Smash their reinforcing units. We are going to crush the enemy in the rear and gobble him up at the front. Yum. Yum.' I opened my eyes and realised the General was addressing me. He was in a happy mood.

'Is this the victory that will end the war, then?' I leaned over the vanity basin and spat blood. Not too red, not too painful.

The General replied, 'That is not an anticipated outcome. War is, above all else, an exercise in the unpredictable. The uncontrollable.'

It was a new day.

My eyes sank into the mirror. I was not a pretty sight.

I had woken up alone on the floor of the bathroom, I must have passed out sometime during the night after the General had finished with me. I ran a bath. The water that surged out of taps contorted to resemble dolphins contained a fair quantity of fine, liverish-looking mud. I disguised the mucky water with some bubble-bath. The General scrutinised my reflection as I undressed. I was wearing the remnants of a lightweight battle-dress uniform and I hoped that the slightly sweet, fetid smell emanating from the outfit wasn't coming from me. It reminded me of something just beginning to rot. When I was naked the General reached out and pressed his fingers against the yellow bruises decorating my breasts.

'There is no such thing as surrender,' he said, 'where there is the skill of deception. You understand this.'

The General had arrived home in the middle of the night. Incapable of sleep, I'd had the lights off and the blackout curtains open, keeping company with the orange insomniac sky, watching a complicated play of anti-aircraft fire and tracer rounds. The light show was some way off but it felt and sounded closer than it had ever been before. I poured another drink. Strategy seemed to be a problem. I wondered if anyone knew what the hell was going on. I was too affected by the failure of my outing to invite any of my guards in for a tête-à-tête, although it was unlikely they would have told me anything anyway.

He came in noiselessly, like an animal. What alerted me to his presence was the sudden slide into silence. All outside noise abruptly drained away, creating a quality of calm which was, in the circumstances, highly unnatural. The ice cubes tilted and clacked in my sweating glass. I had to fight an irrational impulse to break something, to bring back the clamour. Instead I sank back into the plump goose-down pillows bolstering the divan, planting my body in softness until the pressure of a shadow upon my closed eyelids told me that the General was standing directly in front of me.

He appeared to have bathed in a colour which left a glowing crust on him. I had never seen such blood on him before, it gave his skin texture, it most definitely gave him a presence. It spooked me, how the throb of the sky complemented him. After several moments of silence I spoke up. 'This light suits you,' I said.

'You know the allure of death,' he whispered.

'No,' I said, 'I don't think there's any mystery about dying. No.'

'You know it in the same way you know everything else. You know it in the same place. Inside. Deep inside your belly. You have discovered the allure of death the same way you discovered the pleasure of your hole.'

He placed the flat of his hand against my womb. Then he parted my thighs with his other hand and gently felt my labia through the paper-thin negligee I was wearing. Whenever I was touched like that I became wet, despite myself. As it was, this talent of mine for wetness was taken by the General as confirmation of his wild conjecture. 'This is how you know death,' he insisted, kneeling at my feet, running his fingers up under my gown, along the skin of my legs, between the heat of my thighs to the hairline of my slit. After dipping the index and middle fingers of his left hand into my cunt he began to slide them in and out of me in a slow, leisurely manner. 'This is how you fuck death.'

I did not speak. There was no need to. I saw how he was smiling at me so I began undressing him. His uniform was moist, my negligee was soft. When he grasped it in his stained fingers it ripped. I smiled back at him, I knew that one. But then our usual opera was interrupted. He took his fingers out of me and reached into a pocket of his uniform and withdrew a knife, a narrow curving knife, its shape quite elegant. And fabric slid, in tatters. And his colour lanced me.

When did my skin turn hard and hurting like a boil, at what moment did it turn so angry? I think it was a purely reflex action when I grabbed the knife.

As always, it had been what he'd wanted.

As always, I had somehow known.

'You are pure sex, Lady,' he had said as he pulled me down to him. 'Suck me. I want to hear you slurping.'

FOURTEEN

Damage concealment is a tricky art. It takes a little training, it's a process of adaptation. At first it was nothing too obvious. It was subtle, insidious, engaging. The imprint of thumbs could be camouflaged with cover-up stick, an application of Courage makeup and a layer of Radiant Rout face powder. I learnt the art of repairing myself so that in daylight I would pass muster. I learnt the colours which best reshaped and disguised my features and experienced the odd allure of wearing dark glasses indoors. I learnt the usefulness of having the right sort of clothes, the sort that did not display too much patterned flesh, and on those occasions when the damage could not be contained, I required invisibility.

I came to understand this facet of war.

I fitted my sunglasses and doctored myself with the cocktails I found the most anaesthetising and for my amusement the General or one of his proxies would tutor me in the art of playing dominoes. I would be confined, as comfortably as my condition permitted, in a shadowy corner of a room, fingering the smooth rectangles of bone, making my selections from the bone yard, manoeuvring the cool pitted tiles in increasingly complicated versions of the game.

Learning how to win.

I learnt how a domino is divided into two distinct halves by a central line: the separate halves identified either by the indentations which represent the irrefragable marks or a blankness. That a domino is also a term used for a mask gave the game for me an irony that the General's witticisms about domino theory did not.

When I was sufficiently recovered I would indulge in my other entertainment—to be driven around the city in the Mercedes concealed behind dark, bulletproof windows. I would sit in the back seat with a bottle and close the partition between me and my bodyguard. I would think about the possibility of seeing Sol, catching sight of him walking along the street or emerging from the doorway of a building, and I'd look out from my mobile cocoon and it was dreamlike, the way the streets slid by, my transport attracting curious looks from people to whom I was a blank, a gesture, a substanceless form in the back seat of a car that denoted considerable power.

I felt no power. What I was doing was adding dimension to my time alone. Rather, as alone as my circumstances permitted. My hand, although still tender, had healed as well as it was going to, leaving the jagged signature of the General's god. I found myself obsessively looking at it, touching it, feeling the red welt of my raised flesh, the way it puckered the skin and reminded me of its presence whenever I pushed down on the flat of my hand. The General had got into the habit of grabbing my scarred hand and clamping it hard against his face when we were fucking and it had become a signal to me that he was close to coming. The healing of my wound did not, however, bring an end to my surveillance.

'Unforeseen consequences are the by-product of any action,' he told me. 'This is a time for vigilance, of guarding against uncertainty.'

'It is also possible that a bomb could drop on us at any moment,' I argued, 'but that doesn't mean we need live out our lives in bomb shelters.'

'We must act in accordance with the parameters of the situation,' he answered. 'The situation of war inherently contains the possibilities of a strike. This is factored into the calculations of risk, and so becomes an acceptable risk. It is nothing more or less than a necessity of war. I do not classify a random attack of street violence as being within the realm of necessary risk as such. I am not convinced that you are yet out of danger.'

'What danger? You make it sound as though I was deliberately targeted.'

He touched my shoulder with his open mouth, a type of kiss. 'How do you know that you were not?'

I swallowed the bile that my lie about being robbed had produced and resorted to repeating for the umpteenth time, 'Someone seized the moment. Nothing more. Nothing less. No danger. No premeditation. No plan.' He made no response to that. He rolled off me and went over to his uniform, laid carefully over the back of a chair. I felt incredibly light without his weight to pin me down. I felt like I might float up and bump against my reflection in the mirror, gilded by cupids, on the ceiling. I could not avoid seeing myself, there was not a place without mirrors in that damn honeymoon suite. He flicked a speck of lint from a sleeve and began to whistle a military tune as he turned his attention to dressing.

Subject closed.

When I faced the fact that I could not contact Sol on my own I went looking for Juanita. I was at the end of my tether. I knew Juanita could move around the city with relative freedom and she was my only hope. Mei Lien had vanished and there was not one person in my circle I could approach for help. I cursed myself for letting Juanita go so easily when we'd parted but I knew she'd been working the streets near the Eastern Sector so I cruised up and down the beats. The sleek car attracted the women's attention as previously but it took several efforts before I got lucky. I'd been combing the sad-looking streets which flowed into the basin of the Sector—a marginal area, one which made the driver nervous and put my guard on full alert—when I finally spotted her.

She was standing in a gaggle of women. My guard ordered the driver to keep the engine running as he and I slid out of the car in tandem. The little group was huddled too tightly together to be bothered by us, even though my watch-dog was stalking the scene as if he were expecting a terrorist attack. Juanita was in a circle of women, five in all, gathered around a slaughtered pig in the middle of the road. Nearby lay the body of a man, which they ignored. Both corpses had their throats slit from ear to ear and their bellies slashed open. The killings had been executed with relative neatness—it looked like a single slice across the throat and one down the torso. Despite the precision of the cuts there was a lot of blood on the road. There were some flies, but not as many as one would expect. These deaths were recent then. Fresh.

One woman, short and fat with fraying hair, waved ineffectually at the flies. Another shook out a length of material from a back-pack and laid it beside the puddle of blood leaking out of the animal. I remember the fabric had a pattern of purple hibiscus blotting a white background like enormous bruises. Two other women smoothed the material out along the length of the pig, then the three of them flipped the pig onto it and began to tightly swaddle and solicitously tuck the swine up. Their tenderness looked absurd as blood rapidly ate the hibiscus flowers. I shifted forward and called out Juanita's name. She looked up and, by way of acknowledgement, stepped away from the group. The four remaining women gripped the bundle and heaved it into their arms. The strain was evident, one woman made a peculiar whooshing noise between her teeth and another groaned. I could see the outbreak of their sweat. Then they lifted the dripping bundle and staggered off down the street carrying their prize. In all this time not one word had been spoken.

I told the guard to stay put and went over to Juanita. We were left alone with the remaining corpse. She knelt and quickly, expertly, went through the pockets in the dead man's clothing. She found nothing. As she jostled the body his guts slid in their torn envelope. She rolled back on her haunches and poked a couple of fingers into the split belly and, digging deep, pulled out a boning knife. Despite the gore, I could see the thing had an elegant shape. The man's intestines listed and slowly poured out onto the pavement. I heard it distinctly, the plopping. I turned away and signalled for the car and we got in. Juanita did not even ask where I was taking her. For my part, I was distracted by Juanita's smell—her fingers exuded the odour of the corpse even though she had wiped her hands on the dead man's clothing.

That morning the General had gone to inspect new defences at the front. I took advantage of his absence to usher Juanita into the hotel, past the attentive soldiers, along the whispering corridors, until I had her in the privacy of my suite where I marched her straight into the bathroom. When she yelped I realised that not all the burns ornamenting her hands were old. She yanked her hand out of my grasp and I knew better than to ask. I found a tube of antiseptic cream for her instead. 'You smell of blood,' I told her, handing her soap and a towel. 'Take a bath.'

I got rid of the guards and took out a bottle of vodka. When the bathroom door opened Juanita emerged in a fragrant collusion of bathroom vapour, soft surfaces and hard angles. In that moment, with her standing in my doorway in my bathrobe smelling of my toiletries, I was reminded of how similar we were, beyond the fair and the dark, the light and the shade, the blue and the black. How perennially similar.

I had no choice. I had to trust her.

I splashed more vodka into her glass and sat next to her. Close enough to see the large open pores of her skin, to hear the pull of her breath, to measure the pulse-beat in her neck. I tuned my voice to her ear and told her about Sol. 'He's my lover,' I said, 'and he's a resister. I need you to find out if he's all right. If he's safe. And I want him to know that I'm okay.' Juanita's eyes flicked around the extravagances of the room, and she gave me a mocking smile and swallowed her drink. Her lips shone at me.

'What's safe?' she asked.

'I need to know that he's alive and that he's going to stay alive,' I replied.

'Why not find out for yourself?'

'I'll pay you,' I side-stepped. 'It'll be worth your while.'

'Why not go to him yourself?' she repeated.

'You don't know what it's like for me. All you have to do is find him and give him some money and a message. Please.'

'What sort of message?'

'You tell him I love him.'

Juanita didn't reply. She spurned the bottle I held out to her and sauntered over to the sideboard and opened a new one. She didn't believe me. She didn't believe the luxury. She was thinking that it would have been better, somehow more true, if I had been like her—out on a street selling myself like the commodity she thought I pretended I was not.

'What do I tell him when he asks me about you?' she demanded. 'What if he wants to know where you are?'

'Tell him anything but the truth,' I said. The door opened and I saw her freeze. The General was not meant to be in the city, but here he was. I wondered if he had engaged in a little subterfuge to check up on me. Juanita was standing with her back against the wall, which made her look somewhat hunted. Did he frighten her? The General interrogated her in a glance, he was good at that sort of thing. After the initial shock, she seemed to relax, her body yielding in such a way it looked like she was totally available to him.

I realised that Juanita was quite capable of holding her own. I saw approval gather at the corner of the General's mouth. I saw him look at me, then he went back to her, almost sniffing—yes, very much like sniffing her out. He began circling her the way a dog circles a bitch and we all knew it. Juanita knew what this game was about. She glanced at me, I glanced away, the General remained intent. I knew him. He was so absurdly male about it I almost laughed. Juanita saw the tickle of my smile and made a feint towards him.

The General ignored her and swooped on an object on the sideboard. He held up the boning knife, the dried blood giving the cast of rust to the metal. 'Where did you get this?' he asked. His voice was pitched very low. He was growling in his attempt to seem calm. Juanita looked nervous again, however I had the advantage of knowing the General's excitements.

'The body was still warm. The neck had been sliced. Split open from here to here,' I answered, running a slow finger between my breasts down to my pubic bone. 'The knife had been left inside his stomach. Like a message. When she pulled the knife out his guts slithered everywhere.'

'Like spaghetti?' the General asked.

'Yes. Like spaghetti,' I lied. Innards did not look like spaghetti to me.

'And this one found the knife?' he asked, going over to Juanita and pushing the tip of the knife against the skin of her throat.

'Yes. It was buried deep in the pit of his belly,' I replied. Juanita remained tactfully silent.

'You knew where to look for it then?' he asked her. She nodded almost imperceptibly. 'What are you?' he asked, almost purring.

She stood her ground. 'A whore,' she said. The General smiled and took the knife away from her throat and brought it up to his mouth. With his eyes fastened on me, he ran his tongue across the narrow flat of the blade to get his taste of it.

'You can go now,' I told her.

'No,' ordered the General. 'Don't send her away. I want to see you take her. After all, that's why the whore's here, isn't she?' He went and hunched down in the shadows—vague, half-lit, glazed, intent.

I began by undressing her. The bathrobe slipped off easily, her skin smoothed by my toiletries, her body looking pliable, languid, accommodating. Juanita knew her cue. She arched back, naked on the settee, her legs forming a dark inverted V, revealing her cunt with her fingers to the crouching figure of the General. I stood before her and dropped my clothes so that the full extent of me would also be seen without effort.

The taste of a woman's sex is particular to her, there may be a generic saltiness, softness, wetness, fleshiness, but there is always a particular taste. Juanita's cunt-flesh reminded me of mushrooms fresh out of the earth and I forgot myself in that moment of putting my face between her legs. I forgot we were a theatrical event. I forgot not the General so much as the General's need. For a moment, my own desire eclipsed his and that was a strategic error.

Juanita was writhing in my mouth when the General's crop whistled across my bare arse. I thought the whistling was a mortar shell coming closer than ever before, but then it was inscribing the arc of the room and exploding on top of me, streaking across my skin. Juanita's legs held me in a vice. Her cunt spasmed. The crop slashed in renewed assault. Juanita opened her eyes and shrieked, scrabbling away from me. I began screaming. The shrill sound of my screams had the effect I knew they would—an aphrodisiac for the General. Totally aroused and erect, he put the crop in my mouth, like a stick to bear down upon, then he mounted me and sodomised me and made his kind of love to my arse. I looked up and watched Juanita watch me.

Afterwards, when the General had retired for the night, she bathed my inflamed buttocks and whispered, 'I'll do what you asked.' And there was nothing else we needed to speak of.

That night, after the General had made his new imprints on me, I started dreaming of a place of blood. Rivers and deserts and skies and mountains and fields of blood. And not just blood. A place of corpses slashed open at the belly and missing their guts.

FIFTEEN

I had not seen or heard from Juanita since we had presented our little piece of theatre for the General. She had been deposited back in the city late that night by an army jeep. I had thrust a telephone number wrapped up inside money into her hand and my last view of her had been distorted by a vile breeze grabbing her inky mass of hair and twisting it around her head as she was escorted to the jeep. I watched from the buffer of my window as the flimsy-looking vehicle carried her out of sight.

It transpired to be a long night of shrieking wind and the next morning the air was particularly foul, full of debris being hurled from one end of the city to the other in a more equitable distribution of goods and garbage. I felt light-hearted despite my tenderised skin because Juanita was going to try to find Sol for me. We had agreed on a simple code: when she found him she would phone and ask me for extra rations of coffee.

As we said goodbye I also handed her a small ankh and told her to give it to Sol for 'luck'. 'He'll know what it means,' I insisted. It was my practice to give him good-luck charms for the silver bracelet I'd given him. The fact that he continued to wear it was evidence to me of his romantic feelings. It would also prove that I had sent her. I extracted Juanita's promise to keep quiet about my situation with the General. 'You realise you're a positive danger to lover boy, don't you?' she had murmured. 'Assuming I can even find him.'

'I can help him,' I replied. 'Maybe not right at this moment. But somehow I'll help. I can't let him go.'

'And what do I say when he asks why it's me and not you delivering sweet endearments? Presuming he'll even talk to me, that is.'

'Say I'll be with him soon.'

'That'll be a cosy threesome,' she said, 'you, your boyfriend and the General.'

I ignored her. 'I know you can lie and I don't care what you say as long as he doesn't find out where I am.'

'You don't know me that well,' she said provocatively, 'you don't know whether I can lie like that.'

'I'm paying you to lie,' I replied. 'Is it a problem? Yes or no.'

'No,' she answered after a beat.

That beat fuelled my stubbornness. 'I won't give up on him,' I insisted. 'If you can't do it I'll find a way to him.'

'You've seen too many movies,' she sighed. 'You sit in here insulated from what's out there. You haven't got a clue.'

'I know what it's like,' I insisted. 'Out there's where I come from. Out there's what I know. In here, it's … survival, just the same.'

She smoothed the money into her bag. 'It's not the same. You and the General, it's not exactly business, is it?' She lifted up my chin with her finger and looked me in the eye. 'Is it?' When I said nothing she pushed against me and whispered, 'But that doesn't mean I won't do business with you.'

Juanita did not make a return visit to the hotel, nor did she call, nor was she in any of her usual places when I drove around looking for her in the following weeks. She had refused to give me an address, telling me she'd be in touch. Returning to the women's baths where I'd first discovered her, I found the building bolted and boarded over and a crookedly painted sign on the door: 'Closed by Reasons of Hygiene'. I began to worry. I thought Juanita quite capable of looking after herself. It was Sol I worried about. I brooded over the possibility that she was avoiding me because she had bad news. Had something happened to Sol? Had my absence caused him to give up on me? Was he alive? Imprisoned? Dead?

I took to my bed.

The General got in his medico, who admired the ugly scar he had made on my palm and pronounced me anaemic and in need of iron supplements. I was served a monotonous diet of underdone meats and raw liver. I did not care to ask about the origin of this meat during an acute shortage of fresh food and it was only when I was forced to that I daintily ate. Sleeping was difficult after these meals. I would dream of obstructions in my throat—fuse wire, the tongues of belts, shoelaces, lengths of rope, buttons dangling from threads, the opened teeth of zips, strands of coloured braid and twisted ribbons— and I would wake spitting strings of saliva and coughing.

What promoted my recovery was the appointment of a young corporal as my regular guard-dog. Perhaps I was not considered a risk while I behaved like an invalid. During the period spent mooning around in my room I ascertained that the boy was clearly bored with his job, and even more clearly amenable to gross flattery. It was a stroke of luck to have been given someone so young, so eager, with so much potential. His early distrust of me dwindled away under the campaign I conducted to win his confidence. I marshalled my energies. I endlessly eulogised the General, who was the young man's hero. I reminded him in subtle and not so subtle ways that I was the General's blessed intimate. I shared the most glorious projected outcomes of our war with him. I even presented him with small trinkets of the General's—a clothes brush, a canteen, a broken pair of field glasses, a stained cloth which I said carried the mark of a battle wound—and I gave him the slip by urging the General's favourite brandy into him and drinking him under the table. I seized a moment when the General was definitely out of the city. I gagged the boy's mouth, tied up his pliable body and locked him in a closet after divesting him of his clothes.

For the first time I truly understood the fascination for cross-dressing. I was absurdly pleased to note how well his uniform fitted, with some judicious tucking and padding here and there. He was one of those wiry, monkey little men, the sort that often surprise one with the length of their prick. Fortunately, his prick had been the first part of him to go limp before the rest of him joined it in situ. In deference to the cock I rolled up a hanky and stuffed it in my underpants so that a slight bulge showed. I looked rather effective with a machismo swagger. With my nose grazing a pile of army files lifted from the General's study it was unbelievably easy to exit through the hotel's front doors. I planned to be gone only a short while so that if my little soldier did wake, his humiliation might buy his silence, or, at the very least, his racket would come too late to stop me.

There were a lot of soldiers in the city and this was creating a lively mood. Apparently there had been a lull in the fighting. I heard a television crowing that our ground forces had effected a meaningful resistance, that we had sustained a spectacular land success, that the enemy was in retreat. I took the news with a healthy cynicism but still, there'd been no air-raid alerts of late and the sour wind which had been harassing the city for weeks had withdrawn. It was one of those soft, hazy days, the sky shimmering, the giant orange orb of sun throbbing with a comforting warmth. The moment of calm, combined with the news that the General was in the Safe Zone conducting negotiations, seduced people into relaxing their vigilance. The very idea of a Safe Zone was soothing, although misleading for I knew that the General had gone there to oversee the execution of certain uncooperative prisoners.

Moving around without a guard on my tail was a joy, too long untasted. I audaciously, slyly saluted my officers, making the signals of a brotherhood which returned to me streets I had not walked in a while. My spirits soared, nothing seemed forbidden, nothing would be denied. I was myself again, my uniform and my money creating a luxurious sense of freedom, honed by that nice thin edge of risk, of being found out as an impostor. There is no better freedom than the one informed by imprisonment. When you comprehend the fragility of freedom, you don't foreclose on it, you grab it when you can, you revel in it because you know it will close up around you of some accord, sooner or later.

My first port of call was a grungy noodle bar I used to frequent. Juanita had told me that she occasionally worked out of a factory shop-front nearby and I hoped the owner of the noodle bar, a rough-faced woman built like a wrestler who did not hesitate to act as a bouncer when required, might have seen her. The woman shook her head in a mournful manner—no, she didn't know anyone called Juanita. I could tell she was fazed by my costume and she cautioned me when I told her I was dressed like a soldier to win a bet. The mood of the city was so ripe it was going to burst, she predicted, it was no time to be playing games. I stayed a little while, sampling the lousy food and the significantly better home-brewed beer, leaving an unjustifiably large tip. 'I'll keep an eye out for your friend,' she winked.

I was trawling through one of the better known fuck districts when I had a stroke of luck. I had just come out of Falklands Place, pleasantly buoyed by the home brew, the girls out in full force swinging their breasts and their arses at any passing soldier with such provocation that I felt a definite desire. My costume was so successful, I did not consider their ability to arouse me strange. I had stepped into an alleyway to discreetly adjust the little lump I was losing down my trouser leg when I looked up and saw Juanita hurrying along Rommel Street. I zipped up my fly and set off at a run after her.

I was gaining on her when the sky above me began to alter and radically bend. A spot of colour grew; at first it was nothing more than a small stain, but in a matter of moments it assumed the heart-stopping signature shape of an A-bomb blast. There was no sound. The sky was not convulsed by anything other than this elegantly exploding mushroom of vermilion. A colour that grew rapidly, grew exponentially, bloomed in nanotime across our soft, orange-skinned sky. As that vibrant, alarming gush of red effortlessly washed over us the same thought must have gone ricocheting from head to head—that a lethal weapon had been loosed upon the city without warning. The thought contained so much dread that the type of calm born of horror rippled out and the red drifted down to us across an eerie silence. I looked about and saw how people were standing stock-still, waiting to drop like agonised flies. I recall with clarity the realisation that I had no gas mask and that I would die. I struggled against breathing, but when that became impossible I opened my mouth and took a great gasp of air and waited for whatever horror would take me.

Nothing happened.

I experienced no new physical sensation. My bodily processes and mental faculties seemed intact. I took some cautious steps. I felt the same. The air did not smell or taste any different and everything appeared as before, except for the new glow of red. Then the stasis ceased and the panicked city violently erupted into living again. I lost Juanita in the frenzy.

When I returned to the hotel late that night I was appallingly drunk. I'd had no luck finding Juanita again. The city was bedlam and the army was touring streets in tanks and trucks, with machine guns and loud-hailers, repeating over and over that there was no cause for alarm and no need for gas masks. The city had not been attacked. The city was secure. But my disguise no longer seemed safe. To get off the streets I ducked into a watering hole somewhere. I must have tried it on at some point because I remember a round, rather pretty, moon-faced young woman slipping a petite hand into my fly and shrieking in my ear with laughter. When my funds ran out I staggered home. My freedom did not seem very much by then.

Home.

The General was waiting for me. He had thrown the shutters open wide and was watching the sullen red burn that was now the night sky. There was a distant barrage of fire, then colour hurtled across the already coloured sky. Pretty, pretty fireworks that had impact. When he saw me he grinned. It had been a while since he'd had me in uniform. Too long, I could tell. 'My brave little soldier,' he said, 'your outfit is lacking.' He handed me a rectangular gift box, on which was taped a medal. I squinted at it and saw that it was the Cross of Honourable Conduct. I giggled and tore the medal away from the sticky-tape securing it to the box and pinned the medal on my chest. 'Open your gift,' he said. I fumbled with the lid of the box and tore it off. Something lay inside the royal purple satin and as I furrowed in the box the satin twitched. 'A remembrance of the highest kind from the soldier you bested,' whispered the General.

It slid into my hand. Slick and cooling. I stared at the severed penis and carried it over to the light. It rolled slightly in the palm of my hand, kissing the General's favourite scar. I wondered if the organ had been drained of blood, there was so little of it in evidence. I wondered about it in the abstract, this thing so disconnected from me. Was it stuffed? It looked huge. I turned to the General. I must have looked puzzled. 'To complete your uniform,' he explained, 'to make a man of you.' Then he made me poke it out through my fly, but not before I vomited over the balustrade. My ejaculation streamed out and out until I was sufficiently emptied, even of bile.

That night the General danced. He had no need of sleep to dream. He danced in me and around me and with me. Inhabiting the most weird, frightening state, the General danced me until I teetered and dropped. Then he laid me out and continued. Where I was not sore I was numb, and I knew I would be dressing wounds in the morning.

Later that night the soldiers danced in a stream out of the city for the Bitch of Battles.

SIXTEEN

The castration of the corporal was not the only outcome of my illicit outing—guards no longer watched over me. My deceit had intoxicated the General and my return to him achieved what tears and tantrums and withdrawal had not. It had alleviated a notion he must have had that I might shoot through, given the chance.

Now I had a man's blood on me I realised it was something I had no choice but to wear. By implicating me in the corporal's mutilation the General had adroitly initiated me into his manner of war. In one stroke he had forced me to appreciate how there was no longer the luxury of choice.

Now there was merely the logic of acceptance.

The General woke me in the incarnadine light of dawn before he left for Command Headquarters. 'I dreamt of you,' he said, his fingers hovering above my hair, 'I saw how you bit off that man's penis.' Involuntarily I reached between my legs. I was still in uniform but the penis was no longer there. 'He was your necessary sacrifice.'

'Is he dead?' I asked.

'Anyone who knows your touch knows death,' he replied.

I opened my mouth to protest but my throat had closed over. His words were absurd but even so, they frightened me. All the more so after what had happened to the corporal. 'You're still alive,' I finally managed to croak.

'You are my consort,' he breathed. 'We are twinned and I am your instrument.' He kissed the palm of my damaged hand in a slow, lingering way. 'My faith in you will reap me my highest reward.'

'What do you mean?'

'I have seen what is necessary in order to complete the destruction of the enemy. My name will be synonymous with their slaughter and the razing of their cities and in their defeat they shall call for you but in vain.' He was speaking in that elaborate way he usually reserved for making announcements to the media.

'For me?'

'You are what the enemy imagines as his own.' I was completely bewildered. 'You and I and the enemy exist only in the realm of war,' he whispered. 'Before we met, you were waiting for the moment to begin living.'

'You think I did not exist before I met you?' I said, never once suspecting the General of being a romantic.

'I think that you will soon begin to truly live.' His hands had dropped to my shoulders and it was as if they contained his entire weight. 'This war is your liberation. And my salvation. I dedicate this battle to you.' There was a long pause. I wondered what I was meant to say.

'Thank you,' I said at last. I decided to push what appeared to be an advantage. 'But how can I truly live with these guards you've assigned to me? They are unnecessary.' As I emphasised 'truly live' I saw the General's mouth twitch. 'I'm in no danger in my own city,' I added. How many times had he heard me say that?

'Indeed, Lady, consider the city yours,' he smiled.

I did not leave the hotel that day or the next. The guards had been called off as the General had promised, disappearing with discretion. One moment they were obtrusively *there*, the next moment they were not. With the General at his Bitch of Battles, my freedom to do as I wished was relatively secure. And I felt incapable of doing anything.

Outside, the world pulsed with a colour which could not be shaken off or hosed away. It clung to the sky, the sun was a fireball, the clouds sat like scar tissue on the broiled horizon. Everything was newly contoured by the ruby hue. On the TV there was footage of the General looking paternal and beneficent and oddly ruddy, assuring the citizenry that there was no cause for alarm. We had not been attacked by sarin gas or any other chemical weapon. The change in the colour of the atmosphere was an attempt by the enemy to destabilise the city. A harmless, tasteless, odourless gas had been released into the atmosphere. The enemy had been attempting to weaken us with hysteria. The only people who had perished were those who, in succumbing to panic, had put on their gas masks incorrectly. They had suffocated.

Red was the colour of our triumph. Red, the colour of our flag.

Red, the vital fluid of life.

The blood that dropped from my womb on the third day was not red, but thick and dark like the sediment from the bed of a sluggish creek. When I sat on the toilet I watched it fuse with the water in the bowl and sink like the heaviness that it was, falling out of me of its own accord. The pain that attended these clots was sharper than I'd ever had with my period, waves of cramps rolling through me, over me, forcing me to breathe in a new rhythm. This was no ordinary period. I swallowed painkillers and stuffed two ultra-absorbent sanitary pads between my thighs, and still they could not contain the blood. I thought I might be haemorrhaging.

I did not even consider calling in the General's medico. I had no intention of explaining the situation to anyone, I was worried that the General might put me under guard again at the slightest provocation, so I ordered a taxi which took, literally, hours to arrive, there were so few of them left in business, and delivered myself to the nearest hospital. The outpatients clinic was bedlam, full of frightened women and fretting children. I was not the only woman who had rushed to hospital because she was bleeding. Women were sitting with hands pressed to their bellies, against their crotches; curled up crying on benches, grimacing, deep breathing, weeping, calling out for attention, blood on their clothes. Were all the women in the city bleeding? A particularly vicious pain stabbed me as I grabbed a harassed-looking nurse. 'I need to see a doctor too. I think I'm haemorrhaging.' When I said it out loud I felt frightened all of a sudden.

'A doctor will see you as soon as possible,' she reassured me, seeing the fear on my face. She looked at the blood trickling down my legs and sat me on a square of floor. 'You must stay calm, I'll fetch you a towel,' she said, darting off.

The women beside me were too caught up in their predicament to hear me ask, 'What's happening to us?' When the nurse eventually returned with an armload of threadbare towels and positioned one between my thighs I asked her, 'Why are we all bleeding?'

'You mustn't be frightened,' she soothed, 'what you're experiencing is a spontaneous abortion.'

'An abortion?'

'Yes,' she said, 'all the women here are going through the same thing.'

'I'm pregnant?' I said. The word sounded unreal in my mouth. I repeated it, to try to get the taste of it. 'Pregnant?' It still came out as a question.

'You didn't know? I'm sorry,' she said, as if it were her fault.

'Everyone here? Miscarrying?'

'I'm sorry,' she repeated. She began to move away and I grabbed her by the hem of her skirt. I noticed for the first time that her grubby uniform was a palette of blood colours.

'The red sky,' I said. 'The red sky made this happen.'

'Sshhh,' she hushed, looking around nervously, 'no-one is allowed to say anything.'

There was no question of being kept in the hospital for observation. Wards were already overflowing with acute cases. Whatever foetal material that remained in me was excised with a dilation and curettage performed with frank efficiency and without an anaesthetic. I was told to go home and rest. There was a shortage of antibiotics so I must be very careful not to get an infection. Infection could easily lead to sterility, possibly to death. I had already looked into the leaden eyes of a corpse, a woman with a fair-sized belly who had been groaning in a low, continuous voice near me in the waiting room. She had been carted out of the operating room with a vacant expression on her face as I had been ushered in. When I lay down I felt the warm imprint of her final writhings rising up from under newspaper hastily thrown over the operating table.

Lying there with my legs mounted, trembling in stirrups, staring into the jumble of white light, seeing the claws of instruments, feeling that pain—the searing heat—as my uterus dilated, cramped again, dilated; hearing the suck of the aspirators, the wailing and the moaning women; seeing piles of blood-soaked rags, buckets of human waste, doctors and nurses grotesquely garbed in blood-rinsed gowns, it was as if one of the dark horsemen had come riding into the mire and thick of it, bursting through the faint underlying hospital smell, witnessing as the nauseating stench of death was being born over and over again from the body.

It was like being transported to a charnel house.

I do not remember getting off the operating table. I do not recall being in any place called Recovery, nor do I recall leaving the building. I suppose I simply got up and walked out because the next thing I remember is sitting on a bench in a deserted park. It must have been some hours after I had gone to the hospital. I sat there for a long time staring at the scarlet sky. It was impartial and distant from what I had just gone through, utterly removed from the horrors I had witnessed, yet it was responsible, I was sure of it. Something had been unleashed when that colour had arrived. I remember realising that a new sort of warfare had occurred and that the city had been infiltrated.

No, not the city. The bodies of the women of the city.

No. The mothers of the city.

The word 'mother' reverberated then, through my numbness. The notion that I'd carried the seed of motherhood was ludicrous. Incredible. I tried to remember when I'd last had my period. It had been always erratic, dates were so slippery I could not work out with any certainty who the father might have been, but unless my pregnancy had been reasonably advanced, it could not have been Sol.

The thing was, such calculations were as absurd as they were useless. I'd been included in a sterilisation plan for State minors years ago; I remembered the day clearly, it had been my fifteenth birthday. Someone has made a mistake, I told myself. There was a tickle of something against my cheek. I swiped at it, my fingers skated along wet skin. I was crying.

According to the reports blaring out from loud-speakers in the streets, the Offensive, code-named Operation Eruption, also known as the Bitch of Battles, had been launched at 0400 hours and was a masterstroke of initiative, the most decisive action so far in the contest for control of the Northern Sector. An armoured wedge had rammed through enemy lines and was at that moment hammering their battalions to bits. Enemy SAM batteries had been knocked out, the enemy was being routed, the enemy was being crushed, the enemy was being clubbed. The enemy was in retreat and their defending units were being neutralised. Neutralised. Odd word out in the liturgy. A dispassionate word, yet a violent word because of a most particular lack of passion.

Of the pregnancies that had been neutralised en masse, there was no rhetoric, no passion, not one report in the media, not one official word.

It was as if nothing had happened.

When night fell I found myself in Bernanos Street. I saw the place where I'd first met Sol, emptied and boarded over, and a part of me felt like sitting down in the gutter and letting the night curl over me until it rendered me invisible to the world. But this was mere fancy, there was no true night to disappear inside of, only a dense shade of bay, which reminded me of the colour of blood when it has dried and darkened, something I had seen rather too much of.

I needed a drink.

The bar I stumbled into was gloomy, but had that weird combination of a blanket suppression and a volatile excitement, the sort of excitement that partnered a big plunge into battle. War news monotonously scrolled on a screen in a corner around which a small group of drinkers were gathered, caught like moths in its shine. Despite the litany of successful strikes there was a moroseness in the room which suited my mood, as did the dour wood panelling and the moth-eaten animal heads mounted on the wall—a gesture from another time and a different generation of gun-bearers. The place had that familiar, stale smell of beer and vomit which never disappeared despite countless sluicings with soap and water. The one off-note in the place was the lamps with cracked red shades, which threw a mean, reddish light.

That damn colour again.

I was sinking into my cups when someone grabbed my arm and a voice bubbled in my ear, 'I'd wondered what'd become of you.' I looked up into the small, gleaming eyes of Mei Lien. I greeted her with unembellished enthusiasm but I heard the tone of complaint in her voice when she asked me where I'd got to. I told her I'd just got out of hospital, it was the truth at least, but I pushed on something too tender then and I began to cry again. 'What happened?' she gasped.

'I was pregnant,' I blurted out, 'but I miscarried.' Mei Lien tut-tutted consolingly and patted my hand. 'It was a shock, that's all,' I said, taking the drink she urged onto me.

'Very sad,' she commiserated, 'very sad, but it's not a good time to have a baby.'

'No,' I agreed.

'Your boyfriend …?' She paused delicately.

'He doesn't know.'

'Ah,' she said knowingly, 'he came to me at the bar for a message from you but you'd gone. What could I tell him?' Another note of accusation. 'He never came again.'

'We had a fight. I couldn't go with him. It was impossible.'

'Another woman?' She licked her lips, quite unconsciously. I nodded, taking the cue, it was Mei Lien's script now. 'Love is so hard,' she sighed, moving into her favourite story. I motioned for another bottle.

By the time I made it back to the hotel I had stopped bleeding and the throb of my miscarriage was ebbing away. I was ready to maybe, finally, sleep but when I got in there was a phone call for me. It was Juanita. She wanted to know if I had any coffee rations to spare.

SEVENTEEN

The day of my meeting with Sol was marked by the death of the dogs. And the death of all the other animals of the city. Many had already disappeared but there were still some cherished pets, guard-dogs, chickens, the odd horse here and there, the occasional goat or sheep, and, of course, the rats and the mice, but even these populations had radically diminished. I did not like to think of rats as a culinary item but hunger was a raw, palpable thing and there was less and less food for more and more people, the population of the city was swelling with Dislocatees. The issue of food reminded me of the mistake I'd made when I last saw Sol, giving him luxuries which had identified the profound change in my circumstances. I couldn't afford to alienate him again, the thread that tied us was too tenuous. A cobweb.

The General was still busy conducting his Offensive. There had been unexpected developments along the border of the Northern Sector and the Disposables Zone, and a skirmish there had apparently become a retaliation of the highest magnitude—on whose part it was unclear—but the unctuous

with some of the rat-holes where Sol and I had met, but I had so little sense of ease I could not help feeling dismayed that it was to be the place for a romantic tryst.

Following Juanita's telephone call I had gone to Pearl Harbour as arranged. The Pearl was a shopping emporium no longer home to shoppers but to the Dislocatees who had fled the besieged countryside and been relocated in the shell of dead businesses. It had become a district unto itself, redolent with the lamentation of homelessness and the trauma of separation, but for all that, the Dislocatees' losses were glorified by the Department of Civil Revisions as being vital to victory. It was irrelevant that they'd had no choice in the matter. Truckloads of telephone books (there were no telephones), plastic spoons, clotheslines, tea strainers, light bulbs (there was no electricity), and plaster statues of the General on horseback, more fancy than verisimilitude, had been presented to the Dislocatees in an absurd effort to make the ghetto more homey.

I had met Juanita at a refreshment site, cunningly fashioned from cardboard boxes, and sipped something that was supposed to be coffee while she told me she'd found Sol. It'd been a tough job, she said, but she'd arranged everything. She then imparted elaborate instructions on where and when Sol and I would meet. The arrangements were non-negotiable. If I couldn't make it he wouldn't see me again, she said, not mincing her words. Was I sure I knew what I was doing? she asked. Was I sure I wanted to jump back into the frying pan with the man? Yes, I said. Yes.

But when I saw Sol my resolve seemed audacious, disconnected from the reality of seeing him. He was pale and weedy, a plant that had not seen much light. He had grown stooped and reedy. When the smoke curled from his mouth his breath whistled, sonorous. Almost melodious. We had both been inhabited by a type of disorder which had taken its toll. I was plump as I could be with a wealth that was not well-being, while his shape disconcerted and dismayed me. Yes, Sol was in a bad way. When he squeezed me my heart jumped and caused a jagged ache. But he was not embracing me, hugging me, holding me, he was probing, poking, patting me. It took me a moment to realise that he was checking to see if I was wired.

I took his face in my hands. 'I'm clean,' I said. 'You know I wouldn't do anything against you.' I put my arms around him and hugged him to me. He did not resist but there was a languid pliability to him that was like a resistance. 'I've missed you,' I whispered. 'I'd almost given up hope of finding you. I was going crazy, I went back to the bar and it'd been shut down.' I kissed his neck, moving my mouth delicately into his clavicle. 'I can't believe that we're together again.' I ran my hands over his back, over the bony vertebrae of his spine. He felt thin, very fragile, as if he might easily break. The thought of that frightened me.

I realised that he was holding his breath. I heard him release it as he averted his gaze and lit a fresh cigarette from the butt of the previous one. 'What's wrong?' I asked.

He took a moment to answer. 'When we were together last time my friends were taken. Someone informed. I wasn't caught because I was with you, but my friends were,' he said. 'I had a lucky escape. A convenient escape.'

'You suspected me of informing?' I asked. 'But I didn't even know your friends!'

'No. Yes. I don't know. It's hard to know who to trust when you're running, always running and hiding. I didn't really suspect you. But afterwards you disappeared into thin air and the bar was shut. It made it easy to start to think …' He stopped speaking and dug his fingers into his hair. I saw he was wearing his bracelet, I wanted to kiss him. 'To think that at the very least you'd abandoned me,' he finished.

'Did you really think that?' I asked.

'Yes,' he answered. He struck a match and let it burn down until it scorched his fingers.

'I wouldn't abandon you,' I replied. 'I know you think I've let you down but circumstances made it impossible to find you. I didn't know what to do until I met up with Juanita.'

'Juanita managed to find me,' he countered.

'Juanita has contacts. That's why I asked her.'

'Juanita doesn't have a fuck-soldier she has to entertain.'

The silence went nowhere. Sol shrugged and changed tack. 'You didn't bring any food this time.' A lighter note? I got out my hip-flask and handed it to him. 'Nice,' he said. 'Courtesy of your soldier, right? He has taste.' I wanted to shake him.

'I'm here,' I said, controlling myself. 'Just me. Just you. Just us. I wish you could understand how important you are to me. I don't want to lose you again.' He gave a great sigh. I hugged him and felt him fall into me, a type of quickening. We stood there awhile, him locked in my arms.

'What's this?' he asked, breaking free and examining my palm.

'It's where I cut myself on that bottle last time we met. I needed stitches. An inept doctor botched the job.'

'The letter M,' he said. The trail of his finger over my scar gave me goose flesh.

'It doesn't mean anything,' I said.

'It's bad luck,' he replied, 'to have a scar like that. It identifies you.'

'Sshhh,' I said. 'Sshhh.' And then I unbuttoned his clothes and then we made love.

No, I made love.

Sol lay under me and received me with passivity. I wanted to kiss him but his head rolled away from me to one side. His passivity did not prevent his penis from getting stiff, however, or ejaculating into me. When the shard of mirror reported our lovemaking back to us I saw how he shut his eyes when he turned his head aside, and I knew that the swoop of his body was a flying away from me, even though he was imbedded in me as deeply as he could be. When he was ready to come he moved his hands up and gripped my hips hard. He held me until his spasm was over and then he let go of me again. I had forgotten the quality of silence that Sol brought to our lovemaking, yet I, too, made not the slightest sound. I came quickly, through sheer necessity. I would not allow apathy to dominate passion.

But we had gone too long without touching and the strain of it had damaged us. Our bodies did not even make an impression upon that hard mattress. The room we were huddled in was not his room or my room or our room. The usual occupant would reclaim it soon.

I slid some money under a pillow for the use of the room, as arranged. Then shelled out the rest of my money to Sol. 'You don't have much of a problem with money,' he remarked, pocketing the curl of notes. 'Juanita told me you were riding a gravy train.' I felt uneasy as to what else Juanita might have let slip. It was dangerous her knowing so much about me, but I had no choice. Without her intervention I would not be with Sol now. Like any procurer, she'd received a fee.

'My soldier can be more lucrative than Juanita's work, that's all,' I replied. 'It took me a while to get this much money

together. But I made a mistake. I thought it was more important than having nothing for you. I was wrong. What's important is being with you.' I had threaded the truth with yet
another lie, but it was for Sol's protection that I did not tell
him any more about that soldier of mine. I leaned on my knees
against his thin buttocks and began to tease out the tangles in
his hair. 'Don't go yet,' I murmured. My nipples impacted on
his skin as I tilted against him. He remained silent but I saw
how the feel of my breasts and the heat of my crevice affected
him. His cock unfurled and lengthened. I moved my body
around in order to face him and he took my head in his hands,
squeezing my ears.

'You've turned me into a whore,' he said. 'You screw me,
you hand me money, you leave. I exist like a whore.'

'No,' I protested, 'that's not true. We both agreed. It's safer
if you're on your own. You wanted it like this.'

'I never wanted it like this.' He shook my head from side to
side.

'It's the war,' I said. 'It's not us. Don't trust what it's doing.
It's pulling us to pieces. Trust the times we're together. Even
when it's like this. Otherwise it'll claim you and beat us and
we'll lose each other. I need you, you've got to know that.
There's no choice for me. I love you. It's how I survive.' It was
dangerous for me to keep talking, I had a violent urge to tell
Sol what it might be like for me if he broke with me and all I
had left was the General. I squashed the urge.

'This is your love,' he said, pushing my head down to his
erection until my mouth opened for it. 'This is what you love
and this is how you love.' His words were emphasised rather
than diminished by the hiss of his voice. 'Take it,' he said.
'Take what you want to call love. You'll call anything love if it

suits you. Isn't that so? Yes, this is the only sort of love that matters anymore.' As Sol entered my mouth with a vigour missing from our previous engagement I began to weep. Small, choked back sobs. He lifted up my face and put his mouth to mine and whispered, 'I'm sorry, I'm sorry.'

When he slid his penis inside of me it felt like he was making a return to me and I fanned out my thighs for his homing and I drenched him in my cum and when my orgasm came it was equally release and surrender. Afterwards though, when the fever of our fuck had abated, it was strangely awkward between us. We dressed quickly, and in silence. We agreed that Juanita would be our new go-between. We did not talk about the circumstances which made her necessary to us. Neither did we make promises to meet soon. When I gave him a kiss goodbye Sol took my tongue, sucked it into his mouth, bit it so that it hurt, then pulled away, opened the door and was gone. I followed him down the stairs a few minutes later, hoping he might be lingering, but there was no sign of him.

I sank down on the bottom step, overcome by the emotion of the encounter and the physical sensation of Sol's touches fading from my body. A young woman with a long scar running down her face which badly disfigured her right eye entered the building carrying a dead puppy poking out of a sheet of butcher's paper, and brusquely brushed by me on her passage up the rickety stairs. The dog did not have any smell but the woman's sweat reminded me of onions. I wondered if it was her bed I had just come from.

I could not summon the will to move. There had been a new cruelty in Sol. I told myself that it was natural, given the situation. War brutalised everyone's sensitivities. But this rationalisation did not really comfort me. Had I tainted Sol? Had I pushed Sol into a new circle of violence, the violence that I had learned to keep company with?

EIGHTEEN

Some targets are just too tempting.

Or some gods are not easily appeased.

I was sitting alone in the red night with a whisky comforter, watching the moon melting in its orbit, trying to control an unaccountable fit of the jitters when the doors burst open to a blaring light, a mania of voices, and the General being carried in on a litter of unravelling bandages and stink, ranting and spitting venomous foam.

So, the Bitch had been recalcitrant.

At the very moment his troupe entered the room the building began to vibrate. The room trembled uncontrollably then gave a great shudder, as if it had been slammed hard by some larger force or object. I lost my balance and fell to the floor, jarring my shoulder. Objects pitched off tables and shelves, clattering and smashing. Paintings of the General slid off the walls. At first I thought it was the effect of heavy bombardment, closer than I had ever imagined possible. Then someone screamed, 'Earthquake!' and, as if the word were a signal, the building ceased its movement with a horrible screeching noise that was the replicate of an animal or a person in great pain.

I picked myself up from the floor, regained command of my senses, carefully felt the muscle in my hurting shoulder, dusted off, and cautiously moved towards the General, still intact on his litter, now confusing his men with the enemy. He, too, must have thought we had come under attack, for he was in a ferocious fit of snapping violence. Only once before had I seen a person so brutally transported and that had been a woman with a freak infection of rabies. I could see that the General's condition was filling his men with horror, even the medicos seemed defeated by his disorder. They could not get close enough to knock him out with their drugs because he had the strength to hold a gun on them. He was lucid enough to fire, which sent everyone spilling to the floor again. From the streets outside came a tremendous wave of public panic, commingling with the ear-splitting wail of sirens, perfectly chorusing the General's performance.

In the end, I was the only one able to approach him, for he appeared to have no difficulty in recognising me. I quietened him sufficiently to peel back the bloody swabs from his belly. When I saw the hole there, I nearly fainted. The whisky I'd been imbibing rose in my throat and it was the hardest drink I'd had to swallow in a while. I felt his brow and found it was ice-cold. When I touched him an awful stench exploded in the air, a smell of shit and puke and blood gone bad, flesh burnt, flesh disintegrating. Thinking that the stink was rising out of him I ran to the windows and flung them open. The smell was everywhere. Creeping. Inescapable.

The smell was as solid as a shape.

I caught a whiff of something inhuman being released.

Something hotly, utterly animal. The hair on my arms stood on end, parting from the warmth of my body.

As if becoming animal, the General's men doubled over and burst out howling, some falling to their hands and knees. It was astonishing. The noise they made reminded me of hyenas separated from the pack. Fear and anguish. The General let loose a vile round of curses which cut through their racket and brought them to heel. I could not help it, I began to laugh. I was approaching hysteria when I went over to the General and took the gun, a Uzi I think it was, and began shooting up the room. I didn't manage to hit anyone.

In this way I forced the General's men from the room and slammed the door and shot home the bolts. I think I was yelling that I would rather be alone with it. I remember opening another bottle of whisky and lowering myself beside the General's litter. His hands were jerking, palms up, extended to me, and he was saying, 'Look at what is in the palm of my hand,' and he was pressing his hands over the hole in his side and smiling in a beatific manner while his palms were filling with blood and then I was putting the whisky in my mouth and watching him and the smell was of whisky and blood and something bad slowly receding.

Finally the men shot the bolts and broke down the door and took him from me. By then I appeared to be violently drunk. Apparently I fought them like crazy. I believe, however, that it may have been one of my most sober moments in my association with the General.

Later, I let it be known that distress had unhinged me.

I was woken by an incantation. The dawn was young and raw,

the bedclothes soaked with sweat. I crawled out of my wreck of a nightgown—it was torn and full of small holes and looked as though I had clawed at myself in my sleep. It also looked like I had begun to bleed, yet when I slid a finger inside my vagina and felt the tip of my cervix my finger came out clean. Since I had no wounds I surmised the blood was not my own. My shoulder was throbbing, however the degree of movement it afforded told me the damage was only superficial. As the sedative wore off I drifted groggily from the bed, bumping into wakefulness against the furniture. The air was laden with fine particles of dust and already the heat was out of control. I groped for the air-conditioner and flicked it on. Useless. The electricity was out. I blundered into the bathroom and the smell of sickness suffused me, sending me gagging into the hand basin. At least the plumbing worked. I stuck my face under the tap and drank large mouthfuls of warm, brackish water but I did not feel much better for it.

As I stumbled over the mess of broken and tumbled objects obstructing my path I remembered the earthquake. I opened the liquor cabinet and broke the seal and unscrewed the top off a fresh bottle, and again I heard the male voice that had woken me. It had started up again, in a sort of singsong. It was a beautiful voice, but it had an insistent quality that would drive one mad if it kept up for long. The physical poetry of that excruciating voice alerted me to the fact that it was not the General speaking, as I had dreamt and at first thought. After a swig of whisky I staggered back into the bathroom, blocking out the incantatory sound by getting under the shower. I slid down upon the tiles and let the water pound me. It helped obliterate the nasty smell that seemed to cling to me.

After a good soaking and a thorough dousing with a

cocktail of fragrances, I decided I smelt and even looked pretty good, considering. But I could have felt better so I decided on a little more hair of the dog. This time my stomach heaved and I vomited in the basin, and instead of feeling better I felt worse and despite my inclination, I put the bottle down. Those damn medicos and their needles full of sleep had upset my delicate equilibrium when they'd punched me with tranquillisers after wresting the General from me. I spat, rinsed, gargled and finished dressing and rang for a pot of tea.

It was only then that the thought hit me that the General may not even be alive.

The door to his room was under guard but I pushed my way through. Inside he was laid out on his bed as if on a catafalque. He had the pallor of a corpse, however the crisp white sheet covering his barrel of a chest was rhythmically moving up and down. He was comatose, yet there was a rigidity to his form that suggested a withholding of something more than vital energy. The General's repose did not look like the normal relaxation of a body in unconsciousness. Drips snaked into his arms and nose, and a tube twisted out from under the pristine sheet and dropped into a large plastic bottle beside the bed. Muck the colour of sulphur was draining from the General's wound into the bottle. The stench clouding the room almost made me retch again. As high and impure as when I'd had my first sniff of it the night before, the stink was now overlaid with the smell of a disinfectant. I held my perfumed wrist under my nose and began to breathe in shallow little breaths.

A soldier in fatigues sat at the General's bedside in a pose of pure stiffness. He was the origin of the voice, dropped now to barely a whisper. He did not cease in his melodic babble, nor did he pay any attention to my entry. A nurse was in a chair in a corner of the room, sensibly wearing a surgical mask. The woman was an odd shade of pink. The colour of the light insinuating its way between the gaping curtains played odd, melting tricks with her features. She was curiously inert, and for a moment I could not see any of her life signs, but then I caught a soft gurgling noise which I realised was her way of talking in her sleep.

When I returned my gaze to the General his eyes were wide open and staring at me, his gaze as fixed as if he had indeed been inhabited by death. I held my breath, swallowing acid spittle. After a yawn of time his right hand slowly lifted and he crooked his index finger at me. Warily, I moved closer. That finger of his contained quite some power. It emitted a force of energy not evident at first sight of him. It was not that I was afraid of him exactly, but I knew better than to underestimate the General's penchant for presenting scenarios to test one's stamina. Even from a sickbed.

I went over and stood behind the murmuring soldier, who was either deliberately ignoring me or completely oblivious to me. I avoided further eye contact with the General by focusing my gaze on the back of the soldier's neck. He was still a youth, his neck unlined. The pigmentation of his skin was odd, irregular. White blotches marred his natural shade. His incongruous snowy hair was cropped very short, it had the appearance of something spiky yet tenderly soft. Young white hairs grew down his nape into his collar, their pattern that of an unfurling frond of fern. His shoulders were incredibly tense, he was holding himself in such a militarily correct manner that he might have been a caricature of a soldier. For the first time I could hear what he was saying.

'Day after day of it. After my first kill I started vomiting. I couldn't stop bringing it up. It was pouring out of me. Until there was nothing of my own left in me anymore. Nothing left to come up. And the taste of it was the taste of them. They were inside me. Weren't human. No, they weren't human. They poisoned me. But I felt clean, killing them. Kill or be killed. You dig them out. You don't think about it. Kill or be killed. You cut them out. You kill them. You do anything to kill them. Anything. I killed them. Necessary. I could taste them. They were in my mouth. They weren't people. They were in my mouth ...' Here, his voice rose an octave. 'Take more for the whore you're in for the kill cut them rut them shoot root shoot don't stop don't stop chop don't—'

On an impulse I laid my hands lightly upon the man's shoulders. He screamed. His head snapped back, his eyes rolled up and the emptied whites glared at me. The veins of his neck popped out, cords of pulsing blue. I dropped my hands and backed away. The sleeping nurse clattered off her chair and began to scream. The General's limbs jerked as if a hand had gathered him up, exactly as if a puppeteer had grabbed the wires of a marionette to propel it to action. He reached up, ripped the tube out of his nose and he too screamed. That was when I saw the eruption. The wide O of his mouth pouring out its sound as a movement began to bubble upon his forehead.

It was no ordinary thing. I smelled a putrid singeing. I saw the skin pucker and blush violently red. Before the shape was complete I knew it, for I carried its twin in the palm of my hand. The duplication was exact.

A god was making a claim.

As I watched, the forehead of the General was branded with the mark of Mars.

NINETEEN

He dreams that he is the Lord of the Dance. He dreams of marking his territories with dung like an animal, he dreams of his great feet pawing a trembling earth. The imprints of his footsteps are craters, indentations of desecration and loss, annihilation and torture. Across the sky his banner waves like blood dissipated, the blush of it spreading out slow and arhythmically, as if infusing sloppy water. When he lifts up his head and opens his mouth to praise his Kali the red air swallows him like a wave.

In his last battle he glimpsed the goddess moving to be at his side, a four-armed dervish who pirouetted up his enemy's nostrils and twirled into their ears and sent them spinning mad into the fray onto the battlefield in which he had hidden charges, mines and explosives. Clever, quick destroyers, limb mutilators, organ replacers, bone shatterers. He watched line after line of his enemies embrace her in their dance, their leaping screaming prance, and she devoured them for him. He heard her licking her chops and her tongue was long, red and wholly available to him.

He who knows the most modern, the most immemorial ways to step men out of their bodies. He who opens their skins and frees their hearts still pulsing from their cages of ribs. That primitive beat, their first foetal message, is music filling his ears, rushing out of their bodies in expansion and contraction of his new universe.

What pleasant labour to lead them, what pleasure then is the waltz, the *pas de deux*, the tango, the quadrille.

A gallery of jerking corpses is a divine movement.

He holds the bloom of death in one hand in imitation of her gorgeous flower while his phallus in his other hand swells, silken ruddy mushroom, growing huge, plunging through every enemy defence. He, the unstoppable unspeakable dancer of death, giddy in the whirl of her arms.

She favoured him when she penetrated him.

A tear rent the sky.

He fell on his knees in simple prostration and blood sprang from his belly. He knew he had been blessed. Miraculous, the whistle of her blade lunging for him alone through the shrouded confusion of battle. He looked up to see his enemies falling like stars under her dancing feet.

As his blood belled and bloomed he capered and sang light-headedly, giddy-spiritedly.

Lalalallalalalal, he sang.

Lalalallalalalal. Tonight my Lady feeds.

As his blood continues its slick, effortless flow he dreams that it readies the floor for their next dance.

TWENTY

I was determined to get rid of the smell. I ordered in the cleaners but their applications of bleach and disinfectants had a short-lived effect. No-one else seemed to be bothered by it, and since those I questioned denied smelling anything particularly odorous I decided they were either lying or being polite. I drenched myself in fragrances until I was a moving wall of scent but still the smell squirmed up my nose. It entered me. I could smell decay, a rotting of flesh, a body doubling with putrefaction, yet the General was not ailing or wasting away. Doctors did nothing more useful than hover like an annoying cloud of insects: nurses attended him in rather more practical ways with a repertoire of sponge baths and body rubs; intravenous drips slipped fluids into him, machines monitored him, a profound relaxation emanated from him. The General showed every sign of being in a state of deep rest. Nothing disturbed him, not the constant traffic of medicos and heavy brass wearing a path through his sick-room door, not the air-raid alerts, not the sound of artillery on our horizon, nor the cacophony of work gangs in the streets shoring up damage from the quake.

Certain quarters of the city had suffered the type of ruin more typical of a bombardment. There was scant equipment available for clearing and repairs, which meant that the undertaking was gruelling. Gangs of women and children were heavily deployed, labouring with woefully inadequate implements all through the day, some of them singing even, under the watchful eye and direction of the Office of Civil Unification. Prizes were awarded to those exceeding the daily work targets and the whole thing developed into something of a ragged carnival. Military tunes and endlessly updated military success stories blared through speakers in the streets to hearten flagging workers. The tedious excavating and carting and reconstructing occurred to such jolly refrains as '5754 enemies killed, 13865 enemies wounded, 2498 enemies captured, 132 enemy defence installations overrun, 78 enemy surface-to-air missile launchers seized, 596 enemy tanks destroyed', and so on and so forth. Not even these announcements caused the General to turn in his sleep.

I felt no compulsion to discuss the skin-crawling display I'd witnessed at the General's bedside. The blaze on the General's forehead had confounded the medicos who, reassured by his perfect pulse and deep regular snoring, pronounced it a delayed onset of secondary wounding. Of course no-one could attribute this wound to anything that made any sense. I wondered if I was the only person who considered the General's elegantly inscribed letter M an eerie event. Did the General's intimates think that he had been blessed by his god? No-one else had even mentioned Mars to me but surely the medico who had stitched the mark into my hand and seen the same scrawl on the General's brow must be aware of the connection. The man simply handed me more sedatives when I raised the matter, but he hadn't forgiven me for turning the Uzi on him when they'd brought the General back.

The General's debilitation was officially described as an attack of trench dysentery, providing an opportunity for hero-ising his rapport with the common soldiery and partaking of the nitty-gritty of war. The War Council had decided that it would be bad for morale if it was known that the General had been wounded, especially since the cause of it remained a mystery. There was also a matter of diplomacy. He'd been found writhing on the floor of a latrine with a hole in his side. The only conclusion possible was that he had been the victim of an enemy infiltrator. Several suspects had been selected and were in the process of being interrogated.

In the days following the General's inglorious return a pattern had developed: he would wake every one hundred and seventy-three minutes—intervals uncannily mathematical in precision—he would demand to hear the latest reports from the battlefield, issue some very specific military instructions, close his eyes and return straight to sleep, snoring in a delicate but otherwise very ordinary manner. The rapid movements of his eyes beneath their lids indicated that he also, immediately, began to dream. His dreams continued until the moment of his next waking. Throughout this time he did not eat, drink, or in any other way relieve himself. The shunt in his side kept steadily voiding dark murky fluid from the neatly sutured hole in his belly into the plastic bottle that was replaced twice a day. The mark on his forehead looked raw but was not encrusted or scabbed, and the skin was smooth, without scar tissue, as if he'd come from the womb wearing the insignia.

I suppose this was a time I could have disappeared. I kept thinking about Sol and I knew that I could become just another Dislocatee, trying to lose myself in order to find him. But I couldn't accept that being on the run from the General was a solution to the problem of wanting Sol. I did, however, get out of my stinking hotel suite as often as I could, but my wanderings only served to remind me I was locked in the General's circle. Everywhere I went he accompanied me. Portraits of him abounded, seemed to be proliferating. Larger-than-life reproductions of him in best military posture laying claim to new surfaces of the city. His images had been freshly garlanded with plastic flowers, obscene stamen and swollen petals blooming in lurid colour. It was as if the city had become a fake, freak, hothouse garden. The smelly air likewise bloomed with discussion of his trench condition. According to the arbiters of communication the General was, hour after tedious hour, escalating towards 'comprehensive recovery', 'unqualified stability', and 'profound rehabilitation'. File tapes of him flickered on television screens and his speeches were recycled both in full and chopped up into soundbites over the radio, flooding us with his omnipresence.

I visited the parts of the city worst affected by the quake, for there was a camaraderie in the work gangs in those places and I was looking for some sort of comfort in others, I suppose. But comfort was not easy to find and so, after touring the worksites and picking my way around rubble, I quit searching for companionship in a crowd and sought out my old black-market contacts, and becoming businesslike tried to organise another sell-through of masks. But I met with no success. Apparently the gas-mask business had plateaued. One day, after leaving my acquaintances, I realised that an unprepossessing-looking woman was making a good job of following me. I quieted a squirt of alarm and went and sat on the steps of a defunct transit centre, fixing her with my best nonchalant gaze as she confidently walked over to me. As far as I could tell she seemed to be working alone.

'Jewellery,' she said.

'I don't have any.' I stood up. 'You're wasting your time.'

'No,' she said impatiently, her eyes bouncing off mine. 'You'll be interested in what I have to sell, you'll see.' She hunkered down on the step below me and pulled her arms out of the sleeves of her tatty overcoat to reveal an array of watches, necklaces, bangles, bracelets, pendants and rings threaded on chains wrapped around her fleshy arms. I'd heard stories of Sellers' arms being severed from their bodies for booty such as this.

'Why me?' I asked.

'You have the smell of money,' she shrugged, the odour of sweat wafting from the folds of her body in strong draughts, 'you haven't lost everything. Maybe you won't. Perhaps you have the gift for fortune. Perhaps you'll end up with much more than you would have, otherwise.'

'Otherwise?' I frowned.

She winked at me. 'Some cynics say that war is as valid a way of redistributing wealth as any other. Why not have the things that others have given up on? Why not benefit yourself, it's no crime.' The Seller continued to cajole and flatter my prudence at managing such hard times but I resisted her sales pitch until she pulled out a small leather pouch, and grabbing my hand poured out the contents—exquisite lucky charms crafted from wood, ivory, silver, pewter, gold, copper, shell, stone. 'There's a powerful lot of luck here,' she insisted, 'and who can do without that nowadays?' With the charms in my hand I felt an obscure optimism, a quicksilver run of happiness. Closer to Sol. In the end, we conducted business. As we concluded our transaction I glanced up and saw the giant billboard overhead. The General was smiling beneficently in a new portrait, a red jewel shining from his forehead, radiating out airbrushed waves of soft pink light, as if he were bringing the new dawn to the world.

'The General's been asking for you, ma'am. He seems to be … waking up.' The adjutant's tone of voice was odd. Higher pitched than normal. The man needed a break, he'd been at his General's side day and night. He usually held himself in check better than this. His eyes flitted to the closed door of the General's room and flitted away again, then jitterbugged around the room like a burning moth.

'And he's certain to wake again in about another three hours,' I sighed. 'He doesn't know I'm here and he doesn't need to know.' I'd just walked in and I wasn't ready for the General. I took little sips of the air—it was worse than usual— and picked up a bottle of Eau de Parfum Artilleria and squirted it liberally. A sledgehammer scent, but effective. The adjutant's nose twitched violently.

'But ma'am, the General—' A violent sneezing attack rendered him speechless. I noticed that his uniform had rings of sweat.

'Has his condition deteriorated?' The adjutant shook his head and wiped the tears from his eyes. 'Is there a nurse or a doctor with him?' He nodded into his handkerchief. 'Fine. Why don't you fix us both a drink while I clean up.' Seeing his hesitation I added, 'Okay, after you make my drink you can tell the General that I'm on my way. If he's still awake, that is.'

He nodded stiffly and went to the drinks cabinet and loudly sloshed liquids in bottles. God knows what he was concocting.

After scrubbing myself in almost clean water—I'd become fastidious about washing, as if it would somehow help keep the smell off me—and following this with a good sousing of the useful Artilleria, I was ready for my drink. It was sitting on a silver tray waiting for me. I had no idea what it was but it was surprisingly good. The adjutant, however, had disappeared. Outside, the wind had picked up and was kicking things about. I carried my glass over to the window and watched the shapes of things being tossed about in the lurid dark. Were they animal? Vegetable? Mineral? I couldn't distinguish but I could see one of those ubiquitous posters of the General tearing and writhing like a live thing until it flew off the wall and into the night. There was a wildness out there which was exhilarating, and it was with some regret that I finally put down my glass in order to go attend to him.

The smell of a thing provides me with an immediate definition of it and I have learnt that the olfactory clue is invariably a reliable thing for me to go by. I knew at once that there'd been no recent cleaning of the room as I entered the General's chamber. As a very young child I'd chased chickens without heads and had watched the slaughtering of beasts. The smell was a memory I knew well. And it was a real smell, in the here-and-now, it was not the emanation of an old wound. It was the pungent odour of a recent blood-letting.

At close range.

Fresh.

Standing in the doorway I was perfectly lit by the light coming in behind me. An easy target. There was a roaring in my ears and I had to fight against a surge of panic. 'Ah, my

Lady cometh,' bubbled a voice. It was the General. As my eyes adjusted to the dimness I saw his empty bed. 'Come over here. Come closer to me,' he commanded. The fetor was awful. I felt the movement of nausea. I stepped a couple of paces towards the direction of his voice. 'I want to see you in your skin,' he whispered. I dutifully dropped my clothes. The room boiled. Whisky vapour evaporated from my pores in frantic release. I could guess where the General was but I could not see him in the dark. Then I thought I felt something brush against me. Or rather, breathe on me.

It was not the General.

In my panic I blundered against a lamp. Possessed by a mad urgency to cast some light upon the scene, I flicked it on. Even though it illuminated the fact that the General and I were alone it was a mistake. I saw that straightaway.

The General was crouched over the dead adjutant, knife in hand. I remembered that knife, it was the one Juanita had found. It had become the General's favourite toy. He looked up at me. 'My adorable naked cunt,' he crooned. 'I dreamt that you ate my cock and I lived forever. I was immortal. You sucked me up and I lived in your cunt-hole until I was reborn. I came out of you fully grown. I ate your afterbirth. I sucked your titties. I fucked you. I was made manifest time after time by your cunt.' I thought I might vomit. 'My Lady pretends not to know what satisfies her, that she likes to eat dick the most. Would my Lady like a taste?' he purred.

'No.'

I did not expect him to laugh in such a hearty, ordinary way. 'Then I will sit at her feasting place,' he said. He clambered upon the adjutant's thighs and made a long incision in the man's belly. I looked away and saw a nurse and a medico sprawled in a corner. They too, had been gutted, their intestines spilled outside the sheaths of their bodies. It was not very pretty.

'Why?' I breathed.

'They submitted to the knife,' he replied. 'Nothing more complicated than that.' Something fluttered within me. My stomach started to convulse. The smell of offal was stuck in my throat. I could not bear to see any more. I turned and backhanded the lamp to the floor and returned the General to his darkness. 'I feel you always with me, no matter if it is light or night,' he said. When I heard the sound of slurping I backed away fast, slamming the door on the General and his corpses, and ran into the bathroom where I brutally sluiced myself with antiseptic until I had stunned my sense of smell.

The amount of drinking I then did in order to lose consciousness might more aptly have been called drowning.

TWENTY-ONE

Plague and pestilence. Pus and putridity.

Dirty words. Dirty swords. Dirty war. Dirty wounds.

After witnessing the General's recipe for recovery I retired to my room with an assortment of bottles and whenever anyone knocked on my door I refused to open it. I was drunk for days. Unfortunately the more I drank, the less I could sleep, and the less I slept, the more I drank, and my attempted obliteration was not successful. I simply ended up feeling foul. The General must have judged my mood well—after sending one of his men on a reconnoitre, he left me alone. Every now and then one of his minions would persist in knocking on my door to announce that dinner or breakfast or lunch was ready. I did not answer the summons.

In the meantime the General recuperated with vigour. He wore a tube and a little bag like a colostomy patient. Fluid continued to leak out of his punctured side like a weird menstruation but his wound gave him absolutely no trouble. The doctors deduced dead nerves because he felt no pain whatsoever, but the General laughed at them. He was very proud of his wound and he made the tube and bag a part of him with such facility it was disconcerting to some. He ascribed the awful deaths of his adjutant and the nurse and medico to an assassin whom he'd overpowered. Needless to say, this assassin got away. Nothing was made public, but no doubt some innocent was selected, tried, sentenced and executed with appropriate speed.

I did not ever ask.

I understood the processes of power.

When I emerged from my 'fever', which was how my binge was tactfully referred to, I was wan and wasted and too dissolute to care about anything much at all. Removed. Quite some distance from the frightening place I'd visited that night with the General. By then he was up and about, back at the normal business of war. When I finally opened my door a new adjutant presented himself and handed me a bouquet. Obtaining flowers was a near impossible feat. I stared like an imbecile at the idyllic pink roses and the red-tongued lilies and white clouds of baby's breath. I almost missed the General's accompanying note—'I shall crown my Lady with the flowers of battle and gild her with the glories of war.'

His eloquence went into the toilet along with my breakfast. I had to admit that I couldn't hold my liquor like I used to. I took stock of myself, swallowed an anti-nausea pill, vomited again, forced down two more pills and within the hour I had managed a little food, was cleaned up, dressed, and animated enough to want to go somewhere else for a while.

Anywhere else.

I told myself I needed the exercise and that I was not avoiding the General who was busy convening a special meeting of the War Council. When I announced that I was going out alone the men looked uncertain but no-one said anything or attempted to stop me. There were now three security guards stationed in our rooms around the clock, an extra security measure against further incursions of assassins. The adjutant did venture to inform me that the air out was more cruel than usual and advised me to take a gas mask. The possibility of chemical attacks had been minimised but he said it would be wise. I didn't argue. I liked the anonymity, the protection, the guise of the mask.

I was not the only one.

Fires were burning in the streets, a gauze of smoke unravelling from the heart of the city. When I first saw it I thought there had been bombings. It was not inconceivable, I had surrendered thoroughly to my drunkenness and hadn't a clue as to the most recent developments of the war. But on coming closer I could see that these fires were pyres, deliberately constructed, around which knots of people were clustered wearing gas masks. Black, sick-looking clouds puffed up out of their midst, slowly infiltrating the city centre. It was disturbing, the slow, casual drift of dark into the ruddy sky. The glowering colour produced an acute sensation of being under threat, an effect not in itself unusual, but what made the situation seem ominous was the silence of those anonymous citizens circumscribing the pyres. What I could hear with exceptional clarity was the crack and cackle of fire feeding.

I heard the mob before they entered the street, their faces fierce and naked, shouting a slogan I was already familiar with. 'Kill the enemy! Kill the enemy!' To which they added a new refrain, 'Burn, enemy! Burn!' while jabbing firebrands at the sky. As they advanced I felt a throb of panic—who exactly was the enemy here? I'd heard reports of public executions in the city, which the General had dismissed as unsubstantiated rumour, but now I wondered if there was anything the General might not allow in order to entertain and arouse his people. There were even TV cameras there. Before I could get out of the mob's way I was swept into their orbit and rushed towards the pyres. A squad of soldiers were in attendance, hovering on the periphery of the scene, not attempting to keep the crowd in check, let alone moving to restore any semblance of civil order.

A sergeant who recognised me stepped forward, saluted, said, 'Let me assist you, ma'am,' and assuming the role of a bodyguard roughly pushed into the crowd, which parted for him once they saw the uniform. He forged a way for me clear to the front row of the elite crew in masks ringing the fires. He wedged me in, respectfully saluted again and left. I could have done without that intervention. I hastily slipped on my own mask and made it secure—who knew what lethal chemical cocktail might be burning there. From my vantage point I had an unimpeded view of a young woman bound with ropes being thrust forward towards the pyre. She was shrieking and straining away from the flames with all her might, the muscles in her neck bulging. Despite the intense heat I felt a chill. Without any ceremony whatsoever she was lifted and held aloft by a mass of hands. At that point she collapsed like a rag doll, it was as if the fight had been scooped out of her, and without further ado she was flung onto the fire. Her screech was bloodcurdling. Then there was a *whoosh!* as she ignited, her body going up in a gush of flame, fire eagerly eating her clothes, hair, skin, limbs. I reared back into the solid wall of the mob behind me, feeling nausea rising.

Next, an old man was grabbed and tossed onto the pyre in a similar fashion. He, however, went quietly, not making a single sound, not even when the fire bit him. I could not be certain, but when he looked at me he seemed to be smiling. His body spectacularly exploded with a loud *whomp!* and people cheered, a tuneless jangle of cries. There were seven other victims, some trussed and screeching, some in catatonia. They all burned. It was sickening. Held hard in place by the bonding crowd I watched brands of bones and torches of hair and candles of skin melt. When two women fainted behind me I seized the opportunity to punch an opening in the wall of jubilant executioners and I pummelled my way to the perimeter of the crowd.

After getting well away from the mob and the pyre, I pulled off my mask and tried the air. It was harsh and gritty, rasping through the windpipe a little, but otherwise nothing much to worry about. I supposed that those wearing masks were too delicate to smell flesh burn. I began walking away fast to put some distance between me and the barbecue pit. Further down the street there was a kid on his own bouncing rocks off a wall. A scrawny sort of kid with a shorn head and scabs on his knees in decent enough, although dirty, khaki clothes which suggested a uniform. He must have been about twelve, too young for the regular army but carrying a rifle over his shoulder anyhow, an ancient AK47 with 'kill' crudely carved on the wooden butt. I wondered if the gun still worked.

'Do you know what this is all about?' I asked, gesturing at the mob. He slipped a handful of rocks into his pocket and looked me over.

'Gotta fag?' he asked. He had a belligerent air but seemed willing to talk.

'I don't smoke,' I said. He looked disgusted and turned away. 'How about a drink?' I tried. That got his attention. He nodded assent. I tugged out the small hip-flask I liked to keep in my bag and handed it to him. He took a big swig from the flask and drank like it was milk.

'Got any money?' he demanded. I just looked at him.

'So what's this about?' I asked again. The way he hugged that flask against his chest I suspected the flask was lost. The kid thought a moment, gulped down another mouthful of whisky and decided to answer.

'They got the pox.'

'What pox?'

'The infection.' He pronounced this last word as if it were exotic, a word he had recently learnt to use. He looked back at the pyre. 'Did you see her?'

'Who?'

'She was the first one in the fire. I knew she'd scream. She was scared. She tried to pretend she wasn't one of them but she got found out.' He stopped, then said, 'She was my sister.' Then he turned and ran, still hugging the flask. He disappeared in seconds.

I was walking around in circles, happy to be losing myself in a maze of unfamiliar streets, when a sullen breeze kicked me towards a cluster of buildings daubed with graffiti. Getting closer I saw that they had all been decorated with the same thing—the mark of the betrayer, the St Peter's cross. The muddy red stigmata were inverted Latin crosses. The places which bore the sign had been vandalised: doors busted open, windows shattered, furniture smashed and strewn about. Curiosity prompted me to take a closer look when another child, this time a girl, possibly nine years old, appeared in a doorway. Huge dark eyes scrutinised me from under an extraordinary mat of mousy knotted hair. She had that fixed, unsettling stare that children have down to a fine art. She was skinny, badly dressed and very dirty. She looked hungry. She looked like many of the children of the city—and smelt like the most neglected of them. At least her stench was nothing ghastly, merely the odour of someone a long time unwashed.

'Hello,' I said, after a moment of uncertainty. She seemed to be sizing me up. I wondered if I had walked into a mugging. I'd heard of orphaned kids roaming the city in packs, looking for opportunities to survive another day. Opportunities such as myself.

'Go away or you'll get sick,' she said.

'Sick? What sort of sick?' I asked. I was an idiot in the impatience of her gaze. She slowly held out her arms. In the crooks of her elbows there was a constellation of small sores erupting in a pink watery ooze, which had dried to a yellowing crust in parts. The inflammations could have been a crop of infected pimples or baby boils. 'Does that mean you're sick?' I asked, pointing at her arms. She nodded her head. 'There must be something that will make it better,' I offered.

'I'm going to die soon,' she replied. Her sureness rattled me.

'It's probably a rash,' I protested. 'I'm sure you won't die from it.'

'You don't understand,' she said, 'it means the enemy's got you. It means you lost. It means you're dead.' There was a noise of a barrow or some such object being dragged along the street and the girl backed into the shadows of the building. I stepped towards her. 'No!' she yelled, grabbing a broken broom and running at me, connecting with real impact. Luckily it was the brush and not the handle she rammed into my stomach but still the force of it sent me staggering. Tears stung my eyes as my gut heaved. 'Go away,' she cried, 'go away before I kill you!'

When I returned to the hotel Juanita was waiting for me in the lobby. I saw that she, too, was carrying a gas mask. She moved towards me and a trick of the light carved up her face, hollowing out the eye-sockets and highlighting the jut of the bones in her cheeks. I was reminded of how some people are eaten from within, not always by illness, but it made me think that Juanita was sick. When I took her up to my suite her eyes went straight to the table where a meal had been laid out. 'Are you hungry?' I asked.

'Yes,' she replied.

'Sit down,' I said. 'You look like you could do with a decent feed.' I squirted perfume around the room as Juanita sat and ate without let-up until she bolted for the bathroom. I could hear her violent retching through the half-opened door. 'Feel better?' I asked when she returned. 'You want to try again?'

She made a grimace of disgust. 'No. Thanks.'

'Is it the smell in here?' I asked. 'Is that what's making you sick?' The awful stench which had accompanied the General back from the Bitch of Battles had become a permanent presence and it certainly interfered with my appetite.

'Smell?' she repeated. 'I don't smell anything except that perfume you've been spraying me with.' She paused. 'Unless I'm the one who smells bad.'

'No, no,' I assured her, 'it's just that I can smell something … rotting.' That was a polite way of putting it.

'Probably a dead rat.' Juanita sank down on the sofa with a

small groan and rubbed her belly. 'I haven't been eating well lately.'

'Juanita, were you pregnant?'

'No,' she said, 'not me. How come everybody knows about those miscarriages but no-one's talking about them?'

'Because no-one wants to talk about them. No-one in charge, that is. There's nothing like war to provide the proper perspective on what matters and what doesn't,' I said, hearing a bitterness in my voice.

'You sound upset about it.'

'No,' I shrugged, 'not me.' Juanita glanced at a bottle of champagne sitting unopened on the table. 'Apart from food, I gather your appetite is otherwise unaffected?' I queried, popping the cork and joining her on the sofa. She grinned in agreement and a brighter light glimmered in her eyes.

'What a haven,' she sighed, tasting her drink. 'There's madness out in the streets. Have you seen it? The fires?' I nodded. My stomach was still sore from where the child had rushed at me. 'Bloody stupid hysteria. It's bad for business.' She stroked the sofa appreciatively, her fingers close to my thigh. 'You're nice and safe in here. A nice little set-up with the General.'

'You can't afford to talk about it, I think,' I said. I looked at her until her eyes slid away. 'For your sake as much as mine.' I lowered my voice and leaned into her. 'Whatever's outside, whatever violence or madness, it's in here. It originates here.'

'Why stay then? Why not leave if it's so bad?' she taunted.

It was my turn to look away. 'It's either one type of danger or another, isn't it?'

'Maybe you're afraid of finding out this isn't as bad as you like to tell yourself and what's outside is a whole lot worse after all.' Her lips curved in disdain.

'I know what's out there,' I rejoined. 'I remember it very well. It's difficult to compare it with what I have here because in many ways I'm insulated against the worst that most people have to suffer, but in another way I confront what most people couldn't.'

'You're dramatising your situation in order to make it seem like you've got it tougher than anyone else. Or that you've got no choice. You don't have to play the victim of circumstance for me. I'm sitting here drinking your champagne, remember?' she snorted. 'And you wouldn't be party to the General's … tastes if you didn't in some way share them.' Juanita touched the small burn scars on her hands. Before I could ask her about them she lowered her voice and said, 'Is the General here? Is he really sick? Or is it a rumour? Some say he's dead. What happened?'

I didn't think it safe for Juanita to demonstrate such interest in the man who'd put a knife to her throat the first time they'd met.

'He's very much alive. He's away at some heavy-duty powwow. And you're right, I'm here by choice and I can't seduce you into thinking otherwise by whining about it.' I smiled, topping up her champagne, diverting the discussion away from the General in case he made an unexpected appearance.

'Seduce me, eh?' The way she said it was part invitation, part challenge. I leaned across to kiss her but the moment was interrupted by a barrage of noise from outside: a furious flurry of flapping and a soft but definite thudding. Then the siren started to sing. By the time Juanita and I got to the window, the sky was full of birds, mute black butcher birds, diving in kamikaze flocks through the film of smoke, slamdancing the towers and the roofs of the stupefied city, their corpses spinning and falling like chunks of black ice into the streets.

TWENTY-TWO

'The burning of one's enemies has a venerable history. Roman legionaries captured by the Teutons were burned alive before their altars in the ninth century, when the army of Varus was destroyed in the Teutoburger forest. It was an essential part of their victory celebrations. I'm gratified that you felt sufficiently recovered to venture out but perhaps you ought to be more selective about the places you choose to visit.' The General kissed my hand and returned to inspecting the miniature soldiers being painted by his adjutant. I stared at him. The last time I'd seen him he'd been glutting himself on his kill, now he stood before me—rude with health, radiating charisma, the picture of equanimity. In the face of this I momentarily wondered if I was going mad, but a look at his forehead reminded me of the sights I had seen and the thought went skittering away.

'Where's the victory in the people turning upon themselves?' I asked, averting my eyes from the General in order to study the M that had been recently branded on the adjutant's forehead. It was identical to the blaze on the General's forehead except that the adjutant's mark had been burned into his skin. The General's mark looked not so much like a burn as a livid, wholly natural strawberry mark.

'The people only seek a release. They are correct in thinking that intervention is necessary. Who can blame them for wishing to strike at the enemy?'

'They are murdering their own, not the enemy!'

'There are unpredictable circumstances in every war,' he replied. He picked up one of the tiny toys and pointed to a small blob on its back. 'Complete to the Soviet RPG-7 ammo bag,' he smiled, 'an excellent verisimilitude.' He paused. 'Besides which, taking the offensive is preferable to being defeated by caution, even if the response may be somewhat disproportionate. A difficult logic to grasp at times, but a primary logic of war.'

'That may well be considered sound logic but it doesn't excuse the fact that soldiers stood by and watched citizens being flung into the fire by a mob.'

'The situation is under assessment. It is thought that the contamination may well be the work of the enemy.'

Recalling the living conditions in that part of the city where I had found homes trashed and stigmatised I thought a lack of sanitation rather than the enemy might be better blamed. Supplies of mainline electricity and running water were wildly erratic, while the plumbing worked not at all in certain quarters and spasmodically at best in large tracts of the city. In an attempt to maintain some standard of hygiene Edict 33/13 outlawed the improper disposal of waste, and work gangs of war objectors had been hauled from their cells and offered the opportunity to assist the war effort by carting loads of excreta from the shit depots to a dump site on the perimeter of the

Western Sector. A job made hazardous by the lethal showers of debris that fell whenever Patriots and Guardians managed to intercept missiles, but for all that, a preferred alternative to summary execution, which was the only other option.

'This contamination. Why is it called the pox? Is it smallpox?' I asked, recalling those oozing pustules.

'No. It's merely a street term. What it is exactly has yet to be determined.'

'Is it fatal then?' The General shrugged. I persisted. 'If it's not an ordinary disease could it be due to chemical warfare?'

The General pulled the miniature gun out of the hand of his little warrior. 'This isn't right,' he complained to the adjutant who looked up in alarm, his eyebrows working furiously, like thick black lines of paint beginning to run. The man's face was long and lean and extraordinarily furrowed, despite him being not yet middle-aged. 'I believe this is a Colt Commando. An American rifle. And this is a Soviet ammo bag. Wrong.' The adjutant began to quickly search through a box of plastic weaponry that was his miniature armoury.

'Could it?' I repeated.

'It is in the realm of possibility, not probability,' the General answered. The adjutant handed him a substitute tiny gun. The General inspected it and nodded his approval. 'In the meantime, all Infectives and suspected Infectives are being transported to the plague station for confinement and analysis.' The General's hand snaked out and yanked me against him, catching me off balance. I fell forward against the hard rows of metal pinned to his chest and his breath curled into my ear. 'Did you touch one of them?' he whispered. 'Did you get that close?'

Was he going to pack me off to the plague station? I held his eyes and saw his excitement. Then I felt the movement as his sex unfurled against me.

'Yes,' I replied, 'I was that close.'

His head dropped down and his tongue glided into my ear. 'I knew your instinct for death would take you right to it,' he murmured. 'You go to it unerringly, you go in complicity. You divine it in everything. You, who are everything, with everything within you, I know you. I know your smell. I eat you.'

'You don't know me.' I pushed the words out with an enormous effort of will.

'I know what you become, day by day, Lady,' he breathed softly. Ever so softly.

When he entered me I had to close my eyes, even though my wetness signalled my readiness. When he put his mouth to mine I began to avert my head but I remembered who I was with and overcame the impulse. His body felt sharp, as if his bones were capable of somehow puncturing me. This was absurd, but still the fancy took a hold in me and the image of being drilled by his bones emerging from his body, thrusting through his skin and piercing me, became stuck in my head. Behind my closed eyelids blobs of coloured light began throbbing, his fingers crawled over my face, and when he replaced the pressure of his mouth with his hand, the heel of his palm caught under my chin. Strands of his hair fell in confusion over me.

'Make some noise,' he whispered, 'I want to hear you come, I want to remember the times I could hardly stop you from shouting.' My throat was parched. I gave a rather feeble moan. 'Louder!' he urged. 'I want to hear the sound of your whole body.' At that, he changed the tempo of his movements, his penis moving higher and faster, my pelvis flicking in time with his. I opened my mouth and my noise reverberated against him, my lips and larynx vibrating, but I did not come. The pressure of Sol's hand eased off and I shifted my head and eased the crick in my neck. A sense of defeat coursed through me, I wanted to cry. I told myself it was absurd, this gathering of tears. I was simply overwrought, I was still recovering from my recent drinking binge, from my confrontation with the General. The General was in my head but I wouldn't think about him, I wouldn't let him ruin my moment with Sol.

Sol rolled off me with a small sigh and reached for a cigarette and lit it. The flare of the match did a little dance then burnt out. The scent of nicotine netted me and I felt the scrape of his bracelet as his hand trailed across my belly. The charms I had given him tickled my bare skin. I became upset again for the most obscure reason: this was the first time I'd not brought him a good-luck charm. I picked up his hand and kissed his fingers and looked up and saw Juanita standing in the doorway, a silhouette against the scarlet sky. Behind her a sheet of clear plastic had been stretched over a huge hole in the wall to create the effect of a window. Clouds were wallowing in the sky, beginning to boil at a point around her head. The nimbus created an eerie effect.

I wondered how long she'd been standing there. I glanced across to Sol to gauge his reaction but he was looking down at his cigarette. When I looked at the doorway again no-one was there. A disappearance? A delusion? I'd left Juanita sitting in a bar on My Lai Avenue. When she'd invited me for a drink, I'd been expecting a girls' get-together. Instead she'd given me an address and told me that Sol was waiting. The last thing I had anticipated was seeing Sol again so soon. I was flustered. The feeling had persisted. As soon as I'd walked in the door Sol had lifted my skirt and started kissing me in a hungry way but it was as if I had lost a crucial intimacy with him.

The idea that Juanita had followed in order to watch or to spy on us seemed ludicrous, but it made more sense than a phantom watching over us. Juanita was too real, too much rude flesh and blood, to be an apparition. I shelved my thoughts about Juanita and touched Sol's arm, bringing myself back to him, feeling the new bloom of muscles, the hardening tension of his skin, as if the man were reforming below the surface again. There was more strength in him and he was looking much healthier. I pressed against him, wanting to be close, to cross the breach, but he exclaimed and drew away.

'What's the matter?' I asked. He unbuttoned his shirt—we hadn't undressed, his need had been so urgent—and along his left side ran a livid red wound, about seven centimetres long, recently healed. He flinched a little as I caressed it softly with my nails. It looked like a knife wound, sharp and incisive, and began to weep a pink viscous fluid. 'It hasn't fully healed!' I exclaimed. 'How did it happen?' I found a piece of clean rag and fussed over the wound while Sol lay back and indulged my display of concern. My solicitude seemed to relax him, for he grinned at me in his alluring way and slid his hand up and down my leg.

'I got it from a woman with a knife.' He pulled me to him and I felt his erection ride against my pubic bone. 'A small souvenir.'

'You sound almost pleased with it,' I replied, careful not to press against it.

'Call it a badge of courage. A type of war wound.'

'Did she attack you? Were you hurt anywhere else?'

'No,' he replied, his hands swooping on my arse, creeping into my cleft. 'Don't worry, the rest of me is intact and it doesn't hurt much.' He lifted his head and nuzzled my breast. 'I want you again.'

As before, he was not actually brutal, simply not the lover I had known. Or remembered. When he entered me he began to straightaway thrust deep inside me, moving hard, screwing me with a pounding movement, his fingertips biting my thighs. I knew this sort of ride. I concentrated on making my body move in time with his, on trying to make our fuck nice and rhythmic, trying to absorb him without alarm or censure. Sol needed time to be in me again, he needed me to take him like this before he could become slow or gentle. But after a while of this grinding together he did not come and I did not come, and eventually we slowed and he fell out of me, making a wet plopping sound that was above all sad because it was not a sign of love replete, it was a signal that we had not managed to reach each other.

Silence. The strike of his match, the suck of his breath, the cigarette. I laid my hands on him caressingly. 'Let's make nothing matter. Nothing except us, and here and now.' His cigarette brushed oh so casually against my hand—once, then, less casually, twice. I jerked my hand away and looked at him but said nothing.

'Let me kiss it better,' he murmured, putting my hand to his mouth, sucking the burn. When I saw how this aroused him I started to feel afraid. Not the fear of perversion—the fear that I was not with Sol but with someone else. 'I can taste your heat,' he moaned, sliding his tongue against me, his mouth pulsing against my clitoris. 'I can taste it in your skin, I can taste it inside of you.' I opened myself wide as he entered me again, as urgent as before. This time he loosed himself. I, too, began to dance up and down the length of him, dancing out my pent-up longing, my lust, my anxiety, my need, my collection of fears, my love, all coalescing to deliver me of my orgasm, a great shudder dancing out of me, shaking me over and over his burning, twitching body.

Afterwards, when we lay entwined together and I was ignoring the small, smarting burns, lulling myself into the peaceableness of post-coitus, Sol said, 'I want you to do something for me. I want you to get hold of some Ultras. Your soldier is in charge of Supplies, isn't he? They're small and lightweight, easy to shift. The army won't even know they're missing.' It was the first time he didn't say 'fuck-soldier'.

'Ultras? Why?' Ultras were very small, very high-tech mines.

'I've got a contact interested in them.'

'I can give you money,' I said.

'Not enough.'

'What do you need it for?'

'A business proposition.'

'Who with?'

'Why do you need to know?'

'Because I don't know enough about the things that matter to you.'

He stroked my back. 'It's not that I don't want to tell you things but I've got to protect others by not telling you things. It's not just a matter of other people's survival, it's my … honour, and if that goes what's left? If there's no notion of honour amongst us I may as well invite the General to tea and offer him my throat to slit and be done with it.' Sol spoke of the General as if he had a personal bone to pick with him. This talk made me uneasy, it ignited the fear that I'd contaminated Sol through my association with the General.

I pushed the thought of contamination in another direction. 'Is anyone you know sick?' I asked. 'They're conducting spot searches and random checks to flush out those who've got the pox.' Pox. An effortless word. I'd passed a huddle of people miserably stripping at gunpoint in full view of the rest of the street on my way to meet him. 'It's extremely dangerous for you right now, whether you've got a uniform on or not. Shouldn't you be lying low?' After witnessing the impromptu strip-searches I had visions of him being stopped for a pox check and being discovered.

Sol shook his head. 'And who's doing all this pox searching? The military, of course. And have you seen any soldiers being carted off to a plague station? No. The whole thing's a set-up,' he sneered. 'As if there isn't enough for the people to bear without this new hysteria. It's one of the General's malicious little games, that's all. It's merely a tactic to instil fear and hence compliance.' His last comment could have come from the mouth of the General. Sol had been jabbing the air with his cigarette as he spoke and came perilously close to burning me again. I slid off the bed and picked up my dress. I felt extremely agitated. It took three attempts before my dress, a little too tight, slithered over my head. Sol looked at his wrist-watch. Time to go. A small panic began to kick in me. I sat down on the bed again. 'You must be very careful,' I said, gripping him by his shoulders. 'Promise me you'll be careful.'

He leaned in close to me and I felt the heat of his cigarette again as he said, 'I need you to do whatever you can to help me. I need to have you on my side. Get those Ultras.'

'It's going to be difficult. How will I get them to you?'

'Use Juanita,' he answered.

I laid my head in the hollow of his shoulder and whispered, 'Whatever's possible for me, I'll do for you.'

He kissed me on the forehead, leaving the wet mark of his mouth. 'That's what I need to know. That's what I want to hear.'

TWENTY-THREE

Looking down upon the street oppressed me. The usual relief of it being out there waiting for me eluded me. I pressed my cheek against the plastic-sheeted hole and watched Sol grow smaller and smaller until he disappeared. My internal agitation continued long after he had gone. If anything, it grew. And metamorphosed into a numbness, making it almost impossible to pick myself up and get going again. As before, my scant time with him had paralysed my will to move, to return to the other part of my life. What finally stirred me was the motion of the sky. As I watched the contortions of carmine cloud I saw strange, fantastical shapes form and collapse and reform themselves in ruddy vapour. A bizarre lobster broiling of beaks, talons and tails; bovine faces with leering tongues, rolling eyes, contorting mouths; huge roiling limbs; vast, palpitating bellies. An undulating phantasmagoria, shape-changing and shifting too fast to keep a fix on any one cloud having any one characteristic. The show kept going on and on until the shapes abruptly lost all animation and dissolved into thunderfalls of water.

This violent discharge of negative ions got me moving and energy in the form of anxiety began to course through me again, vital enough to shatter the numbness. I virtually sprinted out of that box of a room down the stairs and out the building—again, whose apartment I had visited I knew not—into the drumming rain and onto the street along with others, all screeching and yelling, lobbing containers out into the deluge, scooping up water in their arms, filling their cheeks with it. They were mad with it. This rain was something more than a novel event, it was breaking the bad spell of our parched days and our thirsty nights. Acute water shortages had long ago forced draconian rationing under Edict 15/1. Water thieves were publicly lined up, offered the option of blindfolds, and shot. Now water pummelled the city with the force of fists, pumping the air from gutters, creating whirlpools of garbage, resurfacing the roads, forging new paths up from under the sidewalks, sluicing the ground floors of buildings. The exhilaration was reckless. Palpable.

There was an elemental charm about this normal, natural onslaught. I was drenched in seconds, my dress a clinging obdurate skin hanging between my thighs, dragging against my breasts, a new skin that had the texture and suction of mud, and I was all of a sudden laughing at the rain's stinging slaps, feeling a swoop of happiness until a shaft of lightning shot out of the growling sky and sizzled a woman not two metres away from me. The charm of the moment abruptly disappeared and prudence prevailed over the desire to be elemental. I edged around the knot of people who had instantly closed around the body and ran into a shelter.

A bar.

A favourite safe place from way back.

A room full of flopping, steaming bodies and breathy, high-pitched talk. Already, damp, muddy corners where the music of water was ricocheting into buckets. Already, weeping gaps where condensation was beading walls that were becoming slick under one's palm. Subterranean becoming submarine, and with the metamorphosis a sleepy bar was being aroused to a new vivacity, filling with people brimming with something other than war, losses, privations, the enemy. People transported to sheer, ordinary friendliness by something almost forgotten, the simple fury of a storm. Wringing water from me, I pushed my way to the bar, ordered a beer and found a corner in which to compose myself.

My attempt at composure was shot to pieces within minutes. On a vibrant television screen there played some dated, alfresco footage of the General going about the business of war, and there I was, caught by a camera, plain as day in the back of the Mercedes as the General alighted, the camera zooming in on me and I, as if in response, swivelling my naked face to it, shining with bright luminosity through the open door of the car for a long, exclusive moment before the door swung gently shut and the Mercedes carried me away. As my image blinked off the screen and the image of the General, resplendent in dress uniform and benign before the camera, replaced me and began his studio address to the nation, I put the bottle to my lips and took a long swallow, and heard a dull roaring in my ears that was not the falling of water.

The footage jolted me with memory of that day. I recalled the day because I remembered the outfit. A white silk suit, as virginal as if I were a bride. No memory of looking radiant for the camera. The purpose of the journey had been an exercise in PR. The General had been responding to the issue of the

Southern Sector, the sector which adjoined our most recent land losses at the time. It was filling up with panicked, bullied people deserting their ravaged farms and market gardens with the enemy hard on their tail, desperate to exchange the probability of death for the possibility of it. I had been privy to the War Council's decision to bomb our own area. I had known that deadly footpaths of mines were being laid and forests of electrified razor wire planted in order to contain the fleeing, invading peoples and to provide a buffer between the city and the latest disaster zone.

The War Council had conscionably agreed that the war required sacrificial offerings. These offerings would be passed off as the enemy's mercilessness. The enemy would be blamed for shelling the Southern Sector, which had been hastily declared a refugee camp. The General had thereafter addressed the people in a television broadcast declaring that in accord with the holy principles of humanitarianism these poor terrified innocent needy refugees were first and foremost the brethren of the city. I had been in the car which had taken him to the television studio where he had delivered his address. 'We will protect our own and we will prevail over evil,' he had thundered in his best oratory tones. Just as I had later been at his side when he had signed the order to use this migrating population as a shield for the city. 'There is no such thing as a just war,' he had said to me. The black ink on that document had been thick and wet and it stained the tips of his fingers. Later when I found smudges of it on my body I mistook it for bruising, until I saw that my virgin-white suit was likewise smeared. No longer immaculate.

Suddenly I wanted out of that bar. I loathed recognition. I wanted home.

Home. A hotel.
A place for witnessing horrors.

Chemical agents affect the nervous system and the breathing centres. Working their way in through skin. Eyes. Nose. Throat.

The nerve gases tabun, sarin and soman can be lethal within minutes after contact with the skin or being inhaled. A nerve agent, in general, is designed to kill numerous people or, at the very least, disable them in the short term. Chemical agents can be colourless, odourless, tasteless. They can mean a rapid or a prolonged death. Agonising death. Blindness, deafness, vomiting, diarrhoea, choking, paralysis. Burning the skin, eyes or lungs. Dropping as bombs, spraying from planes, exploding with artillery shells, detonating with mines. Stealthily or explosively. Insidious or clamorous, they were always part of the arsenal, part of the calculation of what might be done to whom, intoned the General from his height above me. I had been laid out on a Turkish ottoman, an antique, exotic touch. 'For instance,' he continued, 'during the Peloponnesian War in the fifth century BC the Spartans used Greek Fire as a primitive method of chemical warfare. Ingenious, no?'

In 1899 the Hague Convention renounced the diffusion of asphyxiating or harmful gases. In 1915 the use of gas was introduced by the Germans into World War One. This first experiment comprised poisonous chlorine, soon after replaced by mustard gas—a vesicant, a blistering agent. The skin bubbled. As did the lungs. It became a gas widely utilised by all battle contestants, although at times was grossly ineffective. 'Gas masks,' he said to my questioning stare, stroking my bound ankles, 'and other effective anti-chemical protection. Nowadays, masks, suits and gloves. And inoculations.'

'Oh,' I said. 'Inoculations.'

'There is also decon powder and the detection litmus paper which provide a key essential response,' he continued.

'Decon?'

'Decontamination,' he replied patiently, as if speaking to a child.

In theory, chem-war was an unacceptable practice and in 1925 the Geneva Protocol prohibited the use of asphyxiating, poisonous, or other such gases, and of all like liquids, materials and devices, although chem-weapons were used in some wars after that. 'For example, in Ethiopia, China, Yemen, Iran, the Gulf, Pakistan, Tibet and Croatia,' the General lectured. A Chemical Weapons Treaty had been ratified in 1997, but by no means by everyone and sooner or later the advantage of not signing was applied in various wars, and chem-war became common for a while because certain parties indeed had the advantage before international sanctions became too much of a disadvantage. 'Politics,' sighed the General, 'getting in the way of war.'

'But von Clausewitz says war is the continuation of policy by any other means,' I said, airing my knowledge gleaned from too many nights reading *On War* to the General. 'Von Clausewitz says the purpose of war is to serve politics, doesn't he?'

'That depends entirely on who is making the policy,' replied the General. 'What I want you to remember,' he continued, plucking at the knots in the cords around my ankles, 'is how unwieldy chem-weaponry is. A warhead may just as easily detonate into a harmless puddle or evaporate in the air as achieve the target. Besides which, there is a very high degree of efficiency of defences against it.'

'Gas masks,' I murmured. 'Inoculations. Litmus tests. Decon powder. Gloves. Sealed rooms. Chemical suits.'

'Good girl,' he smiled, sliding his finger up my calf then breaking off mid-movement to unfasten his jacket. The General then proceeded to tell me that in battle-real terms, chem-war is an effective practice. Meaning that it is a black-mail, a strategy, and an efficient enough method of annihilation when the chemical is delivered correctly. 'What is most useful,' he smiled, 'is that it can badly interfere with fighting and can be a greater deterrent than that of direct casualties. Protective clothing limits field performance. It's good strategy.'

'But the people,' I protested, 'the population who aren't fighting who may be equally at risk, what happens to them? Aren't they vulnerable?' The General slapped his hands together. He was adamant. The city had not been exposed to chemical warfare. There had been no mass onset of symptoms. No blood gases, no vesicant, no phosgene, no lewisite. The amount of chem-war agent required to create a hazardous cloud was entirely dependent upon weather patterns. It would have taken literally tons of the stuff to have had such an effect, it would have meant thousands of observable, and therefore interpenetrable projectiles. 'There is no way, then, that the miscarriages which afflicted every pregnant woman in the city and which no-one deigned to speak about, let alone acknowledge, or the deaths of the animals which also occurred without comment, and now the pox which we're told hasn't been identified, can't be easily avoided or really even be dealt with, are the outcomes of chemical bombardments? No way at all?' I insisted.

'No,' he said, opening the closet. I watched him fastidiously hang his jacket on a coat-hanger and place it on the rack inside.

'What about biological warfare?' I said. As he withdrew his hand he inadvertently brushed the arm of the coat-hanger and the jacket began to rock. Back and forth. Back and forth.

The General tut-tutted. Development, production and stockpiling of biological warfare weapons had been outlawed by the 1972 Biological and Toxin Weapons Convention. Not one nation had since been found guilty of utilising a biol-weapon. Of course there had been inexplicable outbreaks, events note, not attacks as such, in certain disenfranchised parts of the world but nothing had ever been conclusively proven an actual act of warfare. Although biol-weapons were cheap and could affect hundreds of thousands of square kilometres, compared with the coverage of only tens of thousands of kilometres that chem-weapons could achieve, there were significant management problems which had not yet been sufficiently resolved for them to be an effective weapon. Not to mention the fact that they were outlawed.

This so-called pox was a salamander, not a goddamned red herring. Neither was it tularaemia, anthrax, botulism, Red Rock fever, ebola or Streppett's syndrome. The cases of the as-yet-undiagnosed illness were contained, isolated, restricted. Under control. The plague stations were a success, the number of cases levelling off. Possibly dropping. I flexed my wrists in their binds and recalled the steaming concertina of people in that bar in which I had sought sanctuary from the rain. There'd been dissenters during the General's television appearance. True, drink may have given them their tongue, but still, they spoke out. 'I think some people are sceptical,' I said.

'It suits certain imaginations to contemplate the spectre of a plague,' he admonished.

'The threat of the pox is more real to them than war statistics,' I countered.

'Which is why the lesser intelligence takes that path,' he said. 'The vast canvas of war defeats their vision; the more they can reduce the picture, the more in control they feel. A small outbreak of sickness occurs and there is no immediate explanation. No cause. But despite this, the sickness is manageable precisely because it is observable. The sickness consumes them, it fills their heads, it gives them a cause which demands an effect. Not to mention a prognosis, a rationale, a cure, and in one stroke they are reduced to this moment above all other moments, the moment when sickness becomes something more than sickness, when it becomes the symptom of their poor jaundiced search for meaning and clarity in the midst of confusion.'

I looked at the General rocking on the balls of his feet.

Back and forth. Back and forth.

He was staring at my breasts. I had not had the opportunity to change out of my wet clothing and my dress was in all likelihood transparent. I had been shivering with cold for some time. 'Why are they confused?' I asked.

Silence.

The buttons of my bodice opened to the manipulations of his fingers and my breasts were released from the sodden material. 'Why should a contained outbreak of illness mobilise them in this way?' I asked.

'Mobilise?' he said. 'Mobilise? What a unique choice of word.' He gripped my nipples between his thumbs and forefingers. I must have been ovulating because my nipples were extremely sensitive and painful to touch. 'Do you know something that I do not?'

'No,' I replied. 'Nothing. I know nothing. Sometimes when I hear things I jump to my own conclusions, that's all. It means absolutely nothing.'

His finger tracked over my breastbone and lifted the clammy material from my belly, pulling down my underpants and continuing on to my mons veneris, coming to rest in the cleft of my cunt. He hovered over the hood of my clitoris. 'You never say nothing,' he sighed. 'Meaning exists in everything you say.'

'No,' I said. 'No.'

But still he lurched to his knees and he put his mouth to my mound and I heard the familiar and distinctive noise that accompanied that activity. The transmission of rifles and sub-machinery. Ak ak ak. Rat tat tat. Sshhh sshhh sshhh. 'FN FAL,' he raptured, 'MAS36, F88, MP44, L96A1, Beretta AR70, AK47,' my lips vibrating to his mouthings, 'M60, M14, M16, VZ 61, Uzi, Sten Mark 2, Colt Commando …' And my body was making its call, firing under his tongue, worming under his invocation of the killing tools.

TWENTY-FOUR

He, ravenous, dreams of food, he dreams his Lady tosses him a fleshy petal from her lotus. It has the suppleness and texture of a tender meat. It is a pliant skin in his hand. Erotic stretched skin, glowing like a lampshade. It burns inside him in his sleep, animate nightlight lighting up the path of feasting.

He knows she favours him. She uncoils elegant limbs, shows him her red-streaked smile, her strong snapping teeth, her salacious tongue. A garland of severed hands hangs from the delectable curve of her waist. She shimmies, loose-hipped, and beckons him to her table, her hands weaving an invitation.

He alone of all others.

He alone of his sex.

He feels himself surge towards the sword in her hand, that instrument of grace, the weapon which neatly fits the hot curve of their intent. She calls to him by lassoing his neck with her noose, and as the rope burns, his mouth waters. Goddess of unsullied appetite, woman of unmistakable odour. His sex rises to accord with her nakedness and he offers himself to her feet. He is a god who knows where his place is and when to take it.

Endless lines of devotees file past them making salutes of war. Sitting with her like one of her pet jackals decorating her table he sees how she eats by scissoring her legs. He sees how she eats by gesture of her jaws. As her two mouths open wide he sees that those blooded holes are the start and the finish.

Damn and curse.

She who makes heaven and she who is hell.

She who breeds in order to feed and keep feeding the hunger that sends him to reap new fields, reach new plateaus, annex new realms of gourmet delight. The unceasing rounds of the hard and easy slaughters are his promises and prayers to her. He will keep his Kali so entertained, so fed and amused, because his appetite is pure. His carnage is his signal to her, together they will dance without hesitating through the mire of his making.

What a destiny. What a pair. What a world he is conquering, what territories he is carving out.

She, monumental mother of warriors.

She, cunt of conflagration. Princess of principalities.

Squatting like the basest, the grandest of women. Bellowing like the strongest, the most penetrated. Letting him lap the sweet-sour blood from her pap. He can feel his Kali's beautiful fury as her four arms whirl around him, her necklace of skulls knocking against the bone in his breast. His ticking dick sways in divine movement with her. What empires they will conquer, what treasures are theirs for the taking. She, his insurmountable, indispensable companion of war. She, his goddess-fuck.

His spasm is deep and violent, milk in blood, and when he hears her howling he knows that he has pleased her well.

TWENTY-FIVE

It rained for days. Water turned to mud. Thin nasty mud. It became so that water no longer seemed to fall from that huge sore of a sky. It smelt and felt and tasted as though mud were falling, as if the water could not wait for a decent conversion, could not wait for its meeting with dirt or dust. The clear joy of water had gone—no more filling the pans out in the street and happy bathing in fresh puddles. The new misery introduced a new smell, the fetor of water that was brackish and evilly bad. It was as if the heavens were leaving their gift to rot before letting it fall, and if there were gods they were either impervious to an overload of tribulation or too busy giggling at the new chaos to have any other care. There were those, however, who still prayed despite the futility.

People drowned. People died face-down in centimetres of water, the smallest possible amount required for drowning. People fell into mud slides that demolished whole streets; people disappeared, submerging along with all trace of their having had a life. At first the Dislocatees suffered the worst, they had the largest body count, the most catastrophic disruptions, but then more and more waterlogged and muddied corpses kept bobbing up in other parts of the city, places that were salubrious and unused to death shoving its face in their doors in any form other than an official delegation to announce the death of a husband or a brother or a son in battle.

A hastily convened Department of Drownings was inundated by grieving relatives of the wet dead, as they were called. I don't know why, perhaps to distinguish them from the war dead, because like the war dead there were so many of them. And at that time there were far fewer of any other sort of civil dead, even with the spectre of the pox. I remember watching the bodies being hooked and dragged to shore by sodden, slime-covered soldiers wielding a long pole with something very much like a meat hook on the end. The General had taken advantage of a lull in the downpour to personally tour the beached parts of the city. I stayed in the Mercedes and watched the hooking of human flotsam from the tinted window—it was nothing at all like the sport of fishing I had seen in my childhood.

After that demonstration the General must have decided that I needed further inculcation because he announced that we would visit the Department of Drownings. No, I wanted to say, I really have seen quite enough for one day, the one day when there had been the smallest break in the line of clouds and the faintest lifting of the oppressive threat that was the sky, but I didn't say that, or anything much else, and he pressed my hand and moved his knee against mine and I pushed my spine straight and hard into the soft leather upholstery of the car, as if to deny the luxury, as if that somehow made a difference. The thought turned over and over in my mind that this was one way I would not, no matter what, find Sol if he went missing. Sol had been officially missing ever since he'd started running and I don't know why it bothered me all of a sudden, the idea of him going missing. Maybe I'd seen too many corpses being yanked naked and featureless out of water in one day. Maybe that was the moment I comprehended just how impossible it was for me to ever have a claim on Sol, even if he died. Especially if he died. Just another lost one.

It was astonishing how quiet and contained the relatives and friends of the wet dead were as they waited, dripping, in queues to report the losses and vet the dredged-up bodies, but I suppose adversity was well and truly a weight by then. Carried by so many of us. In the past few days, as if in response to the deluge, the war had begun raging on the eastern front, where the world was bone dry and there was nothing much except stones and dirt and desert. The ferocity of that exchange was audible over the radio (the TV along with all other electric gadgets had been sabotaged by the disruptive storms), with bulletins of the battle's gains and losses interspersed with official weather reports and interviews with hemming and hawing meteorologists, interviews that were entirely conjecture because no-one knew what the hell was happening with the weather.

One thing I was grateful for was that the rain put a stop to the public pyres, for it was logistically impossible to host open-air burnings such as I had witnessed. As the damp rose and the mould bloomed and the foul water gushed or seeped into everything, I thought the new calamity would wash away the old but this was not to be. The voice of the nation which flowed with unceasing unctuous smoothness from our battery-operated radios instructed us to boil our drinking water, to avoid public places, and to not share utensils, embraces, or lend out our personal effects. There was little else in the way of advice on how to avoid contamination. The original plague station had blossomed to three, not including the one which had been washed into the river in a torrent so ferocious that there were no attempts at rescue.

'You shouldn't have come here,' Juanita said, 'I'm fine. I've been too busy to see you.' She blocked the doorway with her body. Her voice was shrill and up about half an octave, despite her imperious demeanour.

'Just shut up and invite me in,' I said. 'I'm wet through, I'm thirsty and I haven't waded through streets of muck to entertain your neighbours on your doorstep.'

She gave a little sigh and seemed to sink into herself, so I seized the advantage and stepped inside and slammed the door behind me. Juanita shot home the bolts, all three of them, and sardonically flapped an arm at the room. 'My queendom,' she said. By way of reply I handed her a bottle of vodka. 'I'm sorry, I didn't bring any food,' I added.

'Who needs it?' she asked. It looked as though she did but I didn't say that. Her apartment was small, full of gloomy furniture, the walls flaking paint, the ceiling sagging, but it had, incredibly, a whole wall of intact windows, requiring a huge blackout curtain. It was a fitted curtain with pinch pleats and hooks, hung properly, which lent an elegance, despite the wear. Juanita went over to the windows and twitched the curtain halfway across, obscuring a close-up view of the red-brick geometry of a building. A flooded, denuded park opposite filled the rest of the window space. 'I like looking at the trees,' she murmured, 'they remind me to be restful.' She looked anything but restful, opening the vodka and pulling glasses out of a cupboard in the corner that served as a kitchen with noisy, perhaps nervous, movements. I looked at the trees. They were stumps sticking up out of eddying waters which had submerged the park. A dead, drowned landscape.

A closed door led to a bathroom, I guessed, and another corner of the room had been sectioned off with two huge wardrobes to create a bedroom. I glimpsed clothing strewn all over the floor and the closet doors. By way of decoration there was an abundance of old mardi gras masks pinned to the wall above the bed. Juanita saw me looking and threw me a towel. 'Dry off,' she ordered. I dried myself, feeling oddly self-conscious, her eyes steadfastly on me. Then she handed me a drink. We sat opposite each other on a pair of squashy foam sofas. '*Salut*,' she said, tipping the contents of her glass down her gullet.

'*Salut*,' I responded. The liquor was warm but deliciously oily, a good vodka.

Juanita smacked her lips. 'Yum, yum,' she said. Outside the rain started again, a light steady rhythm against the window. 'I'm getting to hate this rain,' she said as she poured us another drink, 'and I'm surprised that you're here, considering.'

'The weather?'

'That you didn't know where I lived.'

'No-one can work when the streets have been washed away. People are grateful to earn however they can.' I sounded deliberately vague because I'd hired a woman I'd met in a bar who assured me she'd once been employed as a private detective and still had the knack of finding people even though the war had badly interfered with business. The wet dead, however, were proving a lucrative prospect; she was suddenly in demand, even if only for the morbid confirmation of the outcome of disappearances. She had located Juanita and charged me the appropriate fee.

'One day money won't buy you what you want.'

I shrugged. 'Until that happens there's no point in not using it to try to get what I want.'

'Fair enough,' she said, passing the vodka, swivelling her eyes to the windows, pulling back the hair from her face, smoothing her neck, running her finger around the lip of the glass, buckling her feet under her, swerving her gaze from the windows to me, me back to the windows, as if she kept catching glimpses of something out there that I could not see.

'What's wrong?' I said. 'I haven't heard from you.'

'The rain,' she said. 'Why are you here?'

'Remember I told you that Sol wanted some Ultras? Well, I've got them.' I'd had to pull a few strings and entertain a few cocks but I'd got them. She didn't reply. 'What's wrong?' I repeated. Another silence. I didn't want to say it but I had to. 'Has something happened to Sol?'

'Sol …' she began, then stalled. My gut tightened.

'What's happened?'

She looked at me. 'Another close encounter. He wasn't caught and he's safe now but he's not feeling particularly lucky at the moment.'

'Does he blame me?' I asked in a low voice.

'Should he?'

'Of course not! It's just that—'

'It's just that you're going to get him into trouble sooner or later.'

I didn't want to think about that. 'The last time I saw him he was going on about the General.'

She gave a short bark of a laugh. 'And I suppose you took it personally. Don't worry, I haven't told your precious boyfriend who your fuck-soldier is.' Fuck-soldier. That was Sol's word. She slumped back against the sofa. 'Why do you insist on seeing him?'

It was my turn to look out at the rain. 'He's all I have of another life. Of who I was, of who I am.'

'A memento,' she taunted.

'No,' I retorted, stung. 'A lifeline.'

'Do you ever consider what he wants? What he needs?' she asked.

'Wants. Needs,' I repeated. 'I've done what I thought necessary for both him and me.'

She snorted. 'You've only done what you've wanted to do. What's necessary is for you to put aside your self-pity. What's necessary is for you to protect him, not endanger him. You insist on seeing him and he keeps on seeing you. Why should he be your escape from your hardships,' she said 'hardships' bitingly, 'regardless of the cost to him?'

'Don't you think I haven't agonised over the possibility of bringing him too close to me … and the General?'

'Then stop being selfish. Stop seeing him altogether.'

'I can't,' I said. 'It's my necessity.'

'You being the General's fuck makes it impossible for you to be with Sol, don't you think?' Juanita emptied her glass in one gulp and poured herself another measure. 'What if the General had you followed? Can you imagine what he would do to Sol if you were found with him?'

I took in the waterlogged park. 'It seems that there's always something to be afraid of. It's fear which makes me weak. But I need Sol.'

'You don't have a premium on fear, you know.'

'I know.' There were tears behind my eyes, falling into me because I could not let them out. 'Can't I see him?'

'No,' she said. 'That'd be a stupid thing to do. Where are the Ultras?'

'In the bottom of my closet in some shoeboxes.'

'Keep them there until I let you know otherwise.' I nodded. 'You better go,' she said, 'I think the rain's getting harder. You wouldn't want to get caught in it, it's too unpredictable. I don't want you getting trapped here.' Her face was shuttered.

'Something's wrong,' I said. 'Tell me what's the matter.'

Juanita refused my bait and got to her feet, saying, 'These days it's hard to tell wrong from right, especially if it's only a matter of feelings.' When she ushered me to the door I went to kiss her goodbye on the lips and she quickly turned her head, offering her cheek instead of her mouth.

'Last time I was with Sol,' I said, brushing my mouth across her clammy skin, 'I thought you were there with us.'

Another broken bit of a laugh. 'What? Spying on you? Watching you fuck?'

'Yes,' I admitted, feeling it had been a ludicrous thing to say.

'I don't get my kicks like that,' she said. 'I only watch if I'm paid to and you didn't pay me enough for that.' She meant it to be light-hearted, I'm sure, but the words came out heavy and flat-sounding, resentful. Not much of a joke. She stood there, awkward, distanced, her arms dangling by her sides.

I lightly touched her on the elbow. 'I didn't mean to upset you.'

'You didn't.' She made the effort to smile at me. I believe it was sincere. 'This rain, it's really getting on my nerves.'

We decamped in the raw middle of night. I must have passed out on my bed in my clothes, for all of a sudden I was being shaken awake by a soldier telling me I had ten minutes to pack. He had been assigned to assist me. Rivulets of water were running down the walls of the hotel suite and pooling under doors and windows. Water, more and more water. Except this water had been polluted, coloured by chemicals or rust or paint or blood. It was disturbing, the way it looked as if it were flush with blood.

Despite being snagged by the remnants of an unsettling dream—I could only recall birds viciously fighting over bones in a wasteland—I could see that the soldier's elaborate courtesy towards me was a form of contempt. I took a petty revenge by directing him to pack the most feminine items, my cosmetics and lingerie, while the first thing I packed were my shoes. I would be hard pressed to explain several shoeboxes full of Ultras. He was a beanpole of a fellow with a long fine nose and an arrogant face that flushed several shades darker as his elegant hands crushed my underwear into a bag. The fine skin of his forehead was puckered with the same notation I had seen decorating the forehead of the General's adjutant. The mark curved cleanly but was quite inflamed from the slow dissipation of blistering. The scar on my hand tingled with weird sympathy and I flexed it in what had become an habitual gesture.

'Why are you emulating the General?' I asked. My question took me aback. A bra swung in his hand, a fine filigree of black lace, as his pale green eyes narrowed and I had the pleasure of hearing the disdain he had been tamping down.

'I would never presume such a thing.'

'What is the meaning of that mark?' I demanded, pointing my finger at the letter on his forehead.

He clicked his heels together with dignity. 'It signifies that I am a member of the General's Chosen Ones.'

'The General has a new private guard?'

'Yes.'

'And you all wear the mark on your foreheads?'

'Yes.'

'I see.' I'd seen several soldiers with the brand but I'd thought it a crass form of hero-worship. The formation of a new guard was a serious business and I realised I'd been letting things slip not to have found this out before now. 'What else distinguishes the Chosen Ones?'

He flicked his eyes away. 'The uninitiated only receive the flame but once and that moment is not of their making.' Gobbledygook.

'Do you have a special mission?'

He paused, then said, 'Only in annihilation is there truth.'

'Meaning what exactly?'

He replied in a drawling, disparaging manner, 'I am not required to speak of it to you.'

'Call your commanding officer sir, lieutenant!' interjected the General from the doorway.

The lieutenant snapped to attention. 'Yes, sir! Sir!' His expression of disdain now most controlled.

The General entered the room and I said, 'He's loyal, he won't tell me anything about the Chosen Ones.'

'You recognise the mark though?' The General smiled.

'Oh, indeed I do.'

'Consider him yours,' he said. I stared at him as he said to the man, 'Salute your new commanding officer, Lieutenant O.'

The lieutenant baulked. 'But sir, the sign!' The General took my hand and shoved it under the man's nose. His response was immediate. 'Sir!' barked the lieutenant, saluting me. His salute may have contained more seriousness if my bra had not been dangling from his upraised hand. But there was little humour for me in the General's next comment.

'She is the mark itself,' he said, 'she who commands armies.'

TWENTY-SIX

I looked down from the El Alamein Tower and I could make out the scavengers wading through the sludge far below. The bleary red eye of the sun was finally visible again and the water had receded three feet already in the past two days. There was widespread fervent hope that this was the end of it. Overhead, a couple of Tantrum fighter planes zapped by, leaving a faint trace of sound in the air. I wondered where they were going, where they had been. They seemed to be heading south-west. I had been informed that the war had suddenly swivelled away from the eastern front; exactly where it was swivelling to had yet to be determined, the enemy was playing games, the enemy was playing for time. We were the cat, they the mouse. Apparently.

I watched television footage of smoke puffing out of enemy emplacements; watched colourful tracer criss-crossing the horizon and mating in explosive disharmony; observed the ruination of certain parts of our city perimeter; heard the incoming, the coded, heavy breathing of single-minded artillery; listened to arguments over strategy; saw the maps;

listened to the commands; heard the unravelling of orders, and jotted down tactics and counter-tactics on my stash of hotel stationery. On TV the only images of the enemy were the flattened, two-dimensionalised prisoners of war, either compliantly accepting a bowl of food or a blanket or a delousing. Or otherwise useful gestures in the bloody drama—suspended from poles specifically designed for the purpose of public display, sometimes swinging in segments, portions of the body neatly arrayed like choice cuts of beef.

A graphic shorthand for resistance, difference, denial, tragedy.

When the bodies were intact, simply hung by the neck, there were placards hammered to their chests with nails and crude but easily intelligible handwriting on cardboard:

> *I am the monster who mutilated your flesh.*
> *My only happiness is the rape of your land and the*
> *annihilation of your children.*
> *I am an unrepentant murderer.*
> *I do not recant the deaths of innocent thousands.*

The medley of these confessions arising from the ingenuity of the torturers and the not so subtle imaginations of the placard writers.

When Lieutenant O stuck his patrician face in the door to see if I required his services I noticed that the scar of his burn was healing nicely. I waved him away. 'Consider yourself off-duty, go play with the rest of the Chosen Ones.' He looked affronted, but that was his problem. 'Go!' I repeated. 'Shoo!' The last thing I needed or wanted was a personal guard, I'd had dogs on my trail for far too long. I had discovered that the twenty-six Chosen Ones had been given new identities by the General—each man had been named after a letter of the alphabet, from A to Z. I had been bequeathed O. 'How original,' I had said by way of congratulating the General on his cleverness.

The lieutenant saluted stiffly and withdrew. I didn't want to think about the puzzle of what to do with him. Since the night the General had handed him over to me he'd been hanging at my side like a shadow, deferential and expectant. What did he expect from me? Despite the General's avowal to the contrary, I was no leader, or otherwise, of armies. Lieutenant O wouldn't find any glory in mixing me a drink or ferrying me across puddles to the car or lugging my bags, which is basically what he'd done so far. I'd been holed up with him for close company for a week and my supply of patience, jokes, and inclination to play dominoes was well and truly at an end. The General had better things to do than watch the waters rise by my side. He'd installed me in the El Alamein and had promptly disappeared, telephoning me at irregular intervals with basically the same message: everything was under control.

The El Alamein Tower, for which we had abandoned the waterlogged Hotel Fantasia Delight, was a sturdy structure of some thirteen stories. The theory being that no-one, least of all the enemy, would imagine the General basing himself in a densely populated residential apartment block. The theory also went that since we were on a high piece of land with good run-off the water would not infiltrate us there. Soldiers joined the residents on every floor, watched the doors, looked out from the windows, and I was deposited at the very top like a Rapunzel—no penthouse suite, in fact a mouldy, moody little place, reminiscent of other dowdy places I'd had the opportunity to visit, its one decent feature being a good wide view of the streets curving down towards the municipal markets, a view for the most part somewhere on the other side of the curtain of rain.

I was not particularly superstitious but apartment 1400 (I was actually on the thirteenth floor, but it wasn't numbered as such) had a dark atmosphere, deeply inhospitable. I don't know why it bothered me, I'd lived in much worse decrepitude, but there seemed such an absence of light in spite of the view, such impossibility of warmth, that I had to stop myself from paying too much attention to the hideous brown stains so much like dried shit or blood that mottled the walls. I reminded myself of some of the horrible places I'd gone to meet Sol in, but still, that apartment gave me the shivers. In the time following my arrival the insomnia had been insurmountable and the claw which had slipped from my throat had returned nightly to caress me and my agitation that I might choke in my sleep was sharper and meaner than ever. I could not fathom why I was all of a sudden being pushed so close to panic. There was no evidence of horror in the apartment. Quite the opposite, it was a mere shell. Empty.

Yes, I decided that was the problem, its profound air of emptiness, despite the pieces of crappy furniture and the scattered baggage and Lieutenant O lurking in the corner. Emptiness. I took another long, healthy swallow of bourbon to relax the tension of my tiredness, to soothe my knotted-up throat and ease the vibration of my nerves. Evidence of life outside disappeared as the curtain came down, obscuring the antlike scavengers. Rain began falling again, steadily, in a soft but persistent rush, splattering the surface of the window with that ruddy pink, at times almost gelatinous, patina. Scientists had not been able to ascribe the colour, let alone the texture, of the rain to anything in particular. After no-one dropped dead or became ill from drinking it or being soaked in it the initial wariness wore off and the sludgy colour became more ordinary than remarkable. No cause for concern. There were readier distractions than a tint in the water supply.

More jets rammed a path through the sienna cloud. More fighters. It had become a frequent event, listening to the planes flying back and forth over the epicentre of the city. Tantrums, Tornadoes, Mirages, Hunters, Furies, Thunderbolts, and any number of others, busily advertising the war should the people forget.

Forget? How could we forget?

Even with the pox and the wet dead we would not forget. Just as we were always victorious, always on the offensive, always maintaining the advantage, always mopping up, we, with the smart weaponry, we, who had been impelled to take the forced measures, we of the just cause, the right cause, the only cause, we who'd had to perfect the art of killing in order to survive, we who were finally and once and for all closing the door on the debate, we, with our clear-cut objective, our durable claim, our understanding of necessity, our rendezvous with destiny, we the people, the heartbeat of the nation, would never, could never, forget that there was above all else a war going on.

They were on a small concrete square of landing between the angle of stairs. They were half-hidden in shadow, in a grimace of an embrace. Flapping about like suffocating fish. I heard them before I saw them, their bodies looking odd, disjointed in the bleating light. A grunting, double-backed beast. He was on top of her, thrusting, the mad urgent motion of rutting, the rumpy-pumpy, his pale moon arse savage, jerking without caution. He was locked into his lust in a place beyond me but her eyes weren't. They were rolling back away from him towards me, the dark irises rearing in their white orbs, whites gleaming shockingly in a patch of light. The way a slant of light had concentrated on that portion of her face was ghastly, ghoulishly theatrical. Her mouth was wide open beside the bobbing crown of his head but that cavern in her stretched face emitted no sound. I would have sworn she was screaming. The thought that she was mute did not then occur to me.

One of his hands was wrapped around her throat, the other had both her hands pinned to the floor above her head. Delicate hands, tiny wrists with long pianist's fingers. I don't know why I noticed this but it was as if I saw her only in details. Eyes. Mouth. Fingers. Arse pumping between her skinny thighs.

Wham bam whumpa whumpa wham bam whumpa whumpa.

I knew that rhythm. It was the I'm fucking you bitch rhythm, the I've paid for this rhythm, the who the fuck do you think you are rhythm, the you're nothing but a cunt-hole rhythm, the I'm taking what's mine rhythm, the I'll fuck you and you won't walk for a week rhythm, the I'll make you piss blood rhythm, the I'm going to slice you apart rhythm. Not the steady, regular rhythm of the metronome but there was something of that instrument's cadence, intransigence, monotony in those grossly rhythmic pelvic thrusts. And the smell—sulphuric, that raw smell of sex, the penis gone ahunting, the vagina opened, aweeping—I knew that smell. Shoving itself up one's nose, splashing over one's thighs, coating one's skin with layer upon layer of smell. I knew it. It was in my throat like the acid that presaged vomit. As always, it was the smell that alerted me. My nose had known it before I'd heard his noise or seen her eyes, my nostrils had discerned the distinct odour of rape.

It wasn't that I was inured to violence or impervious to the girl's suffering, but for some reason I was fixed to the stair that ushered me down to their writhing bodies, held immobile by the spectacle. Held in that curious space of suspension from one's self that sometimes accompanies particular, usually awful, moments. Despite her silence, I could clearly hear the girl's cries because her eyes were yelling at me, blasting my eardrums with their shrieking, but still I stayed on that step above the two of them. My fascination was not voyeuristic, no part of me was titillated, I was wondering in a kind of dull, stupefied way what I ought to do. I actually don't recall making a decision one way or the other—to turn on my heel and try to ignore it, or to immediately interrupt them and report the man to his superiors and hope something came of it—when I bent down and picked up a piece of debris littering the stairwell, a lump of concrete I think it was, and walked down the last couple of stairs and crushed the back of the man's head with it.

No, I don't recall deciding to do that. I simply did it.

Afterwards, Lieutenant O reminded me that rape was not considered a crime. Neither a civil crime nor a war crime, it was therefore not punishable. 'Unlike murder,' I replied.

'Self-defence,' he amended after the slightest pause. 'It's no crime to defend oneself against the possibility of assault.'

'Ah,' I said, 'then the expectation of assault changes everything?' I kept wiping my hands against my clothing as if something were stuck to them.

'It frames it in a more identifiable context,' he replied, prodding the man's body with the toe of his boot. 'Why is he naked?'

'The girl,' I said, peering up the stairwell as if she somehow might be there, 'she ran off with his clothes. Somewhere. Long gone.' The girl had lain prone under the body for several seconds and then she'd frantically begun scrabbling at the man, unable to get out from under him. I'd taken him by the shoulders and heaved him over so that he rolled off her. His eyes were closed, his mouth was open, smelling of garlic, even though he wasn't breathing. I could feel his body warmth through the khaki of his uniform. I noticed that his limp penis seemed to be dribbling. Had I struck him at his moment of orgasm? The little, the big, death.

The girl looked like a frightened rabbit but she did an unexpected thing: when she got to her feet she carefully wiped her mouth with her hand and adjusted her clothing with slow dignity, then she viciously kicked the man hard in the belly, one, two, three, four, five times, and then she knelt and began efficiently to strip him. She ripped off his shirt, belt, trousers, underpants, socks, shoes with the utmost efficiency. 'Are you all right?' I'd asked her. 'Are you all right?'

'Are you all right?' the lieutenant asked me.

She had completely ignored my question. After she had stripped the body she finally looked at me, a lancing stare of complicity, and then she'd picked up the lump of concrete and wrapped it inside the soldier's clothes.

'I'm fine,' I answered. 'Nothing to worry about.'

'Did you see her hit him?' he asked. I don't know how long

I'd been sitting with the corpse when he'd found me. A while, I can't recall. A part of me had been thinking that the longer I guarded him, the better were her chances of getting away. Another part of me had been fretting that I would miss my appointment with the hairdresser. I don't recall thinking about the fact that I had just killed a man.

'No,' I said. 'I didn't see that happen. No.' After secreting the slab of concrete in the dead man's clothing she turned and disappeared down the stairs. Not a sound. Not a word. Not a look. Just a plain, silent, skinny girl with a long unravelling plait of dirty blonde hair and a bundle in her arms, scratches on her legs, bruises on her body. Utterly ordinary. Totally unforgettable. I felt compelled to add, 'She didn't hit him.' I wiped my hands again.

'Ah,' he said, 'I see. It would be better if you carried a gun.'

'I thought you were my gun,' I retorted.

'As you wish, sir,' he said. And he flipped the body over and withdrew his Beretta and emptied the magazine into the back of the corpse's head. The sound echoed through the stairwell. I felt nauseous.

'Don't call me sir,' I said, tasting vomit again.

'No, sir,' he said. 'I mean, ma'am. How do you wish to be addressed?'

'Not sir.' I concentrated on suppressing the urge to vomit.

'Lady,' he said, pocketing his pistol. 'My Lady,' he said, expansively.

'No. Just lady,' I replied, making the effort to get to my feet to start the long walk back up those stairs. The scar on my hand was burning as if the wound were fresh. The lieutenant made a move to assist me, I pushed him away. 'No,' I repeated, 'lady, just lady.'

TWENTY-SEVEN

In my career I had done many things to many men but until that point I had not actually done one of them in. Not even a justifiable homicide, although I'd had plenty of aggravation and some opportunity in my time. I did not fool myself that death was a painless enterprise. Despite feeling the castrated corporal's blood on my hands I had not sought to be, nor in any literal way had been, the agent of his death. In that incident I was above all else guilty of an extreme thoughtlessness or a reckless naïvety, but I had been able to excuse myself with the reminder that I'd had the right to try to slip my chain, to regain my freedom.

For some time I had lived entirely in the company of professional killers. More than that, I was the mistress of a man who killed with passion and impunity. A man who had vented a blood-frenzy before me without any inhibition and, likewise, with enormous calculation and consideration, was the director of the fighting that had engulfed us in war. The arts and purposes of killing were nothing new to me but the experience of it was. What I observed in the soldiers I saw on parade, the men marching the path of the General, was that they were men either before or after their first kill. There was no pacific middle ground, they were men for whom killing was a reality, a promise, an inevitability. I saw, too, how some of them became addicts, and as with any true addict I saw how the hankering for killing could become a yearning, would be their transformation, could be, also, the death of them.

From the beginning I had seen how the men with whom the General surrounded himself were badly afflicted with this taste for killing. This had alarmed me in the early days, for whenever I had held their eyes or shaken their hands I had seen and felt their desire for death in a palpable, almost physical manner, there was such force behind it. A desire not so much for personal death—although there were those with the suicidal impulse—more an infatuation with death per se, the death of others, the death, of course, of the enemy. Death-speak permeated their conversation and even their polite chit-chat would be peppered with such phrases as 'search and destroy', 'the killing ground', 'terminating with prejudice', 'the blood tax', 'dramatically improved kill rates', 'after we cut it off we're going to kill it', and so on and so forth. People who had entirely lost the idea of what constituted customary social discourse.

'I have been informed that you require a gun,' the General said that night after we had finished dinner. Because he had been seldom at the El Alamein, dining together signalled a special occasion. And he had dressed for the occasion, a midnight blue A-line shantung silk dress with shoestring straps, one of his favourite outfits. Dozens of tiny rhinestones were embroidered on the straps and over the bodice and the way they refracted the light was beginning to give me a headache. I could hear the rasp of his stockinged legs crossing and uncrossing under the table, the sensation of nylon moving against nylon being one of his excitements. He picked up my plate and licked it clean, with long, sweeping strokes of the tongue. I'd had no appetite for the tripe and had pushed my dinner over to him and sat toying with the cutlery, pouring out dose upon dose of wine.

To no avail. The scar on my hand still throbbed. Had I hefted the piece of concrete with that hand? I couldn't remember. I soothed my palm against the crisp linen table-cloth—the General enjoyed the accoutrements of elegant eating, I suspected he also enjoyed the juxtaposition of a beau-tifully laid table with miserable surrounds. In these circum-stances his appetite was enormous and his humour invariably good. Tonight was such an occasion and he roguishly grinned at me and poured us another drink. I decided that Lieutenant O must have given the General a tactfully edited version of recent events, otherwise the General would no doubt have been demanding gory details and carrying on about my rap-port with death.

My rapport with death.

I dismissed that bleak thought.

'I don't know much about guns but I doubt that I need one,' I replied. I thought how easy it would be to use a gun, much easier than picking up a lump of rock like a cavewoman. Too easy. Instant and distant. Time to change the subject. 'How are your memoirs progressing? Your adjutant tells me you've been writing a lot.' Now, when the General wrote, I was not required to hover in a suspended fuck-state, one positive out-come of living together.

'My memoirs are progressing brilliantly and your doubts are immaterial,' he smiled, all charm and courteous pouring of wine. 'It's been remiss of me, not equipping you properly. It's necessary that you know how to handle a weapon.'

I picked up a knife and twirled it in my fingers. 'Why do you assume that I don't know how to handle a weapon?'

He chortled and leaned over and ran his index finger along the blunt blade of the knife. I recoiled when I smelt his breath of garlic. For the first time I noticed what was engraved on the knife, the M was almost indecipherable amongst the curlicues and swirls. 'Then the more weapons you can master, the better, no?'

'No,' I said, dropping the knife.

'Take this,' he said, lifting his Luger from his shoulder holster, strapped, as always, to his body no matter what the outfit. He laid the gun on the tablecloth between us. 'One of the most ergonomic pistols ever designed, the standard German officer's pistol in both World War One and World War Two. A collector's piece. But it shoots very well.' The gun looked solid, efficient, substantial. It gleamed blue-black. 'Feel it, own it, use it however you want. I insist.'

'It's your gun,' I stalled, 'I can't.'

He pulled out another Luger, this time from an attaché case, and laid it down beside the first Luger, twins nestling together. 'You can,' he breathed. 'If it's not one gun, then it's another. There are so many of them; after all, there's a war going on.' How droll. He continued, 'I simply like to know that you have the option if anything happens.'

'What's going to happen?' I asked.

He shrugged, eloquently, elegantly. 'Who can tell? Uncertainties abound in war, that's the nature of it; despite everything, there's always something that can never be taken into account. Sheer whimsy can define the course of a battle.

Naturally, the science of mathematics, especially logistics, plays its part but ...' he shrugged and smiled at me disarmingly, '... *c'est la guerre.*' The General pushed both pistols towards me with the tips of his fingers, perfectly lacquered with Battle Blaze. He was fussy about his nailpolish. 'Choose.' I extended my hand and lightly touched the walnut handle of the second Luger he had laid out. He flicked it across the table to me and it spun into the net of my hand. 'An excellent choice, an excellent gun, it's been my faithful companion, it has never let me down.'

'But this isn't your gun!'

He picked up the remaining Luger. 'I never saw this gun before today. But from now on it is mine. And mine is yours.'

I didn't want it but still, my fingers were curling around the stock of the gun. There was a clatter as the General threw a magazine upon the table. 'And this,' he said. 'You'll need to feed it, for you'll find it's a hungry little thing.' A candle guttered and the blotches on the wall collapsed into a dark pattern. I gripped the gun and felt a sensation jolt the palm of my hand like a small electrical shock. I quickly put the gun down on my lap. It was quite heavy but it nestled there easily.

'I don't like this place,' I said, 'I want to go somewhere else.'

'Why? Do you believe in ghosts?'

His question startled me. 'Ghosts? Why ghosts?'

I saw he was watching me closely. 'Some believe that the dead sometimes haunt the living,' he offered.

'No, no ghosts.' I gave a little laugh to demonstrate my grasp on our here-and-now. 'What about you? Have you seen ghosts?' I felt nervous about this line of enquiry. Would there forever be a ghost for me in that stairwell? I had no wish to find out.

'Frequently,' he replied steadily. 'Nothing breeds them like war.'

'What do they look like?'

'Oh, like you or me, like anybody, anybody at all. It can actually be difficult to distinguish at times.' I was sure he was pulling my leg, drawing me away from my original comment.

'There's no ghost here,' I said with the assurance of the eighth or tenth or thirteenth drink. 'It's the walls, I think they're bleeding.' When I said that I realised that I was drunk.

'How poetic,' he murmured, picking up my scarred hand, 'how exquisitely perverse. Now you've given me a hard-on.' He pushed my hand down to the smooth bulge of his penis. 'Feel it?' I nodded. As the General pulled me towards him his gift jabbed into my belly. His gun. My gun. Our gun. The remaining Luger on the table had somehow multiplied. Now there were two of them. Perhaps I was seeing double. He took up a gun in each hand. Yes, my Luger was definitely in my lap. He then picked up a knife. How many hands? Four. Two hands holding two guns, two hands waving two of those initialled knives. That explained it. I was definitely seeing double.

The stink of drying was immense. It wafted all the way up to the top floor and came in through the windows. When I'd smelt the change during the night I got out of bed and locked every window in the apartment, to no avail. In the morning sky, not a single cloud—just the unremitting glare of rouge, that crazy colour which was normal for us now.

Normal?

Should that be a word used anymore? I supposed the war

had adjusted the meaning of words and things, so whatever had once been abnormal was now normal.

And vice versa? Very possibly.

The very notion of a new normalcy was disturbing; it meant that we were not merely living in straitened or heightened times, we were living life with new standards, new conditions, and with absolutely no guarantees that our lives would revert to those ways which had existed before the war. In fact, it was becoming more and more difficult to recall the ways we had once followed. Present circumstances dimmed them, if not cancelling them out altogether. Too much had come to pass, too much had been lost or irrevocably changed. It was here and now, or nothing. There was no in-between and it could be dangerous to believe there was. It was either survival or death.

After I killed the rapist I became hyper-aware of death. My own death, no-one else's. In the past my nervousness had exploded in fear for Sol but now I was calm about him. My nightmares continued much the same as usual, they were a reliable guide to the fear that could surface in me, but I could forget them upon waking even if they did promote a fear of sleeping, although there were ways to lull this fear. The best being the beautiful blur of alcohol. Drink provided a type of easy forgetfulness when such forgetfulness was required. Drink allowed me to relax, to enjoy what was there to enjoy. Sometimes, to sleep.

Sleep.

Even now the word is like an elixir to me. To sleep and not to dream, to simply sleep unencumbered by dreamscape or unconscious eruptions. How luxurious. Perhaps that is the true victory, the surrender of one part of the self to another, cosily and happily. No ghosts, no outrage. No claustrophobia.

No claw. No vivid imaginings. No remembrance of what was once normal. Or abnormal. All wafted away on the river of sleep streaming over you and floating you off to a friendly shore. My idea of sleep as a means of knowing peace came out of those sleepless days in the El Alamein Tower, drinking away my descent of that stairwell, futilely scrubbing the stains on walls with an aggrieved Lieutenant O, haranguing the recalcitrant General to move us to another safe house, making useless unanswered enquiries about the girl I had aided, watching as the water disappeared once and for all, feeling afraid of the death I sensed all around me, hanging over me, a veil I couldn't rip off.

'*Salut*,' I toasted. '*Salut*.' But still that damned veil choked me when I lay down to sleep at night.

TWENTY-EIGHT

I was doing my face when I noticed a tiny sore on my bottom lip. I examined it carefully, it looked like a small blood blister, perhaps a cold sore, not a pustule. I convinced myself that it was not the pox. The General had probably bitten my lip. I applied another layer of Sunny Squadron lipstick and blotted and it disappeared. The official line was that the pox had been contained thanks to the plague stations. Citizens were urged to continue being careful but the spectre of a rampaging plague had diminished. It had been replaced by a different sort of horror: Infectives were suiciding at an incredible rate. It was as if they could not wait for whatever else might take them. The official line was that suicide was not a symptom of the disease, merely an outcome of frayed nerves and the burden of illness. Since these suicides comprised the only wholesale deaths due to the pox (bar the public barbecues), it was loudly and repeatedly claimed that the danger had passed.

Sol's belief that the pox was one of the General's tactics nagged at me. I knew the General did not hesitate in using the appropriate means to achieve the appropriate ends—the shelling of the refugees in the Southern Sector being such an instance—to intensify public frenzy against the enemy. But pox had not been blamed on the enemy and a tight hold was now being kept on pox hysteria. Death by suicide was useful in this regard, all blame apportioned to the suicide.

I re-examined my face in the mirror: there were hollows and the beginnings of lines but when I smiled I still looked young. Young enough to take my body and its pliability for granted. I scrutinised my makeup and was satisfied. I was young. I lifted the bourbon and drank. I was young. The spirit burned my throat, felt like hot soup, like something nutritious on a bad night. Despite this feeling of warmth, I stopped feeling young. I felt old. I etched in my eyes a little more, some kohl on the inner lower lids. I looked like a mummy. Not young.

Rapport with death.

No.

My Luger.

No. It was in the closet next to my domino set. I concentrated on my makeup. I had forgotten what an art it could be, to look beautiful. Did war make the art of beauty obscene, did war diminish beauty? In general, yes. In specific, no. I carefully dabbed at my colourful mouth.

The General was at the head of a many times decorated table. An impressive table full of unimpressive men. I sneezed and moved the dusty plastic models of fighter planes and tanks aside and did my duty as hostess to lead the brass in a toast. I raised my glass, then my eyes, and then I smiled at my General. 'To our war lord.' My voice as thick as the glorious orange-pink glow of Sunny Squadron. The champagne bubbles got up my nose and for a second I thought I was going to have a sneezing attack, but I recovered with finesse and was given the job of taking the minutes. Quite an honour.

I was fiddling with my bra strap and entertaining the wandering eyes of a lieutenant general when the General spoke. 'We need to take care of the Insurrectionists,' he said, pulling out his Luger and leisurely loading it. That made everyone attentive.

'What Insurrectionists?' I asked, forgetting my role.

'Those who like to call themselves the voice of the people. They must be infiltrated.'

'They are all bluff and blunder,' interrupted an incautious colonel.

There was a silence as the General inclined his head and sniffed at the interjector. Nothing more, but the man was marked. The General then elaborately checked his gun. 'They must be vanquished. Are we not servants of the greater cause of glory?'

The reply was a ridiculous and rousing chorus: 'We are the servants of glory!' I dropped my hanky and scooped to retrieve it in order to hide my amusement.

The General noticed my ruse. 'I have received confirmation that these Insurrectionists are responsible for endangering public health. The pox is their doing, an attempt to destabilise the city and destroy its government, thereby delivering us into the hands of the enemy. They have no aim but the aim of internal agitation and hateful division. It is they who are responsible for the deaths of our unborn children, the slaughter of the animals and the unleashing of a contagion.' He dramatically paused before thundering, 'These terrorists seek to poison our city, to bring it crying to its knees, to break it.

They would mortally wound it in their attempt to take control of our war!' There was a loud explosion of babble from the brass which I did not attempt to note. I was busy digesting the information myself. A group of terrorists?

The General held up his hand and the noise slid away. 'We must penetrate this inner enemy,' he announced, 'and I cannot think of anyone less innocuous, more reliable.' Everyone followed the General's gaze and turned to look at me. The General started clapping. For several fateful seconds he clapped alone, then I heard the table's startled, uneasy burst of applause. Like a round of rapid fire. 'A woman can use not only natural but unnatural weapons,' he said. The men were so astounded, or so scornful, they tittered. I stared at him. 'Consider yourself anointed,' he smiled.

'You're talking espionage, infiltration, spying. The very idea is ludicrous. I'm not a secret agent, I've got absolutely no training, I don't even know how to shoot properly! I know nothing about these Insurrectionists. Besides, I've been seen with you on television, remember?' I slammed down the bottle. That damned TV footage still haunted me. I'd been so careful to steer clear of cameras, all I could hope was that Sol hadn't seen it. The General shrugged, a little act of violence. 'But why?' I repeated. 'Why?' I'd been asking why for the past hour and getting no useful response. Exactly the same response as all that heavy brass had made before they'd eagerly thundered out the door, leaving me well and truly anointed by washing their hands of me. Zero sum game. Their General's gratification would be gained at my expense and I was easily expended.

'You belong in this war,' he said. 'Until you fully enter the battle you will remain incomplete.'

'I don't want to enter any battle.'

'You have no choice,' he replied. 'You have no need to be afraid,' he added.

'Why not?'

'To be at war is to be at peace.'

'How delightfully cryptic,' I spat. The General laughed. I was furious because I was afraid and my fear was so easy for him to read. I knew, also, that he would not change his mind. Stalemate. Thankfully, Lieutenant O interrupted to say that I had a telephone call. So, the phones were working again. He handed me the phone. It was Juanita.

'I have one minute to speak,' she said. 'You've got to come and get me. I'm at Plague Station Number Three.'

'What're you doing there?' I exclaimed.

'Shut up and listen,' she said urgently. 'I don't have the pox but I've been rounded up and put in quarantine. It's a set-up. Someone with a grudge against me. For god's sake, use your influence and get me out of here.'

'But—' I began.

'Or you'll never see your precious boyfriend again.' She hung up. I clicked the receiver. Nothing. Not even a dial tone. The line was dead. I thrust the phone back at the lieutenant.

'Who was that?' asked the General.

'It was Juanita,' I said, telling him the truth, 'she wants to see me.'

'Juanita? Oh yes, your friend. Your fuck. Your folly,' he drawled. 'By all means you must see her. How good of her to stay in touch. Take the car. The lieutenant will accompany you.' I stared at him. Was he drunk? 'It's been a while since she entertained us and I do remember her as being most entertaining.' Did he want another piece of theatre with me and her? He looked at his watch, it seemed a false, exaggerated gesture. 'I really must be somewhere else. We'll talk more about this later.' He wheeled around and left the room. I threw the glass of scotch against the wall. It bounced but did not break. Lieutenant O placed the phone on the table as if it were something fragile and cleared his throat. 'The car is ready when you are, Lady.'

On the drive I tried to push aside the problem of the General's fantasy about me as a Mata Hari and concentrate on something simple, like looking out the car window. There had been changes to the city. Because streets had been eroded or washed away we had to take a tortuously slow, circuitous route to Plague Station Number Three. It had been set up in an abandoned shopping complex in the Yom Kippur District, formerly a high-density shopping suburb. Many businesses had collapsed, but still, here and there, shops did a trade, mainly in the most essential commodities, although one or two offered a bizarre mix of tourist goods such as postcards, tea-towels, snow-domes, letter openers, drink coasters and souvenir maps of the city with the places of import and interest neatly marked. The maps were possibly the most frivolous things to buy, for the city was in a state of gross change, what with the constant fraying of its perimeters due to the bombardments, the ruptures and relocations resulting from the earthquake, the inrush of Dislocatees, and the wholesale disappearing of places that came with the rains. Even I, who had known parts of it like the back of my own hand, was no longer confident as to where streets now led.

*

The light was so harsh as to be interrogatory. When I put on my sunglasses the relief was immediate. The administrator frowned at me from behind his surgically clean desk but the frown disappeared when Lieutenant O protectively moved forward a step, becoming not so much imperious as imperiously threatening. I, on the other hand, slumped back in my uncomfortable chair. I approved of the lieutenant's demeanour and understood that it had been wise to bring him along. It was a definite point in my favour that the administrator could be made nervous, and he kept darting fascinated glances at Lieutenant O's forehead. I had to admit that the lividity of the scar was arresting, as was the resplendent uniform with the brilliant red M embroidered on the black armband, and the intense gaze that could very effectively communicate contempt. I mentally gave Lieutenant O full points for his performance, especially since he'd not been briefed.

Still the administrator tried to bully me. 'This is a quarantine station, not a hostel. If this woman is here, as you claim she is, then she is here for a very good reason.' He pursed his lips primly after his delivery. I was fast recognising this as a habit of his but I'd had a long acquaintanceship with just this sort of trenchant righteousness.

I casually crossed my legs to underline the fact that I was perfectly at ease with this specimen of bureaucratic obstinateness and said, 'I'm afraid that it doesn't matter if she has the pox or not.' The administrator flinched, possibly at my loose use of language. 'I know and you know that this is a holding station, nothing more. I grant that it's an efficient way of keeping people off the streets and out of the hands of the more immediate danger of maniacs and mobs, but can you honestly tell me that this is a contagious infection? Nothing I've heard so far suggests that it is.'

'The method of transmission has yet to be determined, but that is no cause for cavalier behaviour. I would be derelict in my duty if I were to release a possible Infective back into the population. Besides, this is the best place for proper treatment.'

'What exactly is the treatment, given there is as yet no diagnosis and no cure?'

'Isolation, monitoring, nursing if required.'

'Do many internees require nursing?'

He bristled at the word internee. 'Sufficient to regard this contagion as potentially fatal.'

'Apart from the suicides, I thought no-one had died of it,' I persisted.

He resisted answering for a long moment. 'The weak and the elderly.'

'Of the pox? Or of natural causes or other illnesses?'

'Of complications,' he said triumphantly, 'which have yet to be determined as not being directly related to the epidemic.'

I sighed. 'I am not here to investigate whether you deserve to have the job of running a plague station, or even whether there is indeed a plague or not. I am here to rescue one poor unfortunate from this marvellous never-never land of yours.' How I enjoyed being insolent. As if seeking to enlist male support he turned to the magnificently impassive, wholly attentive Lieutenant O, but his eyes swivelled back to me when I added, 'A very important unfortunate.' I paused for theatrical effect. 'An intimate of the General's.' I leaned forward and tapped his desk with a stern finger. 'It's very delicate, this business of the General's intimates.'

'But she's a whore!' he blurted.

I shook my head and tut-tutted, resisting the very strong impulse to slap the expression of distaste off his face. 'No, no,' I crooned, 'she's his paramour.'

'His paramour!' The word literally exploded out of his mouth. 'Impossible!'

'He doesn't believe me,' I said to the lieutenant. 'He doesn't believe the General is capable of such discrimination. How will I persuade him?'

Lieutenant O withdrew his pistol. 'Am I to be your gun …' He paused, very nicely, very naturally, 'again?'

'I doubt that it's necessary.' I smiled at the administrator. 'I'm sure it's not necessary, even for a whore.' I was enjoying myself, watching the man's face turn quite pale and his lips disappear inside his mouth with the effort of holding them still. It was a trite but irresistible revenge on all the officious men I'd dealt with. I did not feel ashamed of that little exercise until a long time afterwards, when for some reason the memory of the man's frightened, bitten, turned-in lips returned to me.

'The fate of this woman is on your head,' he said stiffly.

I smiled again. 'The administrator is only too happy to oblige the General and consign the whore to my care.'

Was that the first time I invoked my own purpose as that of the General's? I do not recall either promoting myself as an envoy of the General or in being in such accord with Lieutenant O before my visit to that petty bureaucrat. At the time, I excused myself with the justification that Juanita was depending on me. But what I now remember most clearly is how much I enjoyed flapping the mantle of power in that man's face. Yes, it was a new and heady pleasure, to assume the power of the General for my own purposes.

TWENTY-NINE

'What a dump,' Juanita complained. She couldn't sit still and kept moving restlessly around the room, an awkward scarecrow reaching out to touch things then withdrawing her hands at the last moment. There were bracelets of tiny burns adorning her wrists. When she saw me looking at them she shoved her hands in her pockets. I'd seen too much ornamentation of that kind on Juanita before now for it to be a novelty. 'Men have all sorts of tastes,' she offered, adding a little barb, 'as you well know.'

'I understand,' I comforted.

'I'm not really interested in whether you understand or not,' she snapped, instantly furious. I held my silence. 'Sorry,' she said, 'I'm taking it out on you. Sorry.' She withdrew a hand and ran it over her badly shaved head and grimaced, 'I'm a mess, aren't I?'

'Yes,' I replied. She stared at me and burst into laughter, which she quickly bit off, throwing herself in a tattered chair. She sprawled there unmoving, then said in a low, depleted voice, 'Could you believe that place, that prison?'

Two grim floors of cages as in an antique zoo, furnished with cots, buckets for waste, and not much else in the way of comfort as a preventative against suicide for those fulfilling the essential criteria of an Infective—pustules, along with various secondary symptoms: coughing, diarrhoea, fever, nausea, lack of appetite and listlessness. Similarly appointed observation enclosures constructed mainly of barbed wire for the suspected Infectives on a third floor—which is where Juanita had been housed—for those evincing at least three of the symptoms bar the pustules. These inmates were released after a lengthy period of quarantine if the pustules did not appear. And finally, for the seriously ill, the opportunity of dying of other complaints in slightly more congenial surrounds than the primitive cells—quiet, windowless, padlocked rooms with better pallets and frustrated care from overworked female attendants (a new form of State employment for women). In addition to these I saw makeshift laboratories for the doctors; examining rooms for the nurses; offices for the officials; soldiers patrolling with machine guns glinting in an ugly yellow light that cast a glow the colour of urine; and the dizzying, astringent smell of disinfectant assaulting all surfaces and lifting in waves above the crackling speakers loudly issuing instructions on mealtimes, sleeping times, self-cleanliness times, or loudly playing patriotic music or dispensing those endless, regurgitated loops of news from the front.

All the inmates were women, children and elderly men.

Where were the infected soldiers?

The administrator had flared his nostrils as if I had asked an impertinent question but he was careful to answer me civilly. He did not know if soldiers had presented with symptoms, but in any case the armed forces took care of their own. 'How very appropriate,' I replied. The administrator affected not to have heard me. 'Do you know anything about this?' I turned to Lieutenant O.

'No,' he'd said.

'No,' I said, 'it was as real a prison as any I've seen. How on earth did you get to use a telephone?' Once inside, all outside contact was forbidden.

Juanita hesitated. 'Bribery,' she breathed. In the receiving depot all new arrivals were stripped, their clothing burnt, their heads shaved, and they were showered en masse, fumigated, then medically examined in the most obtrusive manner before being released, wearing the equivalent of sackcloth, into the cells. Had Juanita secreted money or something of value in one of her body cavities? That suggested she had been prepared for the emergency, not an unwise precaution, considering the temper of the times. Or had she bartered with something else? Probably her body, I decided.

'Why would someone want to set you up?' I asked.

'I don't know! Nothing is out of the question, is it? You can't trust anybody now. All it takes is someone with a grudge, or someone who wants your apartment or your belongings or anything you have that they don't have. The people are turning against each other. When that happens ...' She stopped talking.

'Go on,' I said softly.

Silence.

That was the quality of Plague Station Number Three that struck me the most. I expected a place of such contained illness, misery, anger, distress and trepidation would surely be rife with the calls and curses of its inmates. But the place was inhabited by a peculiar silence. There was the omnipresent noise of the loud-speaker, the moaning and groaning of the fevered, the squalling of some children, but there was no evidence of unrest or rebellion. A dull, chronically debilitating acceptance distinguished the horrible place. Sullen as well as sunken sad looks followed me in my medical guise of surgical coat and mask as I was escorted through the building, at my insistence. The administrator had been all for bundling me back into the car and delivering Juanita to me under an armed guard, but I forbore with him and got my way. I even breached the suicide room, the place bodies were delivered to prior to burning after a successful attempt. Even with the tight security, Infectives were managing to kill themselves. Getting my own way, though, was a victory that disturbed me more than I cared to admit. At the end of my tour I could not wait to get out of the place. The pox was a nebulous, if worrisome, thing, but a concentration camp under the guise of a plague station was a stark, frightening thing.

I crossed the tiny room that was now Juanita's home and took her hand. Her eyes filled with tears but she would not let them flow. 'It's the malice that makes me feel weak,' she said. 'I tell myself they're only being human but that's not much comfort, is it?' Returning to her apartment upon leaving the plague station, we had found her place gutted, every stick of furniture gone, the place emptied of her presence. Nothing remained. It was as if she had died.

I brought Juanita back to the El Alamein and Lieutenant O unearthed a minuscule bedsit on the eighth floor, miraculously empty. The place had been recently abandoned and I thought of that girl in the stairwell, for a woman had lived here, leaving behind tell-tale traces of her presence. I shivered at the thought of ghosts. Juanita shivered also. 'I feel like shit but I don't have the pox,' she said, 'in case you're worried. I've felt off-colour for ages, probably the swill that passes for food nowadays. If it was the pox I'd have the sores by now, wouldn't I?' The initial stroppiness of her tone sliding into entreaty.

I nodded and stroked the goose bumps on her arm and said, 'I'll get a razor and shave your head properly so it will grow back the same length.' Tufts of hair sprouted from her scalp like strange growths, accentuating her wild, sick look.

Her scalp was fleshy under my wet soapy fingers. The razor-blade sensuously slid over the bones of her head, rasping a little here and there. Small dark hairs floated like scum, curling on the surface of the bowl where I rinsed the razor. 'Do you wonder how you would look bald?' she said at one point, gripping my head between her hands. 'I would like to see you this naked.' Her baldness did not make Juanita beautiful, but she was, as always, no matter how degraded, a striking woman. The push of skull bones perfectly pronounced, weirdly accentuating the jut of her mouth, now a curve of bitterness, as if she had sucked on sour fruit. Afterwards, she refused a mirror and lay down without speaking on the camp bed. I was in the act of leaving when her voice arrested me. 'Have you ever wondered whether you're being used?'

'Used by whom?' I asked.

'By the man you reveal yourself to.'

'You think Sol is using me,' I accused.

'Would it bother you if Sol used you?' Her voice was scratchy, like a dry leaf being crushed.

'I know that he uses me, as you call it, to survive. And no, it doesn't bother me.'

'And what about your General, the way he uses you?'

'I use him too,' was my reply. 'How else could I have rescued you?'

'Don't ever think it's equitable,' she said. 'Don't ever make that mistake.'

The siren sounded, right on time. Curfew. We'd been living under a curfew for a long time and curfew-breakers were an unacceptable security risk. The corresponding punishment was death if the soldier's aim was true, or imprisonment and god knows what else if it was not. I thought I heard the sound of running in the streets below. And yelling. And screaming. Straining my ears, I killed the lights and twitched back the curtains and pushed open the window. The wind entered at once, and although I thought I'd passed too much time in the activity of watching the night to be made easily afraid, the gulping lunar wind chilled me inside and out. The moon was in the sky, sick-looking as usual, but huge, which did not seem usual. Ordinarily the moon, the night, did their poor best to mitigate the bloody hue of day, but tonight it seemed as if the rock had fully absorbed the day's colour. Close by its side a red light pulsed, brightly, like a beacon.

The red planet. Mars.

Mars, the god of war, why was he burning tonight? I flexed my scarred palm in the bitter breeze. Something rode in with the wind. Was that a homage, a signal, to flash his stamp on my hand? It was a long time since I had smelled something so cloying, so sweet. I remembered the smell of roses and my nostrils were soothed and my fright somersaulted, became a loose, low nervousness, and I raised my drink, as if in a toast. I quickly drank to dismiss the thought of toasting a god I did not want to know, the heat of the liquor pearling in my gut creating enough warmth to combat the squeal of the wind. There was no need to salute a deity of war. But Mars was more than a figure of war. Mars was inanimate, the fourth major planet from the sun. It was half the size of earth, it had a surface temperature of minus 23 degrees Centigrade. Not burning at all. I shivered and drank anew. I recalled the General's lecture to me about this red god, this planet; he had slipped his fingers between my thighs, along my cleft, inside of me, and his hand had emerged painted with my menstrual blood. '*Mars vigila,*' he had smiled at me, striping his face with my blood, two streams flaring from the bridge of his thick nose out along his blunt cheeks. 'Mars wake up.'

I roused myself and folded back the memory. Thirteen stories below, the streets were silent and empty, no curfew-breakers, no illusive Insurrectionists—about whom no-one had been able to tell me anything—no sniping soldiers. I had mistaken the sound of human screaming for the wailing of the wind but it had not been the first time. I was freezing myself in useless reverie. I slammed home the window and rested my forehead against the icy pane of glass. I wanted to be connected to something out there larger than anxiety, something benevolent, beyond the war. And as I recall that night—me pinned to the cold glass like a stopped moth; the will of the General encircling me like a scavenger seeking purchase; Juanita twisting in her claustrophobic closet; and Sol, as always, as from the very beginning, tauntingly out of reach—I should have seen that shutting that window was a useless preventative against events.

*

Smart bombs are meant to find their way through the dark.
It's supposed to be high-tech accuracy, the way a smart bomb
fixes on the target using computers, laser, infrared equipment.
It's supposed to be so clever, a bomb that will follow the laser
beam down from the aircraft. This laser beam that is so accu-
rate, theoretically taking the smart bomb within thirty centimetres of the target, say, theoretically giving the pilot an
amazing hit with, for instance, a GBU-27 1000kg penetrating
bomb. This bomb will pierce several metres of concrete, say,
to get that much closer to the actual target before detonating.
These bombs are supposed to enter buildings through door-
ways and windows, are supposed to hurtle down furnace
flues and elevator shafts, are supposed to strike so deep that
the damage is not simply superficial or merely structural. A
strike to the very heart of the target, to its nerve centre, so that
the greatest damage is inflicted upon places of greatest critical
and strategic concern. The beauty of it being that hardly
anyone is meant to be killed. Anyone, that is, who is in that
place at that time for anything other than military purposes.
That useful phrase, minimal collateral damage, had been
popularised with the help of the smart bomb during the Gulf
War.

'Did you know that?' asked the General.

'No,' I answered. 'No, I did not know that.'

He sighed and clucked like a mother hen. 'I educate you so
you will know these things.'

'Would you like me to help you remove your uniform?' I
asked, hoping that he would untie me. It was very, very late,
the brittle hour before dawn, and I was tired and my muscles
ached. He looked down at his uniform and plucked at the
ruined fabric. There were dark splodges on it in many places

and the material was torn a little, and powdered with greyish-white dust or ash.

'No,' he smiled, 'I am quite comfortable as I am.' He took a piece of stained cloth between his thumb and forefinger and caressed it. 'The bomb was wildly off target, nowhere near me, but there was a lot of collateral damage.'

'It wasn't a smart bomb?' I asked, watching him lick his forefinger and rub it against a stain.

'Oh yes,' he replied, 'but the smart bomb is far less successful than is widely believed. It's junk technology, very hit and miss.'

'More hit than miss in this case.' The General laughed at my little joke. Despite being at the forefront of a bombing he was in very good humour. He sucked his forefinger clean then applied it to another stain on his jacket. My eyes fixed on the jerking motion of his wet finger against the fabric.

'Is that blood on you?' I asked.

'Yes. Do you want a taste?' he replied.

'No, thank you. I've already eaten.'

The General chuckled again. 'You always go for the jugular,' he said in that growling type of voice which signalled sexual excitement. 'You like those places where the blood jumps.' I wanted to contest that point but the General was sinking down upon his haunches, his knees taking purchase in the curve of my hip, and somehow in the course of this manoeuvre a knife had appeared in his hand. I decided it might be prudent to keep my mouth shut. Squinting into the semi-dark, the flame of candles throwing guttering shadows, I discerned that it was the boning knife Juanita had brought up from the belly of the anonymous corpse in that street a lifetime ago. The General had not played with this toy in quite some time.

'My little pet likes the same places you like,' he said in a susurrant, amorous voice, weaving the knife in a curious, elaborate way above my body. 'It, too, likes the bite that precedes release. It, too, likes the lure of the flesh, the beautiful dark drink, the point at which there is never hesitation, only return.' As the General babbled on, I was fascinated anew by the intricate movement of his hands dancing the knife around me. He was master of his movements, some type of elite commando knife training I supposed. He had entertained me in this way before and I had sensed from the first such time that it was more a private ritual than a threat and I had little fear of being sliced by either accident or design. His version of sweet talk kept flowing on, rumbling over me. 'Arrow of Kali, cock of Kali, cry of Kali, her pet feeds so she might smile—'

'Kali?' I interrupted.

'Oh, queen and consort,' he crooned. 'Oh, crown and cunt.' And the knife whistled past my nose. A whistling like incoming, although the speed would have been impossible, and there was no incoming ripping up the new dawn of another red day. My eyes must have flicked to the window when it happened, I must have been looking away, because I don't remember seeing the cutting. When the drops spattered me I first thought they were large warm dollops of sweat. It had been terribly cold but that's what I thought: sweat. My eyes left the empty pink light and returned to the General. They saw the hail of colour as he cried, 'Rubies for my Lady!' and flung his hot bright gems all over me. I moaned, I think, and averted my head from his offering—the skin of his wrist split laterally by his knife. 'I am your happy servant,' he gasped as he thrust his opened-up wrist into my mouth. 'Eat me, Lady, eat me.'

THIRTY

When he enters his dreaming he is alone on a vast plain. A burial ground. The midnight light is dark, sticky, viscous and sweet-smelling. Sickly. Over his shoulder the moon drops its red load into a cloud. He hears a roaring in his ears he knows is the low-flying formation of fighter planes, but in the sky, nothing.

Emptiness.

Then he sees the cloud mushrooming on the horizon just like the hot bomb but this shape is so much more beautiful, growing impossibly fast, forming the shape of a giant flower.

He knows this shape, this lotus.

Barbs of light spring from the cloud and stab his eyes, wringing tears from them. He weeps without feeling his weeping.

He, too, is a flower. He is beginning to blossom, his feet planted in blood and bone, his new shape pushing out into the heart of Kali's darkness. He, the flower, peeling away from his outer skin, a uniform of some kind stiff with braid and medals weighing an impossible weight.

He, the bud, unfurling, the bandage fluttering from his wrist like a trail of fireflies, like the white flag of surrender smeared with the stain of his toil. His crimson petal calls her to him but he knows only complete obedience will bring her. He sinks down and caresses the dirt of the plain in the basest manner and the excruciation of it is a relief. In the distance a series of bomb blasts occurs, the hollow booming sounds of her laughter.

When his Lady finally stands before him the earth clinging to her feet tastes like something rotting, like nectar. He wants to roll over and offer his belly so she will have somewhere to place her restless feet. Under him in unmarked graves bones begin talking, begin pressing against him, wriggling and popping out of the soft furrowed ground, skulls waggling, jaws shouting out her name. They yell so loudly his ears hear the word like a terrible head-splitting explosion.

Kali! Kali!

One explosion after another.

Her name detonating, the word jumping around him, her word a mine bursting into shrill shrieking shrapnel, screaming and bursting out of the ground, the bits of body pieces flying up into his mouth, filling his mouth, the warm wine and the hot meat, the fragrant cry of her name. For he who knows her name answers her call and he opens his mouth wide in gladness. She smiles and bends to him and rolls him over and over so that her feet have somewhere to dance and the incandescent worm slithers from the skull grinning so happily in her extended hand and greedily it enters his mouth, roiling with his tongue.

Oh! She kisses. She kisses him!

He cries out in his happiness, the warmth of his tongue coating his lips with her colour.

THIRTY-ONE

The taste was in my throat when I awoke. It was a dream of banging shutters that took me from the dream that I was choking on my own hand, and the banging woke me. I awoke spitting and when I saw the russet stains on the pillow I thought that I had bitten my mouth in my sleep, but then I remembered the General's performance and knew it to be his blood. The taste was brassy. The noise continued. Not shutters. Insistent knocking. My bedroom door. Outside, coarse yellowy windborne grit was being flung against the windows with great force. It reminded me of chicken feed. I lay in bed watching the grit appear and disappear, thinking of the possibility of solitary farms in wild desolate places being ripped apart not by war but by wind, until the knocking stopped and whoever it was went away. It hadn't been the General, he never knocked, and on more than one occasion when he had faced obstruction to his purpose he had simply shot the bolt on my door and walked in.

After a while I began wondering about windage. Were missiles being blown off course? Where were the bombs landing?

The General's late-night chat about silly smart bombs had given me the notion that the city might actually face true ruin. Despite his easy countenance and scornful talk it seemed to me that the night's pour of bombs had made happy marks. The Office of Defence, the Office of Telephones, the Office of Applied Military Research and the Office of Infant Registration, which is where, in fact, the General had been, conducting some extraordinary executive strategy meeting, had all been hit with varying degrees of success. Targeting the Office of Infant Registration—and it had been exactly that, nothing more than the Office of Infant Registration—had either been the brilliant luck of the hardware's outright waywardness, a clairvoyant inspiration, or insider knowledge on the part of the enemy.

The enemy.

I remembered all too clearly Sol telling me that there was no real enemy, and anxiety began tingling through my nerve endings. Unlike him I could not honestly believe that the war was nothing more than an elaborate show put on by the General for his own purposes or amusement, and the thought that I had started siding with the General against Sol alarmed me. Yes, the enemy existed, but as far as Sol was concerned the enemy had been redefined. That had been the change in him; Sol had gone from not wanting to know the enemy to knowing it, and once he had a clear, identifiable target, he'd fixed on someone closer to hand, not something fleeing across a television screen, not something in the abstract. I could not stop thinking of the Insurrectionists and how Sol's rhetoric might belong to them.

It seemed, too, that the General had begun extending his notion of the enemy, if his palaver about the Insurrectionists was anything to go by, but he hadn't once mentioned espionage and I hadn't before considered that there might be spies operating in the city. It seemed unreal, but after the thought entered my head I couldn't get rid of it. Why else bomb such an innocuous place as the Office of Infant Registration? The General's meetings with his brass had become increasingly haphazard to the uninitiated. Whole sheaves of officials would trek all over the city to obtain an audience with him at short notice. A new department had even been created for the express purpose of finding locations for the General's appearances while creating efficient smokescreens to shield the information. It was called the Office of Events and one quickly came to learn that announcements of the General's materialisations were reliably inaccurate. It was far simpler for his people to content themselves with the commanding stare of his portraits that dressed the city.

The thought of spies in the city recalled to me with renewed and unrelished clarity the General's demand that I perform the activity of spying for him. The General's ambitions to make me over as an infiltrator of the so-called Insurrectionists frightened me in a new way. I felt inexperienced, I felt naïve. Vulnerable. Very much at a disadvantage. I suspected that it would be a false optimism on my part to hope that the General would forget this absurd new enterprise and I was not long in discovering that he had indeed not forgotten—he had merely, benevolently, given me a brief period of grace in which to attend to Juanita.

When the noisy banging started up again a fury erupted in me and I hurled myself at the door. A resolute Lieutenant O stood before me. 'Is the building on fire?' I hissed.

'No, Lady,' he replied.

'Is the city under attack?'

'No, Lady.'

'Is the General wanting me?'

'No, Lady.'

'Then wait until I call you,' I yelled, reaching for the door.

'I beg your pardon, Lady,' he intervened, 'but today is the day I am to begin your instruction in shooting.' I must have looked at him insensibly. 'Your gun,' he added. 'The General has entrusted me with ensuring your proficiency in the carrying and discharging of firearms.'

I expected to be taken to a shooting gallery; to be given a lecture on the components of guns; to be shown how to load, how to cock and uncock, how to operate the safety, how to sight the gun and point it down a corridor at the child-simple outline of a body with a bullseye at its heart, which might even jerk about and lurch towards me on a track if the gallery was sophisticated enough. Instead, Lieutenant O drove me out to a dry strip of land south-west of the city, in the opposite direction of the fighting. Leaving behind the quagmire of streets that comprised the devious throughways and dead ends of the city, we motored out of town on what had once been the main highway. I remember the sun was a dull bleating red through gaseous-looking cloud—typically nasty-looking, but the heat of it was a pleasant sensation along my forearm resting on the open car window, the burn drifting up from the pudgy bitumen like a slow-spinning dervish. The wind had dropped as abruptly as it had begun and become a soft breeze, deceptively suggesting that the world was a gentle place.

The road shimmered in pink gauze and stretched out flat and emptied before us. The landscape looked as though it had been stripped bare, for there were no trees or vegetation to speak of, just pockets of saltbush stubbornly sprouting from the unamenable-looking dirt, but the sheer openness of the countryside after the press of the city was a revelation. The tension began to unfurl in my shoulder-blades as a feeling of release trickled through me, I'd not been on an open road in a long, long while. We whispered over the distance in a companionable silence, an occasional convoy of military vehicles slipping past us, heading in the opposite direction. The road was rutted and potholed but it was still in reasonable condition and I guessed rightly that it was a supply and troop transport link. According to the lieutenant, the enemy had attempted to soften up the highway but they had been unsuccessful thus far. He hastened to reassure me that there was no need for concern, the area was a hundred percent secure.

Our journey was punctuated by a series of checkpoints set across our path like ordinary toll-booths, with an accompanying straggle of army tents and camouflage canopies and other odd-sized makeshift buildings pitched some distance from the road. I was informed that these nondescript settlements were no-go areas, were mini-battle stations equipped with hidden SAMs, mobile rocket launchers and truck-mounted electronic surveillance systems. Upon approaching the heavily armed checkpoints, the lieutenant insisted on rolling up our tinted bulletproof windows. The car would purr in a low, understated way while I stayed nicely anonymous and he slid our authorisation through the sliver of space at the top of his window. Stiff salutes and a hurried, very respectful return of the piece of paper invariably followed.

After we had passed through several checkpoints, the land began distorting in heat-folds about us. It became progressively lonelier, the occasional sad scatter of abandoned farm dwellings became looser, and the landscape developed a surreal characteristic: distinct, odd-shaped mounds of dirt thrusting from the earth in array. I was informed that these bumps in the landscape were buried tanks, and when instructed to look more closely with a pair of binoculars I could see the guns sticking out of the mounds of dirt like tiny castle turrets. 'If this area is so secure, why all the hardware?' I remarked, moving my elbow out of the trajectory of the now broiling sun.

'There has been a recent shift from the primary set of targets,' the lieutenant replied.

'You mean the area's being mobilised?'

'Not as such. I imagine it's a strategic interdiction, an anticipation of a possible probing operation,' he returned smoothly, as if reading straight from an autocue.

'All that means,' I said, sliding my sunglasses over my nose and returning my darkened gaze to the lumpy landscape, 'is that this is an area well and truly ripe for receiving an attack.'

I did not expect a large quarry, slicing into a hill which had been split apart by mining. Large outcrops of dense grey granite had gone grey-white where the rock had been broken open and left to crumble. The shards of the rock revealed speckles of white quartz which glittered prettily in the light. The heat seemed to crowd into the place and the air smelt of dust and the smoke of a tamped-down fire. We had arrowed off the highway and gone down a well-travelled dirt road, coming to a pause at a security gate set in a high chainlink fence with razor wire along the top—definitely an enclosure. The guards clanged open the gate and saluted us as we rolled into a type of compound. Rusting hulks of mining machinery occupied the grounds along with a collection of low, rectangular, concrete-block buildings. Soldiers were stationed around the fenced perimeter of the quarry and along the top of the gouged-out hill. For such an obscure outpost the place seemed impenetrable and extraordinarily well defended.

As it turned out, we had come not to a bizarre rifle range but to a Judgement Camp.

A Judgement Camp was where political prisoners were shipped after the perfunctory trial which invariably found them guilty of high treason. A Judgement Camp was the place for final judgement, final judgement being a euphemism for execution. The prisoners were delivered to the camp and detained for arbitrary lengths of time: some were executed within hours upon arrival; some lingered in the camp for endless months, being badly fed, badly treated, clothed and housed, never knowing which day or which night might be their last. The strain of this would, of course, encourage suicides, and in the case of an unsuccessful attempt at suicide care would be taken to restore the prisoner to the usual semblance of survival until final judgement occurred.

This information was relayed to me by the colonel of the camp, an overly eager man with an over-anxious air who held a waiting umbrella above my head so as to shield me from the curious sun as I journeyed from the car to his office, one of the box-shaped buildings, where he removed his clammy hand from my elbow and enjoined me to partake of the bottle of champagne he'd been saving for a special occasion.

'I don't drink,' I said gracefully, wiping my elbow against my side. 'Water then?' he enquired, picking up a jar of iced water with tinkling ice blocks. The sound was provocative but I did not want to drink with the man. I'd disliked him immediately; there was something dank about him, despite the arid air.

'No,' I said. There was a silence. 'Why am I here?' I said, turning to the lieutenant. 'I thought you were taking me to a rifle range.'

'I have—' he began.

Only to be interrupted by the colonel. 'This is the General's preferred camp,' he enthused, 'as I trust it will be yours.'

'What's he talking about?' I demanded.

'Target practice, Lady,' replied the lieutenant. 'The General sent you here for target practice.'

'But why here?'

Lieutenant O gave a small cough, as if embarrassed at having to spell it out to me. 'Live target practice.'

'Live?'

'You have the opportunity to be executioner, ma'am,' burbled the colonel. 'You choose who and when.'

'Who and when,' I repeated.

'Yes, after we tour the camp, you nominate the targets and we'll have them fitted according to your needs. Perhaps you'd like to practise on a stationary target then progress to a moving target as your confidence increases?'

'It would be best to utilise your handgun for a stationary target in the preliminaries. The optimum range for your Luger is approximately twenty metres,' interjected the lieutenant.

'Yes,' enthused the colonel, 'and in addition to single-shot mortality shooting you could practise disabling. Here's where a moving target is best considered. It's a useful exercise to have a moving target you're aiming to disable, or at the very least take out slowly, rather than straight off eliminate.'

'You may find it frustrating to focus effectively on a moving target at this stage of your tutorship, Lady,' murmured the lieutenant.

'We have sniper rifles if you prefer to hunt the targets out,' continued the colonel. 'The M98 is a bolt-action rather than a semi-automatic but it's a guaranteed hit—'

'In ideal conditions,' interjected the lieutenant again.

'At up to five hundred and fifty metres', the colonel resumed. 'And it's got telescopic sight so you can harass your target at around about nine hundred metres, which is good for getting the feel of how far your bullet will go.' I held up a finger and there was a small silence as I delicately wiped the sweat from my upper lip.

'Allow me to ensure that you have experience in handling a range of guns, Lady,' said Lieutenant O. 'The General would consider me derelict in my duty if you were not well taught.'

There was a much longer silence as I took out a small mirror and a tube of Bronze Bombshell and fastidiously reapplied my lipstick. 'Very well then,' I said. 'Teach me. But there's one thing: I'm not the executioner. I came here to learn to handle a gun, not to shoot live ammo into live targets.'

'But that's what the camp is for!' spluttered the colonel. 'What else is there to shoot?'

'Earth, sky, clouds, emptiness, space,' I replied, pushing to my feet. 'Anything and everything in this godforsaken place. Anything that isn't human.' I leaned over and plucked the colonel's special bottle of champagne out of the ice bucket. 'How about I start with this, a stationary target, at twenty metres.'

There was a faint gurgling noise from the throat of the colonel.

'I'll fetch your Luger,' smiled the lieutenant.

THIRTY-TWO

It was Martyrdom Day when Juanita tried to kill the General, a day which the city was supposed to celebrate. But the mood of the city was not given to jollity, for what was being remembered were the war dead, who were carted back in body bags, whole or in bits and pieces, or not returned at all, having been lost in the fighting or blown into bits too indistinct to collect. Martyrdom Day was to be a celebration of cemeteries and crematoria, with lurid red flags flapping along streets that led to groaning graveyards where the military bands would keen and ceremonies of exhausting pomp and flash were to be conducted over the mass of new graves. New heroes. New martyrs. Our national flag, a white claw sprouting from a field of opium-poppy crimson, had been newly adorned: a black M had been stamped in the centre of the claw. Clear and explicit and all too easy to confuse it with M for martyrdom, which was the presumption, in accord with the event.

Upon returning from my outing to the Judgement Camp—a successful one, for I had a good aim and Lieutenant O had decided I'd shape up nicely under his tutelage—I discovered a blood-stained bandage laid out upon my bed, one of the General's distinctive messages. His piece of theatre had been more dramatic than the actual slice to his wrist but I'd insisted on wrapping the cut, his manner of blooding himself being typical of his idea of entertainment. At the time I was simply grateful that it was his own blood he was playing with and nobody else's.

Just after I dumped that delightful little communiqué in the bin I received another message via his adjutant: the General was relocating and I was to be ready to leave the next day, following the celebrations. When I asked where we were going I got a tight-arsed, 'I'm not authorised to say. That's a Level One confidentiality and I can't clear that, ma'am.' At least I had some warning, which made a change.

I went down and told Juanita the news straightaway. She'd told me she hadn't managed to contact Sol since I'd brought her to the El Alamein and I was frightened that this impromptu move would ruin my chance of seeing him again. She pumped me for details but I had to admit I knew nothing. 'Don't you ever get tired of being nothing more than the General's fuck?' she accused. 'Aren't you tired of existing like a bought fuck? I mean, I know I sell it but it doesn't define me, the way you let it define you. You don't have to go with him, you know.'

'I know,' I shot back. 'But it's not like I've got any real alternative.'

'You could run away. Now. Tonight,' she urged. 'I could help you disappear.'

'Don't you think I've thought about it? Disappearing won't help anything.'

'You're in too deep,' she sighed.

'Look, you stay put and find Sol. I'll leave you enough money to get by, just make sure you don't disappear. I'll be in touch as soon as I can. It's not as if I'm leaving the city.'

She laughed, a lightning-flash change of mood. 'I guess none of us can jetset out of the city, it's not exactly an option. Can you imagine,' she cackled, 'walking out to the enemy wearing the cutest little two-piece in a stunning shade of surrender white? Wouldn't it cause a scene! A surrender, probably! One of us going to one of them! The end of the war!' she screeched, then pulled herself together. 'Haven't you anything decent to drink upstairs? We must toast our last night together.' She was speaking very fast, spittle flecking her teeth. 'I want to get pissed together like old times,' she demanded. 'But not in this grubby little coffin.'

'It'll be curfew soon.'

'Your place then,' she insisted.

A noisy night followed. The General was not expected back until after midnight and I warned Juanita she'd have to be gone by then. 'It'll be safer for you,' I said, 'he can be unpredictable.' An understatement. The General was not so much unpredictable as downright hazardous. I sent Lieutenant O packing and opened the bottles. Outside, it was as if the ghosts of the dead were being stirred up in anticipation of Martyrdom Day. The wind came up as usual with the claret-coloured moon and the building groaned and carried on under the pressure of it. I felt a healthy respect for the population of the dead who were being invited to the party. For my own part, I was perfectly happy to keep company with Juanita. I had no wish to traverse the stairwell where I had left a corpse. I was not superstitious but I was more than ready to quit the place. For diversion I turned off the lights every now and then and slipped aside the curtains to reveal the tracer fire in the east lighting up the horizon of hills at regular intervals; it provided an entertaining illumination—a nasty, yellow, exploding show of light.

'This war will soon be over,' hiccuped Juanita.

'Dream on,' I replied, pouring her another drink.

'What's the time?' she asked.

'Nearly ten o'clock.'

'In another few hours it'll be over,' she insisted.

'Well, I'm glad the General gets his address in before the war finishes,' I replied, 'he's due to broadcast any moment now,'

'Yes!' she yelled. 'Let's hear the General's last war speech.'

It was a studio broadcast, of course. These days, the General did not appear in public if he could avoid it. He looked expertly coiffed and serene, he enjoyed speaking to camera. His medals were impressive. There seemed to be more of them hanging off his chest, but then the General was accruing medals all the time. The podium was flanked by two Maniac missiles. Some set-dresser's idea of an appropriate *mise en scène*. 'This war has not been undertaken lightly,' he began, in an exceedingly doleful manner befitting a national observance of death. 'This war is, above all, a war of love. Love for our nation. Love for our homeland. This love is a necessary love, for if we love not who we are, then who are we? If we love not our nation, then what is our nation and how can it be valued? This is a difficult love, a hard love, an enduring love, a love that requires the greatest effort, a love greater than any individual love, a destiny-shaping love, as ours is a destiny-shaping war, a necessary war that will defeat the lowly and make our futures bright and clear, true and pure, and that of our children's futures and our children's children's futures.'

Listening to the General talk about children, let alone love, was obscene. The whole idea of Martyrdom Day was obscene. 'This is obscene,' I muttered.

'Sshhh!' quieted Juanita, glued to the screen.

'We will triumph as an entire nation and we will live on in such triumph and our triumph will be passed from one generation to the next,' continued the General in that familiar oratory voice. 'And in this way we shall survive, more than survive, we shall conquer all the forces arrayed against our homes and our children and our integrity and our identity as people of one great nation. But …' here the General's voice dropped to a hush, 'this victory is a hard, difficult victory. It cannot be achieved without sacrifice, without the spilling of precious blood, blood which nurtures us, sustains us, fights for us, protects us and, above all, humbles us. Let us give thanks for this gift of love, for the offering of lifeblood, for the supreme gift of our martyrs who died in order that we may live.'

Boom, boom.

Fade to black.

'Here's to the spilling of blood,' cried Juanita, spilling her drink and starting to laugh again.

When I heard the dogs barking I didn't pay any attention, but after a while I realised that there couldn't be dogs barking because there were no dogs. There hadn't been a single pet or stray left after the death of the animals, nor had I heard the sound of one since. Now, I clearly heard the crying of dogs out in the streets. Streets that had been made deathly quiet by the curfew. Yes, it was distinct, unmistakable, a ragged chorus of barking intermingled with high, drawn-out howling, as if there were a pack of dogs out there, loping through the city, calling to each other. Hungry. Hunting. These were the sounds of big, agitated dogs, not the itty-bitty yapping of little dogs. I scanned the streets with a pair of infrared binoculars, but I saw no animals. Only my ears registered their presence. What made it worse was that Juanita claimed she couldn't hear a thing.

Events get a little blurred after that. I was a little drunk. I remember Juanita kissing me, then I felt the sharp point of a knife at my throat, then I was kneeling on the floor while she jerked my hands behind my back and tied them with fishing line. 'Don't pull or you'll cut yourself,' she admonished. I flexed my wrists and the nylon bit into me. All the while I was saying inane things like 'Juanita, you're drunk'; 'Juanita, untie me'; 'Juanita, stop this please'; 'Juanita, you're hurting me.'

She pushed me into my bedroom and laughed and tickled me with the knife. I thought she was cutting me. 'This is for your own good, so your skin is safe.' She pushed me nose-down on the floor and ripped off my pantyhose and hog-tied me, then wound the fishing line around me. I'd been shackled by the General too many times for it to be a new experience but I was starting to panic. She hunkered down beside me. 'I don't have anything against you, understand, I don't admire you too much but I like you. I like you a lot and we go back a long way and I don't want to hurt you. I wouldn't hurt you, understand. You've been extremely useful, getting me in here, getting me this close to the General.' She wiped sweat off her face, it bubbled up again. Her breath fumed with that distinctive odour of ethanol. And something else, something bitter. Earthy, even. 'You're going to have a bit part in history. Of course, I don't know what'll happen to you after I kill the General.'

'What if you don't manage to kill him?' I pleaded. 'He's an expert. He'll kill you.'

'Do you think I would've come here if I couldn't face that?' she replied.

'Why?'

'Did you think he'd go on and on and on? You know,' she whispered, leaning in closer, 'this is all my idea. I'm the one in control here. I'm the one making death matter for a change.' She picked up the pantyhose. 'I've noticed you like black pantyhose. Don't you think you're a bit of a cliché? Mistress of the death-dealer. Lady in black,' she mocked, stuffing them in my mouth and tying them tight around my head. 'Happy Martyrdom Day.'

I couldn't see what she did next but it sounded like she was trashing my room. Clothes and shoes went flying. Domino pieces bounced off the walls. After a while of this, she turned the lights off and shut the door. All I could see were the tips of furniture and the shadows of things strewn on the floor and the sliver of light beneath the door.

I heard a few small sounds as Juanita moved about in the next room but she did not check on me or speak to me again. I didn't know if she was ignoring me or had forgotten me, either way it didn't matter, I was incapable of affecting her decision to kill the General. At one point someone knocked on the apartment door but after a few minutes they went away. It was an agonising wait. The noise outside intensified. No more dogs, but the usual ripping and keening of wind. The crazy man, the wailing woman wind. A bad thing to be listening to while waiting for something awful to happen. As I lay there in paralysed discomfort all I could do was hope this was one of those nights when the General didn't come home.

*

It was a bomb that killed him. To be precise, it was a V100 Ultra, an anti-personnel mine. She had placed the Ultras under a rug just inside the front door. A couple of steps inside the door. Others were found hidden around the apartment—under the General's mattress, beneath the sofa cushions, in his boots, even under the toilet seat. Lethal little metal shapes. An ultra-slim, ultra-efficient mine, easy to set, with precision sensitivity, ideal for toting in a lady's shoulder-bag. Or a shoebox. Designed to kill, not wound. He got it coming in the door. He didn't die straightaway but slipped away a few hours later.

Slipped away.

It sounded gentle, effortless, as if he'd had a choice. The experts pronounced it an amateurish job but still, Lieutenant O was dead and another of the General's Chosen Ones badly injured. As I told the General's Head of Security I had no idea what time Juanita left the apartment. I did not hear anything worth noting after she had shut the door on me. I'd been left on the floor for hours and I must have slept or passed out for a period. When the first explosion happened light was clotting the sky. My first thought was that we were under attack. Because Juanita had harassed me with a knife I hadn't considered that she would employ another means of disposing of the General. I had chosen to forget the packages I'd been keeping for her to pass on to Sol. In the bottom of my closet in some shoeboxes, as I had told her.

No, I said, I have no idea where she got the Ultras, or how they'd been smuggled through the security checks routinely conducted in the foyer of the building.

I was reminded that I was the only civilian excluded from such checks.

I was reminded that I enjoyed unprecedented security exemption. Despite certain advice the General had received.

The General, of course, was safe and sound. He'd been downstairs in the car waiting for Lieutenant O to collect me for a select dawn graveside ceremony that was scheduled to launch Martyrdom Day. He'd been rushed from the scene on code-alert red. It was communicated to him that I was unharmed, and soon afterwards I spoke to him on the Security Head's mobile. 'How apt,' he said, 'how ingenious of you to celebrate this day in such an auspicious way.' I couldn't tell if he was being ironic or angry.

'Please …' I faltered. I did not often beseech the General, he did not admire pleaders. He encouraged proudness, non-capitulation; wilfulness, even. He did not always allow these qualities but he admired them. 'Please don't kill her. I endangered you. It was my fault.'

'There is no fault. This has been a necessary moment. Did I not say you were the one to bring the Insurrectionists to us? You, with your cunning.'

'No,' I said, 'I was used.'

'Yes,' he said. 'But not in the way you imagine. You are the implement of righteousness. I had every faith that you would reveal the inner enemy. You needed only to discover your possibilities. You are the howl that illuminates my darkness, the fire that feeds my night. I am guided by what you see, by what you know.'

'Where is she?' I asked.

'The little cunt is with me,' he replied. I heard a muffled sound.

'What was that?' I cried.

'Blood,' he answered and hung up.

THIRTY-THREE

Juanita was being kept in a cell in the bunker complex. The door was unlocked by one of the Chosen Ones, who bowed down towards me slightly in salute. He was a blond giant of a man with massive limbs. I remembered him from Lieutenant O's burial, he had been one of the guard of honour, standing a clear head above his comrades. The lieutenant had been delivered to a hole in the dirt with the appropriate military honours. A widow had wept lightly, stoically. A small daughter not at all. I felt tears, but watching his silent child cured me—who was I to put on a display? Still, I felt the loss of the lieutenant. Afterwards, I touched his widow's hand but could think of nothing to say. I hadn't even known his real name. I had known nothing at all about his private life, despite the time we had spent in each other's company.

The other man wounded by the explosions had also died. I had only met Major B once or twice but still I observed his going and watched the Chosen Ones close around the remains of another lost warrior. Two were now missing from the General's private alphabet. Knowing the General's distaste for disarrangement, I suspected it would not be long before his alphabet was made complete again.

Juanita's unsuccessful assassination attempt was not, of course, reported upon. In any case, there were other more newsworthy things; Martyrdom Day turned out to be a good day for someone to up-tempo the standing status, as the adjutant explained. The city's inner districts were strafed and bombed and the incoming wiped out the celebrations. It was the first time the city had been targeted so extensively, and our Guardians and Hunters and a whole host of other defensive weaponry with equally catchy names didn't seem to do so well by way of interception. Aircraft were flying overhead and unloading all through that day and the shells kept landing without let-up, eating into the city at a worrying rate and with a frightening rhythm. I'd been hustled away from the El Alamein Tower and taken to a bunker before the attack had begun so I was insulated from it. The attack had been repulsed but not before a great deal of damage had been inflicted. The very fact of being in a bunker meant the situation was turning nasty. My readings of war stories suggested that the leader only moved into a bunker when in serious shit.

Was the General losing the war?

I walked the complex of corridors trying to find an answer to that and other related questions, but the doors were closed to me and no-one was willing to discuss anything. The General would call at irregular hours to tell me he would be with me soon; however, soon had not eventuated. His absences were nothing new but I perceived that I had become a security risk, because no-one would tell me where he was. He could have been thirty metres away for all I knew—there was a lot of security, a lot of heavy brass in the place; the

bunker was a large, concrete rabbit warren, profoundly impersonal. In every respect, a military establishment. Uniformly
grey, enlivened with touches of army-green. Fluoros emitting
a bluish, flickering, humming light; air vents sucking and whispering; the concrete walls dank and damp (the place had probably been flooded by the rains); the sound bouncing around so
badly you felt at times you'd become prey to aural hallucina-
tions; and the smell that stale, congested smell of something
closed up for a very long time, a place where the only air was
regurgitated and thin. For some reason I kept expecting to see
the flash of rats in the shadows, but of course there were none.
It was without doubt the dreariest accommodation the
General had thus far lodged me in. My quarters were generous
enough in size but minimalist in every other way. The worst
thing was not having a window. A good place for claustrophobia.

It took me several days to discover that Juanita too was
there, and since there occurred another lapse in communications from the General, it took several more days for his adjutant to convey the message that I had permission to visit her.

When I entered the room Juanita was standing facing the
wall, leaning her forehead against it. She did not turn or in any
way acknowledge my entry. A meal with a stainless-steel cover
over it sat on a stool next to the door. There were flies buzzing
around it. I wondered how the flies had got in. The room was
considerably smaller and more spartan than mine, but with the
same basic principle of design. 'Hello, Juanita,' I said. By way
of reply she started banging her forehead against the wall.
Bang. Bang. Bang. Bang. Bang. I took her by the shoulders and
pulled her away from the wall. 'Don't do that, you'll hurt
yourself.' She was entirely passive. As I turned her towards me

I saw the scarring on her forehead. The letter M had been carved into her brow. It was not a particularly clean job. The banging had caused the wound to bleed and blood-was trickling into her eyes. I grabbed a towel and dabbed her face with it. She looked awful, the hollows in her face were frightening and her breath was putrid. She submitted to my fussing without speaking. 'What else happened?' I asked.

Juanita pulled away and went and lay on the bed, the blood began seeping down her face again. I knelt beside her and held the towel to her forehead. 'Where else did they hurt you?' She simply looked at me, I wondered if she recognised me. 'Why did you do it?' I tried. 'Are you an Insurrectionist like they say you are?'

'It hurts,' she whispered.

'Where does it hurt?' I asked. She gestured at her belly with a limp hand. I eased her dirty shirt up over her torso. As I lifted the material she groaned in pain. I felt a little nervous at what I might find. I steadied myself, then looked. Nothing. Her belly was distended, a bit swollen, but the skin was smooth and unmarked. I'd been expecting something awful but there were no bruises, no cuts of any kind. Still, she bit her lips and moaned in pain.

'It hurts,' she repeated.

'Did they rape you?' I asked.

'A pain in the belly, inside my belly.' At least she was talking to me, if not answering me.

'Have you eaten?' She shook her head. 'Perhaps it's a hunger pain. You look starved.'

'I don't know.'

'Isn't this your food?'

'Food?' Her first spark of interest.

I went and got the tray and brought it over to her. 'When did you eat last?'

'I don't know.' Juanita's voice was slow and blurry, as if she were drugged. At least the blood was beginning to dry on her forehead. The wound made her look quite ghastly. I felt the sweat slide under my arms, the room was overheated and stifling. I began to crave outside air.

I propped her up with pillows and settled the tray across her lap. 'Eat.' I uncovered the food. Lumps of raw pink meat swam in a lake of red … sauce. I hoped it was a sauce. God knows what sort of meat it was, it looked—and smelt—utterly dreadful. Now that the food had been uncovered the flies were going crazy. I expected Juanita to push the plate away, it was so awful, but to my astonishment she attacked, literally attacked, the meal. I moved out of range as she picked up great handfuls of food, smearing it across her face, ramming it into her mouth, making bestial sounds as she chewed and slurped and swallowed. When she had finished she sank back into the splattered pillows, covered in whatever had been her meal. I hurriedly dumped the tray outside the door, picked up the towel, swatted the flies, and cleaned her as best I could. 'Did you talk to the General?' I asked.

'I am the General's sign,' she whispered.

'No you're not, you're his prisoner.'

'His symptom,' she continued. This was certainly the General's manner of talking.

'What sort of sign are you, Juanita?'

'The curving of the way.'

'What way?'

'The final way.' Juanita grabbed my head with sudden strength and yanked me closer towards her. Our mouths were almost touching. 'I didn't tell him.'

'Tell him what?'

'That they were yours.' I knew she was talking about the Ultras. 'You're wondering about Sol, aren't you?' she said, all of a sudden cogent.

'Yes.'

'Did you let him burn you?'

'No,' I replied.

'Liar, I saw your hands. That day you came to my apartment. It was his message.'

'What message?'

'He gave you my mark.' I tried to pull away but she clung fiercely. 'You're in it, you're in the heart of it.'

'The heart of what?' I asked.

'The heart of blood,' she hissed. More General-speak.

'Where's Sol?' I whispered.

'Waiting for the sign.' She closed her eyes and turned her head towards the wall and refused to speak to me again.

The General was waiting for me. A candle was burning, the one I kept beside my bed for the difficult parts of the night, and he was standing before it. I could have done with more time to gather myself, my talk with Juanita had frightened me. When I saw him I faltered a moment then stepped into the part. 'I've been waiting for you to come to me,' I purred. Sexually. Provocatively. Automatically. I had learnt early on the usefulness of slipping into sex talk whenever a certain reassembling, a little necessary realigning, was required. It allowed those few precious moments to get myself into a place where it was easier to manage things.

The General swivelled towards me and said in a soft voice, 'Do not concern yourself with Juanita. She is weak where you are strong.'

So he knew I had just left her. I pushed into the opening. 'She's wearing your mark.'

'Self-inflicted. She aspires to be chosen but it is a vanity.' More likely, off her head with starvation, pain, or torture, or all three. 'She is your handmaiden,' he continued, 'she has never been anything more.'

'She's her own agent,' I said. 'I knew nothing about her intentions.'

'Another expression of her vanity.'

'What will happen to her?' He shrugged. I knew that gesture of dismissal. Time to change the subject. He would not tell me anything he had gleaned from Juanita if I bored him with her. I did the usual, I took off my clothes and waited. He held out his hands, I laid the garments in his arms—neatly, the outer clothing underneath, the underwear on top—and he proceeded to sniff them as I knelt between his thighs. I unzipped his trousers and entertained his cock with my tongue, in silence up until the moment he screamed, 'Take me, Lady!' and gave me his cum.

Afterwards, the General was unusually merry. We ate together, one of those dinners with the starched white linen, the Sevres china and the Waterford crystal at a big table in a cavernous room. Somewhat like the room into which I had followed the General the first time we met. I don't know what reminded me of that room in the bowels of the Department of Insignia Supplies, perhaps the lack of windows and the stale quality of the air. The food was rather poor but at least it wasn't what Juanita had been fed. The wine was infinitely better. After we had emptied the decanter the General insisted on displaying his shooting prowess. I obliged by standing at one end of the room and holding the china so that he might crack it with his bullets. The thought flickered through my mind that this was an excellent opportunity to be shot, but I resolutely held out the dinner plates and closed my eyes against the shattering of the Sevres. I could feel the onset of a headache.

After he'd worked his way through the dinner service he said, 'Let's play a game.' I thought this meant he wanted to fuck but then he said, 'Get your gun.'

I went to my quarters, got the Luger and touched up my makeup. When I returned to the dining room the General was opening another bottle of wine. 'A test of skill,' he said. 'We take a gun, a glass of wine. We undertake a small duel. The first one who shoots the glass …' he held up the Waterford goblets and flares exploded in my eyes, 'out of their opponent's hand will be the winner.'

'Naturally,' I murmured. I felt in no jeopardy myself, I had just witnessed the General's aptitude, but he was putting himself at some risk.

'I have complete confidence in you,' he smiled, as if divining my thought. Bully for him.

'All right,' I said, 'but duellists always duel for something.'

'Precisely,' he replied. 'Something that involves their honour. Tell me, what do you think is worth dying for?' I did not like the turn the conversation had taken.

'Victory,' I said in a teasing way. He usually liked that sort of talk and it could distract him from certain unsavoury trails of thought.

'That word in your mouth makes me absolutely rigid,' he conceded, 'but it does not quite provide us with the rules of play. Come, give me something to shoot for.'

'Would you release Juanita if I won?' I ventured.

'Ah,' he crooned. 'I perceive a line of thought akin to my own.' I somehow doubted that. 'But let us up the ante. If I win, you will execute her. If you win, I will not execute her.' The room tilted, I am sure of it. In the quiet that followed I heard our breathing, twinned.

'Why should I accept such conditions?'

'You have no choice but to accept the conditions because I am the one setting them. And because you are curious. And because you cannot resist duelling for death.' That was a thought definitely not worth pursuing.

'What if there's no winner?'

'There is always a winner,' he smiled. 'Charge your glass. I insist.'

I could feel the panic, the claw touching my throat. I could barely swallow. I had played games of chance and made wagers with my body on many occasions but I had never played for such stakes. I eased some wine into my gullet, we saluted each other by raising our glasses, then we turned and stood back to back. 'Wait!' I cried. 'When do we fire?'

'On the count of ten.'

'Who'll count?'

'I will, of course.' Of course. 'One,' he began. We took a step away from each other. I tried to breathe. 'Two.' The fluoros began to flicker. 'Three.' My palms were sweating. 'Four.' My ears were ringing with the General's tread. 'Five.' The word was nonsense. 'Six.' I began to fiercely itch all along my spine. 'Seven.' The centre of feeling had shifted to the middle of my back. 'Eight.' The word came at me like a very fast train and I spun around towards it and fired.

Did I try to kill the General?

I think I aimed at him but my shot went wide. Somehow I hit his glass. What a fluke.

'Nine.' He kept moving, still holding onto his stump of glass. 'Ten.' He turned and trained his gun on me. 'You cheated,' he smiled.

'All's fair in love and war,' I riposted. Absurdly. Shakily. I realised I was covered in the spillage of wine and my glass was no longer in my hand. I must have tossed it when I'd fired. The General walked towards me until the muzzle of his Luger was grazing my belly. He was smiling. 'You are becoming me,' he said. I swallowed convulsively. 'You understand how nothing can deflect you.'

'Deflect me from what?' I asked.

'From your course. It is in your eyes. It looks out of your eyes all the time now.' I pulled away and went over to the table and picked up a bottle and took a long drink. I couldn't taste it but I could breathe.

'Did I win?' I asked.

'Certainly,' he said. 'There were no rules against cheating.'

'Well then,' I said.

The General went to his attaché case and took out a long thin black velvet box. 'A gift for my Lady. Victor. Penetrator. Whore of hardness. Mistress of might.' When he put it in my hand I thought it was a piece of jewellery because of the velvet case but when I snapped it open I saw that it was a boning knife. 'For the feast I have prepared for you.'

When I went to Juanita there was no guard and the door was ajar. I pushed it open and was confronted by the sight of her hanging by the neck from a light fitting. Her body was gently moving, as if eddying in a breeze, although the air in the room was absolutely still. This movement gave me the hope that she was still alive, so I righted the kicked-over stool and jumped up on it and used the General's gift to hack at the cord strangling her neck. We fell onto the floor in unison. I then gave her mouth-to-mouth and pumped her chest, but after many minutes of unresponsiveness I realised that Juanita was dead.

Dead.

I rocked back on my heels beside her, not able to touch, only able to look. And I rocked for a while and I thought of nothing much in particular, merely that she looked solemn and sad and dirty. Slowly, I closed her eyes, and moistened the hem of my dress with my spit and rubbed away the tracks of dried blood from the ugly M on her forehead. It was when I straightened her clothing that I noticed the beginnings of the blisters in the crooks of her elbows. The small pustules that were the signs of the pox.

I was not afraid. I was emptied.

I picked up the knife and sliced off a piece of her pubic hair. The stubble on her head did not afford so much as a curl of her normally luxuriant hair, but that twist of pubic hair had a bouncy, resilient texture and was the most beautiful colour of blue-black. I laid the knife beside her and opened the velvet case and placed the swatch of hair in it, and since I could do nothing further I left the room.

It was not until later, much later, many drinks later, that I was able to cry.

THIRTY-FOUR

In the dream it was night, and Juanita was outside scratching at the windows trying to get in. She was a mosaic of shadow scraping methodically against first one window then another. A fire was eating the moon and the sky. I was alone in a bombed-out building, everything had been destroyed except the walls, the doors, and the windows. It was only a matter of time until she realised that there was no roof and came in that way. I was naked, hugging the floor as if in supplication, but it was a posture of fear. All I knew was that she mustn't see me. She knew I was inside, somewhere, but I mustn't betray my presence. I heard footsteps thudding towards me. I was unbearably frightened. The footsteps stopped behind me. I couldn't raise my head for the fear. There was a hot breath on the back of my exposed neck. A hand crawled over me. Two hands cupped my breasts. Another hand settled on my belly. Yet another hand opened my labia and began to enter me. I whimpered, trying to resist. A voice said, 'She's mine.' My fear was so strong it broke through the dream and woke me, but when I opened my eyes I didn't know where I was, whether whatever had touched me was there or not, whether Juanita was out there or not, whether or not I was in the dream.

When the General gripped my shoulder I cried out in shock. 'Where are you?' he demanded. 'Who was with you? What have you seen?' His questions punctured the moment of confusion. The dream released me and I knew where I was and who I was with. I wiped away the sweat and shakily composed a story.

'I was on a hill watching soldiers fighting on a plain below me. But they weren't fighting a battle, they were fighting a fire. A huge wall of flame.'

Eating the moon. Eating the sky.

'A cleansing. A conflagration.'

'Yes, a conflagration. Then a formation of bombers appeared, they were flying very low.'

'They filled the sky with her roar.'

'Yes, the sky was full of noise. Anyway, they began to drop their loads but they weren't dropping bombs, they were dropping ... bones, and when the bones fell on the army they stopped fighting the fire and began picking up the bones.'

'Then what happened?'

'I woke up.'

'Why were you frightened? Tell me.'

I heard ... footsteps. Coming towards me.' The truth this time.

'It was Kali, wasn't it?' he whispered.

'No,' I said. 'It wasn't her.' I didn't want to tell him what he wanted to hear.

'It was Kali.' He looked smug. 'You mustn't be concerned, there is no reason for fear.'

I looked around my secure bunker bedroom. 'Right,' I said.

After the dream I kept thinking of Juanita and the fact that she was now dead and the fact that despite all the death I could barely imagine her dead. It was a mournful thought. I opened the velvet box and took out the piece of her hair and it helped me to begin thinking of it. Her body had been zipped into a body bag and taken away for cremation. No last rites. No final goodbyes. Just the carbonising of the corpse and ashes to ashes. Juanita's demise had caused little excitement, and in spite of the inexplicable urge to suicide that the pox frequently engendered it was only too easy to imagine the General arranging her death as an amusing adjunct to our little duel. I felt angry in an unfocused, obscure, wholly unrewarding way and I cursed her, then I cursed the General, then I cursed myself. Self-pity swept through me. Juanita was gone and, with her, Sol. Claustrophobia began to rise. I had to get out of that underground chamber, it had been weeks since I'd been outside. I'd almost made it to the door when the adjutant caught up with me. I was required.

About turn.

The General was sitting in a darkened room, the one source of light a large video monitor over which images played. The picture was mute. Since there was only one chair in the room and he occupied it, I stood. He was intent on the screen, a jumpy long shot of what looked like buildings. Shimmering above them was a beautiful blue blur. It took me a moment to realise that it was the sky. A blue sky. Looking at it made the claustrophobia ease. It had been a long time since I had seen a sky like that and the longing for it was sharp and immediate, like a bad homesickness. The sheer, extraordinary normalcy of it shook me. It seemed to promise something, I don't know what, something almost forgotten, something lost. 'Where is that place?' I asked.

'It is an enemy settlement on the edge of the Last Zone.'

'What's the Last Zone?'

'A no-man's land. A place that belongs to no-one, a place no-one controls.' Somewhere beyond control. 'Not yet, anyway,' he concluded, killing the picture. The grey shape of the screen remained imprinted on my retinas for a few seconds, then it throbbed away into a profound darkness. I pushed against the wall for orientation. Darkness did not alleviate my claustrophobia, quite the reverse. I was attempting to steady my breathing when I felt a hand on my breast. My dream returned to me with a shudder. Another hand glided between my thighs. I was frightening myself, waiting for another, and another hand, but instead I felt the General's tongue squirm in my ear. It was almost a relief. 'You are my message,' he crooned, 'and you have an assignation.'

The assignation was in a church. From the outside the building looked intact, but like the place in my dream it had no roof. When I pushed open the door I saw that the interior had been trashed or bombed and partly resurrected. The pews that were not smashed up had been neatly realigned amid the piles of rubble and a wall decorated with columns of dates and names with little crosses beside them—war dead, I guessed—written in a very nearly illegible script in an unpleasant shade of red paint. At least I hoped it was paint, I did not wish to look more carefully. Another wall had been transformed into a zone of crucified figures painted in a crude but graphic testament of awful suffering—the artist's, if no-one else's. The altar was perfectly preserved, which added a nice surreal touch, as did the intact stained-glass windows that continued the violent theme: saints and martyrs engaged in hacking and stabbing, or being hacked and stabbed.

This had never been a peaceable place.

Even though I had never been a follower of religions the church disturbed me. The fact that it abutted a graveyard and was swamped by a stench entirely suitable to an abattoir assisted in creating the indelible impression that it was a site for obnoxious ceremonies. I took shallow sips of air and daintily picked a path through the rubble. Overhead, the scarlet sky darkened with the passage of bombers throwing their shadows down before the red sun. The noise of the distant incoming did nothing to ease my jumpiness, the splashes were uncomfortably close, the mortar fire was a constant chorus, and I carried my gas-mask kit by way of a prophylactic although it would not prevent me from being vaporised by a missile or being blown to pieces by shells. Upon emerging from the General's lair I had realised that it was a risky proposition moving around the city now.

A situation had developed which had every hallmark of being unstable.

Definitely fluid.

I was in that place of worship as a sort of offering. A player in the General's game. I understood that when I learned I was being sent in lieu of Juanita. If she, or someone in place of her, didn't show it might prejudice the situation. Just what the situation was, nobody would tell me. I had been told that Juanita hadn't had much to tell her interrogators. A place. A time. A date. Nothing, really, about the Insurrectionists. Just that she had an assignation which the General had decided I ought to keep in order to assist the flow. 'This is your war,' he had explained, 'I want you to play your part in it. As Juanita played her part, it is necessary for you to play yours.' So there I was, walking down an aisle strewn with wreckage, carrying the Luger, going to my moment of war. My instructions were simple enough: I was to meet the Insurrectionists and plausibly load the scenario. I was to say that the General was dying as a result of Juanita's action, that chaos reigned, that morale in his camp was non-existent. I was to provide the whereabouts of his bunker. Needless to say, the General's men would be ready for the Insurrectionists when they arrived to finish him off.

'Why should these Insurrectionists believe me? If that's who I actually meet,' I had demanded.

'Why wouldn't they? You are relaying the writing on the wall. The words they long to hear.'

'Don't you think they may decide to shoot the messenger?'

'You jest, Lady,' he had admonished. 'We both know the impossibility of your death.' The General's philosophy about my immortality had flooded me with disgust, and anger did a good job of replacing anxiety. But it was anxiety that accompanied me down that aisle.

Was I surprised when Sol stepped out of the vestry and into a shaft of the nasty-coloured light?

No, because I wanted it to be him.

No, because I knew it would be him.

He gave you my mark.

I bit down on the part of me that was suddenly hurting. 'You've put yourself in a lot of danger coming here,' he said.

I could not prevent myself from saying, 'Does that worry you?'

He smiled then, a courtesy smile, a smile that was not really a smile. The sort of smile I knew well.

'Of course. I never wanted you to be hurt.'

I did not smile back. 'You were expecting Juanita. I've got bad news.'

'I see.' He lit one of his signature cigarettes and I had the smell of him. He exhaled. 'I suppose we're being watched.'

'I was told I was on my own.'

'And you believed that?'

I shrugged. The General had been most determined about my initiation, as he called it. 'I have complete confidence in you,' he had said, 'you are the agent of change. There is no need for any other insertion in the situation.'

'Tell me what happened to Juanita.'

I told him. It wasn't in the script, of course. I was supposed to say that Juanita was being held hostage in order to improve the imperative. Instead I told him that she was dead. I faltered when it came to telling him about her hanging there, about the pox.

'It wasn't meant to go like that,' he said. I bit down harder on my hurt. My confusion.

'It never is,' I said cynically.

'It was her idea, to put herself in the plague station. It was a way of getting into the General's camp. She said it was a calculated risk. She said it was a sure way of getting in close to him because she'd make you take her in.'

I knew then what I'd been frightened to know. 'You know about him.' I could not say 'the General'.

'I suspected. I knew for certain the moment I saw you here.'

So Juanita had kept her promise to me. I did not want to stop there so I pressed on into other dangerous territory. 'Was Juanita an Insurrectionist?'

'Juanita always had her own ideas.'

'Is that a yes?'

'No. She sympathised but wouldn't join us.'

I took a deep breath. 'So you're with them?'

'Yes.'

'All along?'

'No. Juanita brought me to them. If it hadn't been for her ...' He paused. 'Who knows?'

'Juanita was your lover.' I had to tell him I knew.

'Love?' he frowned. 'I don't know, it was a needy thing I guess.' I well knew that needy thing. 'It wasn't the main issue.'

'What's the main issue?'

'Taking control of this war.'

'I thought you were against this war.'

'I am against the General. I am for the people. A crucial difference. The biggest resource is the people, it's their willpower which ultimately must stand against and behind the firepower. That's what must be tapped, channelled and put to the cause. The people are what gives victory meaning.' Déjà vu. I'd heard these words before, from the mouth of the General. Sol had been watching too much television. But he had more words-of-the-General to say. 'The one who endures the most sacrifices is the one who will win. I sacrificed my freedom, my dreams, my beliefs and my hopes. I have fought this war from within, I have suffered this war like a common civilian, like an embattled soldier, like an unwilling conscript. I have been pursued and attacked, hunted and reviled. I know this war well. This is a war the people did not choose, but a war the people must manage if they are to have any power, any control, any collaboration in their destiny.' A nice speech.

'How many Insurrectionists are there?'

'Enough of us to remove the General.'

'There's more to this war than removing the General!' I shouted. I calmed myself. 'I think it's a bit bigger than that.'

'His removal is essential,' he replied quietly. 'Can't you see that the General has conjured this war? He'd have no power if it wasn't for the enemy. The enemy exists in direct proportion to the General's need for the enemy to exist. The enemy's an extension of him and this war will continue as long as he continues. We're prisoners of his war, no matter what. Do you realise that without the General there would be no enemy? He's the true enemy of the people and he must be fought. That is the real war.'

'You want to be a hero too?'

'This is a war the people did not choose, but a war the people must manage if they are to have any power, any control, any collaboration in their destiny. Once the General is vanquished we can proceed towards peace.' Peace. Could I believe in it? 'It's possible to exist without the General. It is necessary,' he said with calm insistence. I closed my eyes. I felt Sol press against me. 'Fight my war with me,' he whispered, his hand sliding over me.

I could feel the erection his new principle of erotics was giving him. As my body made its response a passivity flooded me, a particular type of excitement. I heard him unzip his trousers. He had me kneel on a pew, then he parted my clothing and delivered himself into me, doggy fashion. After the first few thrusts I climaxed quickly and began to violently shake. I opened for him even more. He was moving deep inside me, so deep it was pleasure-pain, when missiles whizzed by overhead. On the fifth impact Sol had his orgasm. I felt him shudder in unison with the walls. Danger close. He pulled out of me with a wet plopping sound. I opened my eyes. He stepped away from me and zipped up his fly. I readjusted my clothing. My cunt was crying semen. I could feel the tears on the inside of my thighs.

'I didn't come here of my own accord,' I said. 'The General sent me.' I didn't want to play the game.

'I know,' he said.

'What do you know?'

'That you're our path to him.'

'Do you think I'm as much your pawn as his?'

'You're not his pawn, you're his prisoner,' he replied. I had a memory of saying something like that to Juanita. 'Choose now. Join us.'

THIRTY-FIVE

In the beginning, as in the end, there was a choice. The right choice, the wrong choice, no choice. I'd thought I'd lost the ability to make choices but Sol gave me the opportunity to choose again. It had been a long time since I'd had the dilemma of having to choose no. Or yes. I'd got into the habit of acquiescing, of thinking that there wasn't any choice but to continue on a path that I had chosen. Or which had chosen me. I had never been so naïve as to think that I could govern my circumstance by simply making the right choice at the right time, there were always mitigating factors, variables, random events, coincidences—lucky or unlucky—outside influences, external forces, internal pressures, and the malevolence or the whimsy of the unnameable, the unknown. The General had part-mapped that unknown for me, he had illuminated whimsy and malevolence. I never used the word 'evil' in association with him because that would exempt him from his humanity and I was always wanting to remind myself of that humanity. In him. In me. In us. Because there was an us, because that was the choice I'd once made.

Could I unmake it?

A temptation, to unmake, undo. To wipe the slate clean, maybe come up battered and heaving but come up clean of him and his breath in me, and the horror hanging before me like a noose. The single thought of it and it was slipping around my throat. The noose, the claw. Interchangeable from the moment I'd seen Juanita swinging as if dancing, with a light breeze pushing her like a happy partner. Juanita doing a little jig, something I'd not seen her do before; a happy, lively little jig, nothing solemn, nothing at all like death with its unimpeachable rigour.

I could choose to remember her another way.

I could choose another way.

I chose.

The General was in one of his odd moods when I returned. It was an arduous, awful return, the shelling had stopped and the shower of missiles had ceased but fires had broken out and the city was convulsed by acrid black smoke. I was on foot. Any other transportation would have been useless in getting me back, many streets had been reduced to a landscape of rubble. I didn't know about the rest of the city but the areas I passed through had suffered badly. I stopped at times to help others pull debris from buried people but our hands tore and were invariably no match against the weighty stone and tumble of brick. After uncovering several corpses, some of them children, all of them grotesquely broken, I hurried on.

The damage, collateral and otherwise, seemed considerable and the atmosphere was one of desperation and dangerous confusion as hasty salvage and fire-fighting operations were mounted and people were shepherded about in a panicky way by the authorities. My nostrils were assaulted by the stench of combustion and fear and my ears were blasted by the wailing of the living for the dead and the keening of the air-raid siren which had somehow slept through the missile attack but had woken to shriek outrage after the event. Things, it seemed, were really starting to fall to pieces. Or rather, in the General's parlance, things were OBE: overtaken by events.

But the General was not conceding any such events. I found him sitting where I had left him: alone in front of the video monitor, his adjutant guarding the door. But rather than studying the usual intelligence data or computer footage, the General was watching a war movie. 'History shows that the army which remains true to the original objective is the army most likely to succeed,' he said, a fairly typical opening, although I somehow doubted that an old Hollywood movie on the Vietnam War had much to do with pursuing the objective, let alone being instructive in successfully achieving the objective, but I let it pass. I also doubted that there was any meaningful connection between what the General was doing and what was occurring at that moment in the streets, but it seemed too late in the day to take that on either.

'How did your mission go?' he asked, eyes glued to the simulated fire-storm on the screen.

'The Insurrectionists believe you are the real enemy and they're set on taking control,' I replied.

'Yes, they are determined to make war against their own. This assault on the city did not come from the outside, it came from within.' I thought I saw him smile.

'Are you saying the Insurrectionists bombed the city?'

'There is no doubt.' The rest of me felt relatively calm but the palm of my scarred hand began to throb and thump like a crazy pulse, I must have hurt it pulling bits of broken buildings away from the bodies. 'They will attack here?' he asked.

'Yes.'

'Good.' He seemed pleased. He returned to his video watching. I was waiting for more questions, for a debriefing; none came. After a while I decided I'd been dismissed. I turned to go but his voice arrested me. It was a low growling, the sound I associated with him becoming sexually excited. I looked at the video screen, a movie field was strewn with movie corpses. Many, many movie corpses covered in many litres of movie blood and attended by plaintive movie music. 'Tell me, Lady, did you use your gun?'

'No.'

'A pity.'

'Why do you say that?'

'It is necessary for you to be blooded,' he said. Blooded? I could not help but remember the rapist in the stairwell whose skull I had crushed and wonder if that qualified me as being blooded. The General paused the video on the image of a solitary red flower poking out of the dirt in the movie field. 'I sent you forth in that hope. It would have been auspicious.'

'It wasn't required.' I sounded defensive.

'Now an offering will be required.'

'What sort of offering?'

'You will divine it, Lady, you with your knowledge.'

'I'll do my best,' I said, taking my leave of him.

Later that night the fever took me. It came without warning and the sweat kept rising despite my efforts to stem it. I had been expecting it, I was not a fatalist but when I had discovered the sign of it on Juanita I began to wait. Not everyone who came into direct contact with the pox contracted it, it was an unresolved mystery, as were the suicides that attended its appearance. Under the guise of fucking I had subjected the General's body to intense scrutiny but he was free of marks, and now, when I examined myself yet again, there were none of the tell-tale pustules. The small sore on my lip had healed and had not made a reappearance. I had marks on me, yes, but they were not evidence of a contamination, they were merely inscriptions of fingers and nails. Both Sol and the General had marked me according to their fashion.

I did not feel ill so much as curiously transported. The fever was a fog that fell over me, cleared, then fell again. It made me light-headed and slicked me from head to foot with perspiration but it was not unmanageable. Despite my best efforts my makeup kept sliding off my face and I had to content myself with a type of nakedness that was alien to me. It had been a long time since I had presented myself without a mask and the exposure was something I felt keenly. As I drifted through the grey corridors of the bunker soldiers kept brushing against me as they buzzed past. I was reminded of insects flying into the light. Slowly it dawned on me that this was not mere fancy, the General's soldiers *were* heading for the light—they were evacuating the bunker.

This was not in the plan. I went looking for the General.

He was in the room designated as his private study. He had just finished adding the final touches to his memoirs, he informed me. I couldn't work out why he was calmly working on his memoirs when his people were abandoning the place. He snapped shut his attaché case and locked it, then handed me the key. 'I want you to wear this,' he said, 'I want the key to me to be with you.' I took the slender gold chain the key dangled from and clasped it around my neck and dropped it onto the wet slope of my breasts. It reminded me of the tiny charms I had given Sol. 'Now the circle is complete,' he said.

I discreetly wiped sweat from my face. Something was bothering me. 'Where's the adjutant?' It was rare to find the General without his adjutant. Or, for that matter, a gathering of brass.

'He has gone on.'

'Gone on without you?'

'Gone on in my name.'

'Is that where everyone else has gone?' This was one of those times when it was necessary to slip into the General's manner of conversation rather than ask a simple question like, What's going on?

'No, they have not reached that place as yet. But it awaits them.'

'Are we going also?'

'Indubitably. The kingdom is yours, Lady.' Dead end. More sweat rose. I wondered if he was finding this amusing. 'Come,' he directed, as he stood and moved to the door, 'let us survey your land.'

Before going to survey my land I excused myself in order to collect the Luger. I also pocketed my few personal items. The set of dominoes I had no qualms about leaving behind. On my way to the waiting car, I returned again to the General's study. I was looking for an answer to the question he would not answer. Communiqués, I'd thought, faxes, battle plans, orders, directives, memos, a diary, anything that indicated what was going on. A hint as to the new plan. What I found did not explain anything but it was a clue, a portent, a potent reminder of a consequence of being in intimate association with the General.

I discovered where the adjutant had gone.

In the third drawer of the General's desk sat the adjutant's head, thick black eyebrows risen in frozen surprise, the M on his forehead a grimace, the fleshy mouth twisted, a smile aborted. I slammed the drawer shut, but not before I felt the shock like a punch to the stomach. Then the retching started.

The city was on fire. We got in the Mercedes and drove to the top of a hill to look at the blaze. Two Chosen Ones accompanied us, clearly alarmed at the General moving about with so little protection. The rest of the Chosen Ones we left at the bunker. Not a complete abandonment, after all. It was a long, slow journey to Patriot's Hill, once a premier tourist spot in the time when the city at night had been likened to a bowl of stars. That fanciful moment had well and truly passed. I walked to the edge of the look-out and stared at the angry glow. Hot spots, the General had called them. The city is presenting with hot spots, he had said. 'They're very pretty,' he added, 'despite being a most regrettable development.'

'Yes, most regrettable,' I echoed. The words sounded loud in my head. The heat in the air was bringing on the sweat again and I was feeling light-headed, as if a little tipsy, but it had been hours since I had taken a drink. A faint aftertaste of vomit lingered in my mouth and my throat felt raw. The dun-coloured night cloaked the smoke but the fires were leaping merrily. The General came and stood behind me and placed his hands on the small of my back. I could not help tensing, it was a sharp incline in front of us.

'All this is yours,' he said. Burnt and all. He seemed to be waiting for a reply.

'Mine,' I replied. My answer seemed to suffice. He removed his hands from my back and stepped to the very edge. The thought occurred that he was inviting me to push him off the lookout. 'Why is the city burning?' I asked.

'Because the Insurrectionists are followers of the flame,' he answered. 'It was not until I knew this that I understood their mission.'

'Are you telling me the Insurrectionists have deliberately set the city on fire?'

'It is their way to the necessary moment,' he answered. Something had been bothering me, I now realised what it was. 'Why is the sky so still?' I'd spent night after night watching tracer fire, listening to the incoming, the heavy breathing of single-minded artillery, and hearing the screams of the sirens. These sights, these sounds no longer filled the air, were vanquished by the inferno. 'Where's the war?'

'The war is within.' The General gestured to the sight before us.

'But the enemy ...' I trailed off. What was the enemy to me? A cipher, a television image, a rhetoric, an unknown.

'A cease-fire.' I had never thought to hear that word on the General's lips. 'Temporary only,' he added. 'A tactic to assert inner order.'

'Of course. A tactic,' I repeated. 'How long will this cease-fire last?'

'Until I make the sign. Then the final battle will begin.'

'Are you talking nuclear?' I demanded, diving straight down to the worst possible point.

'Nuclear. Chemical. Biological,' he shrugged. So nonchalant.

'These are but fruit. The tree of Mars is laden with his bounty. One requires only the strength to commence the harvest.' It had been a while since the General had mentioned his god. The last time he had invoked Mars was when he had scribbled the letter M all over my body with his favourite lipstick, Scarlet Strike. When I was sufficiently inscribed he had me dust him with white powder and take him in the corpse position. 'The god lives,' I remembered him saying.

'And Kali?' I'd said.

'She annihilates,' he had answered. 'She burns.'

I looked down at the burning city. *She burns*. 'Come,' he said, 'it is time to initiate the next phase.

'What phase is that?'

'Our rendezvous with destiny,' he replied. His hand was on my back again, propelling me forward.

THIRTY-SIX

Why was I not surprised to end up in a graveyard? It was in keeping with the lurid night, after all. It was not only a place of tombstones, there was a garden of rest, an acreage where flowers must have once bloomed in nicely fertilised plots. Now it was a sparse, spare allotment of sad, withered grass. Only a scattering of plaques connoted where you stood. Or rather, what you stood on.

On bones. On ash. On forgetting.

On remembering.

The General spoke in a low voice to his two Chosen Ones, and to my astonishment they got in the car and drove off. For the General to be out in the city alone, without his guard, was extraordinary. He saw my surprise. 'A small errand,' he murmured. We then entered the graveyard through the garden of rest. 'How peaceful,' he sighed, striking some unknown's grave with his foot and dislodging the earth. At that moment a spectacular burst of flame speared the horizon. 'That was a petrol refinery,' he explained. That was possibly in the plan but my being in a cemetery with the General was not.

The plan had been that the bunker would be attacked by the Insurrectionists at 1100 hours. Sol had stressed that it was necessary to take the General alive. I did not dissent. Nor did I say that I felt incapable of delivering him any other way. We did not otherwise discuss how I would make the General vulnerable—possibly a seduction in true Mata Hari fashion, followed by a trussing and gagging and a brief but brutal illumination of the score would be the modus operandi. Or perhaps I was expected to drug the General? Or bash him over the head with a lump of two-by-four? Sol did not see how ludicrous my role was, but he did ask if I had a weapon. 'The weapon is not the problem,' I had replied.

After the General had been taken there would have been a telecast to the nation, with the defeated General in evidence, and the assumption of a new order.

That was the plan.

I had been assured that all I had to do was disable the General before their attack commenced. They were confident of victory. 'You do believe it's necessary, don't you?' he'd asked.

'Yes,' I had said.

But the plan had changed.

The General had not stayed where he had been supposed to stay and the bunker had been all but evacuated and I had not seduced him or brained him and bundled him into a cupboard, but instead was standing in a graveyard with him at some time around 1100 hours. He was admiring the effects of flame in the sky. I was feeling a surge of fever. We had already moved a long way away from what was meant to happen. 'What are we doing here?' I asked, my voice sounding too loud. Nerves.

'Sshhh,' he whispered, putting his finger to his lips in a gesture more suited to the theatre. 'We are here to wake the living, not the dead. We are here to honour the gods, not question them.' I debated pulling the gun on him, since we were alone, but I didn't know what I would then do with him; no-one knew we were here except his bodyguards, who could return at any moment. Besides, the General was better than I with a gun. We were also, relatively speaking, isolated in the hilly outskirts of the city, which afforded a nice view of the fires but not much in the way of ready back-up. Even the graveyard had an excellent vista of the burning city. The sky jutted through wreaths of cloud, the moon was full. 'Mars rides tonight,' said the General. 'He mounts the sky to survey his world.' The General's babble was hard to take at the best of times, and this time a rage began to move through me. It was a thick, heavy, viscous thing. A lava.

We ended up on our knees in an artfully arranged semicircle of graves, the General pushing me to the ground then following suit. 'Are we supposed to be praying?' I asked with sarcasm.

'We are invoking,' he replied.

'I am not invoking anything!' I yelled. I was furious and I began to shake, badly. I tried to take some deep, steadying breaths.

He extended his hands and stroked the scar on my hand. 'Lady, you have already done so. And I am here as a tool of your will.' Then he pressed my palm against the matching blaze on his forehead. My palm burned—literally—I felt as if I were being branded, and even now I do not understand either that pain or the fury that filled me. I screamed. Rather, the rage screamed, bursting from me in a scream like a geyser.

My entire head was burning and my tongue was a river of fire and when I opened my mouth the noise rushed out and the lava started to flow.

I do not recall how long I screamed. That is one of the lost moments.

I do recall the white space, not a blur, but a clear white space; perhaps it is the space of obliteration, when all is subsumed and all else is forgotten, when there is no colour, only the space, a moment that is obliteration. Or perhaps it is the moment of the rage and the moment of the scream. Everyone has the moment of the scream. Some screams are heard in all their extended horror; others are stifled, are nothing more than a backdrop to the noisy routine of living, a little tachycardia, causing a small pause in the talking or in the swallow of coffee or the tying of shoelaces or the bathing of children, and into that pause washes a sound—chilling, indescribable—that just as quickly, thankfully, washes out again.

I screamed.

I screamed.

It must have been my moment. As a child I must have screamed, a childish scream of ego thwarted and needs denied. But since leaving early childhood I had never once screamed, and whenever I have opened my mouth since that night in order to scream there has been no scream within me.

My scream has been spent.

The General took it from me. I have been cauterised.

When he removed my hand from his forehead the scream stopped. I heard it stop as if it were something distant, unconnected to me. A blast of sound cut off, almost surgically, so abrupt was its cessation. The General fell to his belly in prostration. I reeled back, soaring to my feet. I felt immense, magnificent, unwieldy. I glared at the tilted tombstones in the half-red light and wanted to wrench them from their anchors. My rage had set. Like lava turns to rock, it had crystallised, transformed, I felt it within me, a sharp pure wedge. A sword. So clear.

A sword.

'Where is my sword?' a voice hollered. It didn't sound like my voice but it must have been, for a different voice answered and I recognised it as the General's voice. Maybe the scream had changed my voice.

'Here.' He scrabbled beneath his belly and withdrew the boning knife with which I had cut Juanita down. I'd left it lying on the floor beside her body. I took it from him and it felt familiar in my hand.

'I am pleased.' I did not intend to say that but I did. It seemed to be my voice.

'Thank you, Lady,' he grovelled. I felt like stepping on him, it was very appealing to me, to think of him beneath my feet.

'Roll over,' I said, 'I want your belly.' He promptly rolled over, spreading himself before me.

'You have tempted me,' I said. 'You have aroused me.' Sweat was pouring off me. My head felt giddy but otherwise I felt magnificent. Alive.

'Dance, Lady,' he begged. 'Do your dance on me.' I kicked off my shoe and put my naked foot on him. The surface of his belly was solid, firm. It felt like the most natural thing, to want to dance on him. I had lifted my other foot from its shoe and also placed it on him, surrendering my weight to him, when a loud shout arrested me. I looked up and saw a Chosen One with a gun in his hand moving towards me. 'Stop!' yelled the General. The man stopped. The General's voice penetrated the vicious pleasure that was coursing through me and the pleasure snapped and I, too, stopped. 'Continue, Lady,' said the General in his odd, pleading tone.

Amusement replaced the pleasure, was the new pleasure. 'No,' I said, squatting down on him and laying the knife against his throat, 'I do not dance on your order.'

'Everything I have done, I have done so that you may dance,' he said. 'And everything I shall do is for that and only that.' The General stared at me and the feeling of immensity returned.

'No!' someone shouted. I swung my head around and saw a man standing in the illumination of moon and fire. I saw his hands raised above his head forming a dark arc. It was only when a flare of light showed me his features that the name entered me and the immensity drained away, like water running down a plughole, leaving confusion.

'Sol?' I said in a voice that was wholly my own.

'Yes,' he replied. 'It's me.' I took in the two Chosen Ones and Sol: a tableau, with the red night pulsing around them. I heard heavy breathing and became acutely aware that I was atop the General. I wanted to get off him, and fast. As I jumped to the ground the Chosen One who had been coming for me moved on me. He grabbed me and locked me in a hold, wrenching at the hand that held the knife. As he did so, there was a shot. I felt his weight slump against me, a profound relaxation of his body, then he fell to the ground and was motionless. His eyes were looking through me with the sightless gaze of the dead. The General was on his feet with his gun in his hand. 'He did not have permission,' he said.

A pause. A heartbeat. Two. Three. Five heartbeats. I could feel my own heart, the thumping. 'He's dead,' I said. There was not much purpose in saying it but I said it in lieu of anything else.

'You, too, are dismissed,' said the General, pointing his gun at the remaining Chosen One. Another shot rang out. Another dropping. Another silence. 'They pledged themselves to me,' he said. 'To the death,' he added.

A thought began to clear a path through my confusion, the thought that I had blood on me. I could smell it and I could see dark stains on my hands. I knelt and scrubbed my palms vigorously on the stubbly grass and the smell of dirt soothed me. I straightened and looked at Sol. His hands were bound with rope. 'What's happening?' I asked. 'What are you doing here?' I could not shake the dizziness.

'I came because of the General's demand,' he replied. 'When our forces reached his bunker we were met by his private guard. We took the bunker but it was empty. Then two of his men arrived with the message that he would speak only to me. The city is ours,' Sol addressed the General, 'you know that, otherwise you would not have abandoned your men.' The General surprised me by laughing.

'Why him?' I asked the General.

'He is your choice,' he smiled. 'He is the one whose tongue danced in your mouth.'

'You knew about him?'

'I have always known. I sent you to him so that you would know what I knew. I have merely waited for his purpose to be fully revealed. You have been his means of approaching me, and I have been patient, allowing him to come to me, bit by bit.'

'What's he talking about?' interjected Sol.

'I think he's saying that I've been a bait.'

The General remonstrated gently. 'No, Lady, I am in your service. I do what is best for you.'

'In that case, the General has miscalculated. The only thing that matters here is that the city is mine,' said Sol. The General tut-tutted.

'Yours?' I asked.

'Yes,' Sol replied. I felt a terrific rush of heat. 'Mine and the people's.'

'What about the people?' I said, mopping my face with my hanky, the white of it seeming to gleam. 'What about all those people burning up down there? Are you responsible for bombing the city?'

'Some intervention was necessary and of course some people have died. How can you expect otherwise? This is a war. It's a necessary war, that's the difference. It's a war for the people.'

'You bombed our own people,' I said, 'and these fires are your doing.'

'There are always casualties,' he replied. 'It is unavoidable. It was a necessary strategy.' Nausea moved through me.

'There doesn't seem to be so much difference between you and the General,' I retorted. 'I thought you were against him, against his way.'

'I am. I'm here now for the good of the city.'

'Bravo!' responded the General, dangerously waving his gun about. I was reminded of my own Luger tucked away in my shoulder-bag. I also remembered the boning knife I had let drop when I scrabbled to get the blood off my hands.

'I have to warn you,' I said to Sol, 'the General is accomplished in this game. He's playing with you.'

'The General may be holding a gun but he's not in a position to play with anyone,' said Sol. 'He's a man, not a god, and the people are tired of gods. They're tired of not having a choice.'

'And you, what is your choice?' enquired the General.

'My choice is to live in a world without you.' In the distance there was a massive explosion.

'The bunker,' explained the General. Sol said nothing. 'The city is not yours, as you think it is.'

'There'll be no city left!' I yelled.

'I'd rather see it burn than let it be his any longer,' replied Sol. 'I will burn it to the ground myself.' A feeling of desolation swamped me. Sol stood on one side of me, the General on the other. What I had feared had come to pass, I had brought Sol into the circle of the General. If not for me he wouldn't be standing here facing the General's gun. He may have joined the Insurrectionists anyway, but the General had focused on Sol because of me.

'What are you going to do with him?' I asked the General. 'Why is he here?'

'I have brought him to you in order that you may fully touch him.'

'Meaning?'

'He is your chosen one.'

'You're going to kill him,' I said. My head began to pound. My voice sounded surprisingly calm.

'No. That is your pleasure, Lady, not mine.'

'And if I refuse?' I replied.

'There is no alternative, you have stepped beyond the moment of choice.' I looked at the General. Would he shoot me if I did refuse? I looked at Sol, he seemed unconcerned. Did he believe that it wasn't possible for me to kill him? Even to save my own skin? I slowly bent and picked up the knife. I hefted it in my hand as if weighing it, considering it. I did not look at Sol.

'This is for carving, not for killing,' I pronounced. 'This is for eating. Give me your gun.'

'Where is your gun, Lady?'

'I didn't bring it,' I lied. I walked over to the General and held out my hand. He took it and raised it to his lips and his tongue traced the line of my scar and the vestiges of blood from the dead man I'd been unable to wipe away. His tongue felt hot, or maybe it was the fever in me bubbling up again. When he put the gun into my hand I felt more than anything else the promise of release.

As I approached Sol he whispered, 'The General can't contain it. He's lost. You don't have a choice, you'll have to kill him.' Another huge explosion ripped the sky. I saw Sol smile at the flash of light and I saw, too, that Sol did not doubt that I would preserve him and sacrifice the General. That I would do this for him because he knew that I loved him. For it was what I had told him the last time we had parted.

'I love you,' I said. 'But I will not kill for you.' I leaned against him and brought up the knife and sawed through the rope. 'If you want him dead, you do it,' I whispered, pushing the gun into his hand. 'You're the one who has the choice now. If you want what he has, you take it from him.' Then I turned and walked away.

I did not look back.

I heard the shot just as I reached the car.

THIRTY-SEVEN

He wakes to find himself alone with the corpse. Blood shines in great dazzling globs.

It was logically necessary, a voice in his head tells him.

It is logically necessary.

When he looks down at himself he sees a man coated in blood. It is warm on him, another layer, a new skin. It is not unpleasant, it is a comfort. A protection. He turns his gaze back to the city and sees the fire vaulting towards him. Blazing yellow light bursting into flares of red, elegantly descending. The wind begins blowing harder, fanning it. Sparks explode like fireworks, so pretty. Fragrant smoke curling through him like perfume.

So pretty.

He picks up the knife and patiently, methodically begins to carve up the corpse. It should be difficult but no, it's the easiest thing in the world. It makes him incomparably happy that it's so easy. Yes, he has the necessary touch. The knife slices as if into butter, skin and muscle parting as if they were waiting for his touch. The bone is another matter, the bone will require a heavier, sharper blade.

The red sky throbs as he works, he can feel it breathing above him, stretched tight across him, feverish against his naked back. He does not remember becoming naked, his new blood-coating fits so well it is only when he feels the sky's breath that he realises he has somehow become naked. He experiences a moment of confusion but then he sees the uniform laid out beside him and his confusion disappears as the medals, the gold stripes, the braid, the insignia, the epaulet of stars, shine at him.

Into the midst of this shining comes a greater shining, out of the fire jumps the hottest flame, its lick the most exquisite tongue of heat. A sear of ecstasy penetrates him.

Mine, whispers the flame. *Mine*.

He sees first the darkness that is her face, then the redness of her mouth and the whiteness of her teeth. Then he sees the hands—four of them—then the breasts with the excited nipples, then the whole burnt black curve of her, her naked, fuming cunt, her legs stark as scorched trees.

Beauty incorruptible.

Unimaginable, immense.

Around her waist a girdle of severed hands quivers as if excited and between her breasts a necklace of tiny skeletons jumps as if embodied. She holds out her hands to him: in one hand the hangman's noose is an incandescent halo; in another she twirls a sword of flame; in yet another there is a burning lotus; her fourth hand is a claw, making a sign he cannot read.

Take the heart, she crackles.

Her arms begin whirling, the force of her movement sucking the air from his lungs like a desiccating wind. He does not hesitate, he steps into her circle and touches the sword with the palm of his hand. He has never known such heat, it melts his skin, pierces his bones, it enters his blood and ignites him.

He is the son of light.

He is the father of fire.

Now eat, she commands. *Eat*.

He eats. He dreams, he eats.

THIRTY-EIGHT

There is memory and there is fear. These two things I carry regardless of whatever other freight. I carried them from my last moments with Sol and the General, the end coming so quickly I had to seize it when it was blurry, still moving, full of momentum. I think, when I walked away, I expected a bullet to stop me. My going had not been a premeditated action, it was just the way it happened.

When I got to the car and saw the keys in the ignition I slid into the driver's seat, where I had never sat, and I had one thought—blue sky—and I pointed the General's powerful, useful Mercedes towards the Last Zone. I was already on the city outskirts but I could not have managed the checkpoints if not for the chaos, the General's car, an attaché case emblazoned with his name and, of course, my lies, although I did not have to say much really, I was known as the General's mistress. His messenger. My Luger was still with me but it probably wouldn't have done me much good if things had gone badly.

When I left it in the car I did not have any regret that I had used it only once, to duel with the General.

It helped, I think, to be fevered, it gave events an odd, chopped-up, surreal cast. Events had the quality of night sweats. I passed out a few times, pulling over just in time to avoid running off the road. The roads, surprisingly, were intact. Rutted and damaged, but manageable. I travelled fast. There was an abiding sense of urgency.

I bought petrol. I think I used my body for that. I remember peeling down the zip on a man's trousers and taking out a penis. But I don't remember anything else about it, perhaps it was an hallucination.

Eventually I reached a point where I could not drive any further. On my map the road continued but there was nothing but the chewed-up earth and a sea of barbed wire. Nothing but a sea. I waited until dawn. I waited until I saw the first bit of blue sky then I entered the sea.

People consider it a miracle that I came through the Last Zone, it's heavily mined. I hadn't even thought of mines. I just picked up the General's attaché case and started walking. It was the second time I expected a bullet to stop me. As a preventative I shook out my crumpled white hanky and held it above my head.

'I surrender.'

I felt an incredible release when I said those words.

The General's attaché case and the key on the chain around my neck were taken away by this government's intelligence people. His memoirs proved to be of little use. I think for the first time, the General's sanity was questioned. I had no desire to read his remains even if they did help provide my passage and my refuge here.

At first it seemed the cease-fire might hold, but in no time at all, the war recommenced.

Another cycle has begun. Sol has assumed extraordinary power.

I thought I could never confuse Sol and the General but now I find that I do. At least in my dreams I do.

I have my grandfather's gold fillings, my grandmother's gold wedding ring, a tiny horseshoe lucky charm, a piece of Juanita's inky hair, my scar and my memories to remind me of my old life. It is sufficient. I take care to keep the scar well hidden even though here Mars is a planet, not a god. It's a disfigurement that causes questions and there are some things I do not wish to answer. At least no-one calls me Lady, for which I am grateful. I left that honorific when I left the General to his fate. His Kali.

I have become the enemy now.

I look like anybody else walking in the street or shopping for food. The language is different but not difficult to understand, the customs are almost identical. The sky stays blue most days and that makes it much easier for me. Most nights my fever rises. It has a curious empathy with the moon and I am teaching myself to not wait for the last sign, the pustules. The fear of it is within me. Tests reveal nothing, still, I feel something inside of me, threading its way through me and it becomes difficult to want to remember.

But I cannot let the fear get the better of me.

The bird will have the worm.

I heard a rumour today that fighting is expected to start very close to here soon.